EARTHSTUCK

ALSO BY THE AUTHOR

THE STARSTRUCK SAGA

Starstruck

Alienation

Traveler

Celestial

Starbound

Earthstuck

AIX MARKS THE SPOT

NOVELLAS

Miss Planet Earth (Pew! Pew! - The Quest for More Pew!)

The Horrible Habits of Humans (Pew! Pew! - Bite My Shiny

Metal Pew!)

Miss Planet Earth and the Amulet of Beb Sha Na

Head over Heels (Starstruck Halloween Short)

BOOK SIX OF THE STARSTRUCK SAGA

EARTHSTUCK

S.E. ANDERSON

BOLIDE

EARTHSTUCK

© S.E. Anderson 2020

Cover design by Sarah Anderson

Editorial: Michelle Dunbar, Cayleigh Stickler, Anna Johnstone

First published in 2020 by Bolide Publishing Limited
Bolidepublishing.com

ISBN: 978-1-912996-23-0

FOR HUGO, AGAIN
CAN'T STOP, WON'T STOP
DEDICATING BOOKS TO YOU

PROLOGUE

THE SECRET TO GOOD COFFEE?
ALIEN ABDUCTION AND IRISH CREAM

MONA BELIEVED IN TWO THINGS: ALIENS AND GOOD customer service.

Not everyone who came to the Jitterbug for a fresh pot of coffee was entirely *of this world*. Well, that's what her ex-manager, and ex-fiancé, told her before he got—most likely—abducted and she got his job. Which meant Mona was next in line for a wondrous interplanetary adventure, if she held out long enough and treated her possibly alien patrons right.

The thought kept her going when life became incomprehensible and stress tried to drown out her thoughts. Maybe, just maybe, one of her customers was from outer space, and she was damn sure she was going to smile and treat every single one of them with respect just in case. It was why she opened the coffee shop every night of the year, including Christmas and

EARTHSTUCK

New Year's Eve. Her travel bag was packed and stashed in the café's back room waiting to go, though it was just gathering dust at the moment.

While waiting for the aliens, Mona focused on the customer experience part of the deal. She perfected her pies. Made the Jitterbug a safe haven for those who felt lost or like an outcast in the world. Like flocked to like, and she built a community. And some, like her, were longing for the stars.

Most of her regulars fit easily under the label of "possibly alien, keep an eye out for them." Take, for instance, Sally Webber: so normal it hurt, yet surrounded by the oddest people on all sides, like the gorgeous androgynous beauty and the potential Woman in Black who came in on New Year's Eve. Or the fact that she disappeared the day the spaceship broke the atmosphere, but nobody noticed since there was a *freaking spaceship* in the sky. Nobody but Mona, anyway. That night, she had stood on the roof with her dusted-off satchel and Christmas lights spelling out "take me with you" at her feet, as her staff and customers hid in the café with paper bags over their heads. It was during that stupidly long wait that she realized Sally wasn't with them.

When the news hit that it was a bona fide hoax, the whole world let out a collective sigh of relief. Mona closed the café for the first time since taking over as manager, cried into her pillow for a good twelve hours, and then opened the Jitterbug the next day, putting the satchel back in its rightful place by the emergency exit.

A week after the biggest disappointment in Mona's life, Sally waltzed back in.

Though it wasn't the same Sally she had seen before the hoax. The first clue was that she was wearing a t-shirt in negative-degree weather. That, and Mona had never noticed how buff the girl was— her arms were straight out of a Hollywood movie, all muscled and skin practically glowing. Her hair shone with the light of a thousand suns, which only highlighted her bright smile.

"Oh my god," said Mona, her jaw dropping as she took her in. "It's you."

The smile widened. Mona fell in love instantly.

"What?" Sally laughed, her voice light, birds landing on her arms as she spoke. At least, that's what happened in the version Mona wrote down later when she got home and tried to make sense of the whole afternoon. "I've only been gone a week. Well, it's been an exciting week, for sure, but I haven't been gone all *that* long."

"You know what I mean," she replied and hoped that would be enough. She didn't have the energy to keep staring at her; the glowing hurt her eyes. "It's good to have you back, girl."

"Glad to be back," Sally said, and it sounded so deeply from her heart. "Can I have a latte?"

"Of course you can!"

She worked her magic with coffee and cream, thankful for the excuse to turn her back a little. There was something magnetic about Sally today, something that made the air around them come alive. Was she flirting? No, this was something more. It had to be.

"I brought you something." Sally reached into her purse. "Here. I found this in a little shop in Mexico."

"Mexico? That's where you were?" She handed the coffee over just as Sally reached across to deposit two dollops of gold into her hand. "Oh, it's heavy! This isn't real gold, is it? Where on earth did you get it?"

"Oh, a small town named Aquetzalli," came a voice from the back of the café, in a booth so out of the way that no one ever sat there. Sally's eyes widened, her new smile wavering as she turned to face the stranger. Her dark, James Bond-esque suit came into sharp focus. "Nice to see you again, Sally."

There was a scream. Sally's mug slipped from her hand, tumbling to the floor in slow motion. The latte sloshed over the rim, and with a sudden, yet anticipated, crash, the glass shattered, leaving a mess on the floor.

And Sally was gone—glow, scream, and all. Anyone watching her would have sworn she had disappeared into thin air, like someone had flicked the channel and taken her with it.

"This never happened," said the woman in the suit, rising smoothly from her seat. "I'm sorry to say that this café has been compromised. There is LSD in the water, and you're all *tripping balls.*"

Mona didn't believe her, but the next thing she remembered was waking up in her bed, her phone vibrating up a storm as it filled with alerts. It was 3 a.m., and her mouth tasted of peaches. It made sense that the whole thing was one very strange dream, even if it meant that the Men in Black hadn't really infiltrated her café.

When she drove up to the Jitterbug to check on the alarms, the police were waiting for her. On the floor, almost exactly where the mug had shattered in her dream, was a trail of sand and bloody footsteps. It led through the back door, the footsteps disappearing in the parking lot, lost in the snow.

"We're lucky we have so much to go on," said the uniformed man crouched by the stain. "Blood, tire treads, DNA? The hard part is figuring out the chain of events. Anything seem out of the ordinary today? It might give us clues to what led up to this."

Mona wanted to tell them about Sally's sudden dematerialization and the strange woman in the immaculate suit, but it had all been a dream, hadn't it? Even as she opened her mouth to deny everything, a figure in the alley caught her eye, and she snapped her mouth shut.

There. The Men in Black *were* here. They were real. And the secret agent lady was more than just familiar; she was the woman from New Year's Eve. The one

Sally had shared pie with. Mulder, Scully, and Agent J all rolled into one.

A finger to her lips. A hand on her hip, but not her hip—no, on the thing hiding under her blazer. Mona gulped. Being in the center of an alien conspiracy suddenly wasn't all that fun anymore.

"Nothing at all. Nothing strange; it's just a café," she told the cop, and the woman from the shadows nodded, striding forward with her hands at her side now, thank god.

"You are to cease this investigation at once," she ordered bluntly, waving a government ID for the cops to see. "We'll take it from here."

"Agent Felling!" one of the officers exclaimed. "I haven't seen you here for a while. Not since—"

"Now, no one needs to hear about that," Felling replied with a curt nod.

"Is it one of *those* cases?" The cop rolled his eyes. "Spooky-dooky?"

"No, no. But you know the rules. Also, what the hell is spooky-dooky supposed to mean? That's not a word, Blake."

The cop rolled his eyes again, a master of eyeball cartwheels. "Is Cross with you?"

"He's out back with the footprints. He'll tell you the same thing, but don't go bringing up spooky-dooky around him. He's a lot less interested in expanding the dictionary."

As Blake and his colleague slipped back into the

night, a chill ran through Mona that had nothing to do with the snow.

"Did you... did you drug me?" she asked, trying to brush the goosebumps from her skin. "Did you seriously drug me? My patrons?"

"Go back to sleep, Ms. Hanks," the agent replied. "It's been a long day."

"I deserve an answer!" Mona reached for her shoulder, the goosebumps giving way to actual tremors. "What in the hell happened back there? And don't tell me any of this LSD bull. I've seen you before."

The agent let out a sigh, rubbing her temples before dropping her hands to her hips again. She didn't look defeated, though admittedly it was hard to tell with all the scowling.

"If I gave you a check right here, right now, would you please go home and sleep it off?"

"I won't be paid off that easily." Mona was getting somewhere. The tremors branched out into excitement, which was, all in all, exciting.

"Nonsense. Everyone has a price; we just need to find yours."

"Give me a trip off this planet, and I'll never tell a soul what I witnessed today. How's that?"

The agent laughed. "You and me both, sister. Take the money, go home, and sleep. Tomorrow, everything will be back to normal."

"And what about Sally? You can't possibly deny what happened in there."

"Who are you going to believe?" A ghost of a smile played on Felling's lips. "Me, a certified government agent, or your eyes? Because, believe me, I'm not prone to lying, and eyes can play tricks on the best of us."

ONE

AND NOW, A WORD FROM OUR SPONSORS

ALL I WANTED WAS A HOT LATTE. INSTEAD, I WAS the next great gladiator of the XIX Pontafarious Games X-treme Edition, and they weren't letting me go without an autograph.

Things like that happen when you panic and dissolve down the cosmic drain of the universe. One minute, you can be in your favorite coffee shop, and in a heartbeat, you're in an arena filled with pink sand, standing halfway between an ancient stone warrior and a pig the size of a hippopotamus, and neither seem the least bit friendly. Your best bet is to grab a sword and defend yourself in any way you can.

If no swords are readily available, that means running away as fast as possible. Screaming and flailing your arms are an additional bonus. Apparently, you get extra points for dramatic flair.

EARTHSTUCK

The arena was ovoid and didn't seem to have an entrance, but the running and screaming sure did cut down my field of view. There was no missing the crowd in the mile-high stands, the floating screens that showed a lovely close-up of my face, or the talking moon in the sky above us, lazily ranting about drinking more Sgagglin.

At least I think it was a drink. It was unclear with all the running and screaming.

So, I cut that out. The one place I needed to run back to was Earth, and I couldn't do that without extreme calm and focus. Not much room for mindfulness here, what with a roaring crowd and two very angry gladiators who were furious I was stealing their spotlight.

"I don't believe it! We have a surprise contender!" The commentator's voice came from nowhere and everywhere, drilling into the center of my skull. I threw my hands up to my ears, trying to block out the sound, but there was too much happening all at once: the noise, the lights, the heat on my skin. And all the while, every detail of the world was brought into sharp focus and every sound amplified until I could hear a fly buzz halfway across the stadium, behind the two teenage blobs sneaking that stuff the lazy moon was trying to sell their parents in the stands. Too much going on at once, and I was now screaming again, screaming for them to make it stop. Make it all stop; make it go away.

Instead, someone tossed me a laser saber. Which made my terrible evening just a little bit cooler.

"Beings of all genes," proclaimed the announcer, "we have a new contender! Our mystery fighter will attempt to take on our two reigning champs, Carlotti the Rhegaf and Jjjjjjjoliiiii!"

"Um, no!" I shouted, but it was no use. The crowd was going wild. Wild for a girl in faded Ugg boots, whose only weapons were a pretty dope laser saber and maybe her headphone cable as backup. "I'm not here to fight. I'm lost!"

"Gladiators! Fight!"

Giant white orbs filled the air, spraying from canons deep below my feet. The moon above my head drawled a lazy "Yeah?" as my face was added to the leaderboard. A hastily taken snapshot between two alien headshots popped up, their stats scrolling past my row of question marks.

Come on, Sally, jump. Reel me back in, Earth. I slapped my face, hard. My skin tingled before bouncing back. No pain, not even for a second. But if I didn't jump right the first time, Earth could be lost to me forever. I had to do it right—or not at all. Why was this so damn hard? Jumping halfway across the universe because James-flipping-Felling is stalking you is one thing. Easy. Instantaneous. A knee-jerk—or jump-jerk—reaction. Getting back should have been the same.

If I had to defeat two gladiator beasts to get a

second of mindfulness meditation, I would push through it, dammit.

I flew into the air and came down hard against the back wall of the arena. The stone warrior had flung me a good fifty meters with one punch, and I actually felt my spine shatter as the arena wall crumpled around me.

I would never get used to the feeling of bones mending themselves, fusing, strengthening, as I stood. I wasn't used to not having a heart pumping a mile a minute when I was scared either. That or the fact I shouldn't be scared anymore.

I laughed. Because what else can you do? You've got a shattered spine on the mend and a laser saber in your hands. *You're immortal, Sally Webber. It's time to act like it.*

The stone gladiator didn't seem phased by my spontaneous recovery, though it was hard to tell his expression, seeing as how he was quite literally stone-faced. Boulders clumped together to form his four-meter tall figure, currently poised on three legs, his face only distinguishable by the ornate, hot pink, tiara-shaped crown he wore.

I was so focused on trying to make out the gladiator's expression that I entirely missed the hippo-pig. He didn't miss me, though, as he rammed me in the hip and tossed me in the air like a rag doll. I fell face-first in the arena sand, breathing in dust and shattered bone.

The pig turned to rush me again, but this time I managed to roll out of the way, covering my shirt with gross, bloody sand. Where was the laser saber? I spun on my heels, seeing its red glow at the other end of the arena. Of course it was all the way over there. I willed myself to appear at its side, saving myself the trouble of running, but the jumping still wasn't happening.

Running it was going to have to be.

I dove into the sand, missing the rock that flew over my head by an inch. The boulder gladiator could apparently pull himself apart, which was a terrible thing to know. If I did that, how quickly would my own arm grow back? And why was I thinking about that now?

"Sgagglin! The drink of warriors!" The moon lazily intoned, and gold bubbles filled the arena, blocking my view of the others. Perfect. I grabbed the hilt of the laser saber and held the weapon high, feeling like the Jedi I was always meant to be.

The saber flickered then died. *Dammit.* I slapped the hilt as I turned it over, and the blade returned for a split second, then arena sand poured to the ground as it faded again. There was dirt on the inside somehow. How did these things work, anyway? I stared into the depths of the device as it flickered back on and cut a hole clean through my skull.

I thought losing an eye would hurt more, but the scream that came out of my mouth wasn't of pain; it was shock. My brain recognized the pain but ignored it, focusing instead on what a dumbass I was. Any idiot knows not to stare down the barrel of a gun, and here I was staring down a laser saber. If I weren't immortal, I would be dead now. That would probably become my personal mantra.

I had to take this seriously. It wasn't a game. Just because my life wasn't at stake didn't mean I could do whatever the hell I wanted. Okay, sure, it meant exactly that, but there were supposed to be rules, right? Zander was supposed to be walking me through all this. Zander should be by my side. Zander should be...

Perks of immortality? No panic attacks. I could still function. But I was still allowed to freak out. There was no way I could win this fight; I would get pummeled again and again until the crowd got bored of me.

What would Zander do?

"Boycott Sgagglin!" I shouted, spinning around and raising a fist into the air.

Nothing happened. Which made sense, what with all upbeat music pumping in the air. The cameras focused on the rock monster punching a fistful of bubbles, which exploded over the arena in golden rain.

"Boycott! Sgagglin!" I shouted again, pushing my lungs as far as I could, allowing them to fill and release past the point where I once would have felt pain.

"Did she say 'boycott Sgagglin?'" asked the rock monster, with a mouth that was apparently exactly nowhere. It stopped poking the bubbles, turned to the hippo pig, and continued in what could have been a very loud whisper. "Or 'boycott, Sgagglin?'"

"Is there a difference?" the hippo pig asked, pulling off his helm with a stiff hoof.

"Well, one is her asking us to boycott Sgagglin," he said, shrugging, all the boulders rolling as one. "The other is asking Sgagglin to boycott something."

"Boycott what?" The pig put the helm back on. "Is this that water thing again? Dude, just fight. Don't bring politics into this."

"There is a serious issue with them pumping the last moon of Gilnea," he insisted.

"We're in the championship fight. Can we talk about this when one of us has won the title?"

"True, true."

"Plus, Gilnea is getting fairly compensated."

"Seriously? You realize why they're called the *last* moon, right? What do you think happened to the others?"

"Shut. Up!" The pig seemed livid. "Neither of us will walk out of here with any prize money if you don't stop talking crap about our sponsors. We can boycott Sgagglin after one of us is rich and famous."

The crowd wasn't too happy about this, and that was putting it mildly. I hadn't realized Sgagglin was such a point of contention or I would have tried a different tactic, but there was no denying it was effective. In an instant, I had a crowd divided, rising in their seats in anger, if they were even sitting in the first place; the two gladiators fighting on screens larger than their already larger-than-life selves; and a disgruntled moon telling everybody to calm down and get drunk.

It still didn't solve my problem of getting back to Earth, but no one was expecting me to kill anybody anymore, which was a relief. That and my eyeball had grown back, which was such a good feeling I couldn't put it into words.

Bubbles flew into the arena, hiding the gladiators from the now-rowdy crowd and hiding the pink hippo from sight until the last second before it charged.

My stomach dropped, a fall from a roller coaster the size and shape of the universe. Everything spread before me, and the walls of the room became tangible, something I could feel, like the movement of the thousands in the grandstands or the motion of the bubbles. And on a grander scale, the tilt of the planet—of the *planets,* all of them—caught in a dance so complex my breath hitched in my throat.

And in the midst of it, my planet. My café. My place in time. *Imagine a cord,* Zander had said. *Feel your way back.* Like a diver in a cave pulling my way through murky waters, stealing small breaths to keep the claustrophobia from taking over—only with the infinity of the universe falling away from me at every side.

I opened my eyes to a darkened Jitterbug, punching my suddenly whole fist in the air. And by the lack of texts on my phone, I hadn't been gone long enough to be missed.

Behold Sally Webber, master of time and space!

My body was aflutter with endorphins, nerve endings happy to have been reconnected. The jump had been oddly easier than I had expected. Maybe that had something to do with instinct. There's something to be said for not overthinking things.

"Try not to flake out on me this time, will you?"

My elation turned to panic as her voice echoed through the empty café. Felling was in the same booth as earlier, in the same suit, as if she hadn't moved since I'd left hours ago. Totally ruining my groove.

I didn't know what was worse: disappearing to a gladiator-style fight or staying to talk with the woman who knew too much. There was probably still time to jump back.

"Hey, Sally. It's good to see you again." She stood and straightened her blazer.

I slapped the laser saber against my thigh, but it didn't turn on. Too bad. It would have been badass.

"Felling."

It came out more sour than I would have liked. Then again, I didn't know how I wanted to sound. James Felling had helped me save the world. But I had changed since the last time she saw me, and I knew that she *knew* everything.

She loosened her collar and motioned to the seat across from her. I shook my head.

"I'd rather not." I pointed to my sandy boots. "I'd like to go home and change if you don't mind. A shower wouldn't hurt either."

"Nice to see you too. Hope you had a nice trip?"

"Uneventful. Then again, which one are you referring to, exactly? Wait, no, ugh, I don't want to do this."

"Then go home, get cleaned up. We can talk in the morning."

"I don't want to do this *ever,* Felling." I strode across the floor, cringing at the crunch of sand under my boots as I pushed against the employee exit. The suede was stained red and gold, which probably wouldn't wash off any time soon, even as I stepped out into the snow and added water to the mix.

All I had wanted was a latte.

"And you just set off the silent alarm," said Felling, following me out. "Way to go. Here, I thought we could let Mona sleep this off."

I stopped in my tracks. "What the hell did you do to her, Felling?"

"Woah, easy." James threw up her hands defensively.

"Why would she have a silent alarm? This is a café, not a jewelry store."

"For the aliens, of course. I was just cleaning up your mess for you. *Again.* She'll wake up thinking it was all a weird dream. All the patrons will."

I shuddered. My mess. I had jumped in front of a crowd of people—friends, neighbors. People who knew me had seen me disappear into thin air. I couldn't be trusted to even step outside of my apartment on my own.

"No, this is your fault." I spun on my heels. Felling frowned, the shadows of her face accentuated by the streetlight.

"My fault? What, no thank you?"

"If you weren't stalking me, I would never have... ducked out like that."

"Oh, sure, I'm to blame that you can't control your new space powers. Well, excuse me for trying to keep the government out of your hair!"

"I saved the world. They owe me that much."

"You know they don't operate that way." Felling crossed her arms over her chest, her frown turning into a scowl. "The only reason you don't have twenty-four-hour surveillance around your apartment right now is thanks to me."

"You being my twenty-four-hour surveillance?"

"It's not like that."

"How? How is it not *exactly* like that?" I stuffed the laser saber into my pocket, lest I start using it as a baton. "I have been living in absolute terror since I got back from saving Earth, all because of your letter.

You can't leave notes like that and expect me to be happy with you as my government-assigned stalker."

"I sent you emails."

"I never replied. Wasn't that enough of a clue that I don't want to talk? I have enough to deal with without you or the government and shit like that."

"Trust me, if I weren't around, you would be knee-deep in their shit. I'm not joking around, Sally. I'm trying to help you. My partner is outside right now keeping the cops at bay."

"You have a partner?" My hands curled into fists. "No, I don't want to know. The best thing you can do right now is give me some space, okay? I have a lot to figure out."

"Fine. It's not you I need to see, anyway."

I didn't think I could ever feel cold again, but her words proved me wrong. The chill was bone-deep.

"I know Zander and Blayde are with you." Her words turned freezing air into ice. "We need them."

"Who?"

"The FBI."

"Which you are totally a part of," I said through gritted teeth. "Dammit, Felling, is that the deal you're offering me? Turn over my friends in exchange for keeping me out of it? Terrible idea. Firstly, I wouldn't do that. And secondly, you know Earth doesn't have the means to contain them."

"It's nothing like that." Felling almost looked like she was ashamed. She shifted her weight to her other leg, and I realized she must be freezing out here without a coat on.

"Then what?"

"We need their opinion on a case." She pulled her crossed arms tighter around herself.

"A case?"

"We're stumped, and they're the only ones who know enough about, well, everything to help. No one has to know."

"A case."

"Murder." She nodded. "Three with the same MO. I need the siblings' unique insight. Stop this from happening again."

"So, when you say we… the real FBI? Or that shady agency you're a part of?"

"Me, Sally. I need their help."

I said nothing. Felling was shivering small, controlled shakes, her lips forming a tight line as she waited for me to answer. I still wasn't sure if I was going to; the sand in my boots was starting to irritate me, too rough on my toes, and there was a lot of grievances to go around.

"What happened, Sally?"

"After the thing with the Youpaf? Or right now?"

"I'm trying to pin down the moment you started hating me."

"I don't hate you." And it was true. I wasn't quite sure what I felt toward Felling, but it wasn't hate. Not after all we'd been through together.

"You don't trust me, though."

"Are you kidding me? I don't even know who you actually work for!"

"Have I ever given you reason to doubt me?"

"Not the Sally I was before, no." I shoved my fists into my pockets. She wasn't who I was angry at. A young boy, his memory tarnished by the man he became, had stripped me of these relationships. He's the one I should have been directing my anger at. But my anger was too big for just one person. I had tasted nothing but bitterness since I had broken his neck. "I'm different now."

"I can tell." She unclasped her hands, one reaching across the divide, reaching for my fingers. I took a step back. "But *I* haven't changed. I'm still here for you, Sally."

"Just give me some time. Please?" I asked, and she nodded.

"Of course. But we need Zander and Blayde. Tell them, please? Tell them that innocent people are dying. I know it's a lot to ask another favor of them, but they're good people. They care."

"If I tell them, will you stop stalking me?"

"Sally, I'm going to deal with these cops, and then I'm going to my hotel to pack. I'll be gone when you wake up. You know how to reach me."

Which would have been a perfect way to end things, but the stranger turning the corner right in the middle of our heart-to-heart ramped everything back up.

"Oh, shit, it's you," he said, freezing like a deer in headlights. "It's really you!"

I could have jumped again right then and there. His eyes were wide and fixed right on me, like he knew me. My body wanted to tear me from this world, to take me far away, but a gentle hand on my wrist kept me grounded.

Felling inhaled deeply. "Sally, this is Agent Cross, my partner."

The man strode forward, almost giddy, the mask of training slipping just enough. "Call me Dustin. And I know everything about you, Sally Webber. So nice to finally meet. Felling has told me so much about you!"

I shook his hand gingerly. It was a massive hand. In fact, the whole man was massive, tall and blond and built like a brick wall. The type of guy who played football in high school, college, and whatever sports team his secret agency surely had. Because even if they didn't have one, they would have made one up just so he could play.

"Um, hi." My hand burned in his grasp. "Felling, since when have you had a partner?"

"Who do you think was managing the media end of things during the invasion?" She glanced at her watch. "He's the one who came up with the Buzzfeed quiz."

"And you told him about me."

"He's privy to the same information I have, yes."

"How many people know, Felling? This is exactly

why I didn't want to see you again. I don't want to be on your radar or anyone else's. I just want to be left alone."

"I guess we can talk later?" said Cross, the unfortunate third wheel. "Sally, you need to get out of here. The cops are on their way to respond to the alarm, and you shouldn't be here when they arrive."

"No, I shouldn't."

I uncrossed my arms, stuffing my hands deep into my jean pockets. I could feel the hair raise on the back of my neck, as if eyes were staring from the shadows. They could well have been. How many of them knew my secret? How many people had Felling told?

Further reason to never trust her again. I was out of that parking lot like a bat out of hell. Or, more accurately, an alien out of *The X-Files*.

TWO

SOMEBODY MARKET MURDER THERAPY
BEFORE IT BECOMES THE NEW TREND

IT'S AN INTENSE ACT OF CONCENTRATION TO STICK
to speed limits once you've piloted a spaceship. My
brain was faster now, and none of the warning signs
that used to pop up when I was taunting death were
there to bother me. Another thing I'd have to get used
to. At three in the morning, roads devoid of traffic,
the rush of adrenaline still in my veins, a faulty laser
saber in my pocket, the only thing I wanted to do is
press on the gas and just go.

Fly away from the panic, from the arena, from the
faux-FBI agent who wanted my alien roommates and
her superfan partner who wanted an autograph.

I took long, deep breaths to try to calm myself
down, but it was no use. My feelings of panic were
just my muscles acting out of habit, the way my body
would normally react in this type of situation. But

somewhere deep in the back of my mind, I knew my body wasn't the least bit phased by what should have been a near-death experience. If I wanted the panic gone, I could switch it off, as easy as that.

I just needed to remember how that worked.

Agent Felling. James. My friend from before. Was she ever a friend? Before I offered myself up as bait to trap the Zoesh, she had been my guard, keeping me in that stupid hotel room in case I needed to be sacrificed by the government. I had said all I wanted to say, at least for now. Eventually, I would figure out what to do with her, but for now, I had more pressing issues to deal with.

I swung the wheel, spinning my car into a perfect parallel park that would have made my dad weep for joy. I gave myself a minute to admire it as I locked up, wondering if these skills would convert to space flight. Probably, but I'd need a jet to test it out. Right now, I had to get my story in order. Zander was probably worried sick I was out this long and this late.

I could hear them before I even made it to the stairs, and it wasn't thanks to my newly enhanced senses. The clash of steel against steel carried far, loud enough to wake the dead. Never mind that my neighbors were people who didn't even wake when a mysterious group of black-clad men had tried to kidnap me from my apartment only a month before. And now, I had just shooed away the only person who could have kept the cops at bay.

Beyond my apartment door, a sword fight was in full swing because what else are two space-traveling immortals to do when you step out for a few hours? Two days on Earth, settling in for a good, relaxing break, and they were still sparring, with swords from who knew where. I certainly didn't own any.

I thought the no-swordfights-in-my-apartment policy would have been a no-brainer, but, apparently, I should have made a list of appropriate activities to go along with the wi-fi password. I hoped they knew better than to bleed all over the Derzan-damned carpet. Not that either of them would ever slip up so badly.

It was less of a ferocious sword fight and more of light fencing, especially by their standards. I had seen them do much worse with what anyone would call non-weapons. Left hands behind their backs, right hands swashbuckling up and down my living room. Zander with a hopeful smile plastered on his face, Blayde frowning, a feature that had been permanently etched on her face since we returned from the library empty-handed.

So much for no blood. With a gentle slice, Blayde lost the fight, along with a cute blouse of mine in the process. Her brother knocked her over the sofa with a well-placed jab as he turned to me, smiling.

"Swords? Seriously?" I chided, cutting off whatever Zander was going to say. He snapped his mouth shut. "Do you have any idea what time it is? It's so late it's early."

"I promise we didn't damage the furniture." He offered a hand to Blayde, lifting her easily off the floor. She blinked incredulously at him.

"I have neighbors, you know," I said, hands on my hips, trying my best to be imposing, which was difficult when there were two swords in the room and neither were in my hands. Though, admittedly, I had a malfunctioning laser saber in my pocket.

"I thought Jules was cool with this."

"Sword fighting? What kind of neighbor would be cool with sword fighting?"

"A pirate," Blayde scoffed, stuffing her hands in her pockets, though I knew she could have come up with a more poignant irony if she put her mind to it.

"Jules is not a pirate."

"Then what's with the...?" Zander made a loopy sign by his ear. "Gold earring?"

"What? Everyone likes earrings. I like earrings, and it doesn't make me a pirate."

"Dang, this makes your planet even less cool," said Zander. "I remember when sword fights were all people talked about. Yet I haven't found anyone who wants to give it a go."

"Stop reminding me. Now where on earth did you get those swords? They look sharp." I eyed the cut through Blayde's shirt. Though the wound had stitched back together, the blood on the blouse was still there. No point in bleaching it; I wasn't going to be able to fix that fabric. "Not something someone would sell on any street corner."

"Yard sale," said Zander, throwing a glance to the kitchen. His eyes widened as he saw the clock. "Sally, where have you been for, *veesh,* seven hours? I was worried sick!"

"No, you weren't. You were sparring. And you can't seriously tell me you have been sparring since I left."

"Well, it took a lot of time to track down a good dueling pair, you know. Blayde and I..."

The guest room door slammed shut. Blayde had slipped out of the conversation without either of us noticing, closing herself off in the small room, the same place she had been hiding every day since our return. I exchanged a look with Zander.

"You actually got her to go outside?"

He nodded. "A few hours. We mostly walked. I'm happy we found the swords. It distracted her for a bit."

My heart sank. Of course. Stabbing her brother was practically therapy in Blayde's book. My anger could have set back her recovery who knew how far. My face flushed.

"Zander, I'm so sorry—"

He shook his head. "Don't be. You're right. Sparring at this hour wasn't wise. I was just happy to see her up out of bed."

"We'll get there. One day at a time, right?"

EARTHSTUCK

It was impossible seeing her like this, as if the centuries were suddenly catching up to her, leaving her dull and dreary. Was I like that before therapy? It was hard to remember the weeks after John's death; the memories that did remain felt as if they were made at a distance.

I knew what it was like to lose someone, but I'd never known a loss like hers. I'd lost family; she'd lost her world. Her entire history had gone up in flames at her own hand.

"Are you deflecting?" His tone suddenly shifted. "Distracting from your disappearing act?"

"How did you know? Did someone from Jitterbug call? Oh crap, Mona doesn't know you're alive, does she?"

"What are you talking about?"

"Shit. You meant that figuratively, didn't you?"

He froze in the middle of putting the swords back into an ornate case propped open on the coffee table. Looking back at me, his eyes bulged. "Is that blood?"

"Yeah, got into a fight with a short-tempered alien space pig and his rock buddy. But, hey, at least I got back on my own, right?"

Zander bit his lip. I stuffed my hands into my coat pockets again and, finding my laser saber, chose to fiddle with that instead.

"Stars, Sally. If you had gotten lost out there... it's not just space, it's—"

"It's time, too, I know," I said, letting out a breath.

"It's not like I wanted to jump. I ran into someone who shouldn't have been here. It's okay, though, right? I'm back, and that's what matters."

"Someone scared you into another dimension, and that's okay with you?"

"Well, no, but I'm trying not to dwell, all right? It's been an awful day, and I just want to—"

"I'll make some tea."

In moments like these, it was hard to imagine he had ever left me. It was as if Zander had never jumped from the apartment, had never been away from my life for as long as he had been. That maybe I was still entirely human, and my life still had a chance, however slim it may be, to return to normal.

But, then, my alien boyfriend checked the water by boiling his own finger, and that illusion went out the window.

"You're going to have to learn to control it," he said, avoiding my gaze. The boil on his finger formed then faded in an instant.

"So far, easy. Don't shock me."

"Emotionally or electrically?"

"The former. Though let's avoid both."

"That's what triggered it? Fear? Panic?" He opened the cupboard, sorting through teas and picking one with soothing chamomile. "Give me one good reason not to hunt down this person."

"Because that's exactly what she wants."

He paused, putting the box of tea bags back on the counter. "She knows about us?"

I nodded. "She knew about you before I did. And a surprising amount too."

I was surprised Zander wasn't more shocked hearing this, but he didn't seem fazed. "Someone was bound to track us down eventually. What does she want?"

"Apparently, they need you to solve a murder. *They* being the FBI, but more likely the real-life Men in Black."

Zander froze, tea bag in each hand, and laughed so loudly it could have woken up not just my building but the entire neighborhood. I sank further into the couch.

"*Veesh!* I was expecting you to say something like alien testing or shady government experiments. Not, you know, Zander and Blayde, private investigators!"

"The worst is that we used to be friends. She trusted me; I trusted her." I paused. "At least, I think we did. A lot has changed since, well, everything."

"Nimien, Matt, Sky People, and World Eater—all that." He nodded, returning from the kitchen with two steaming mugs. "What's that?"

"You tell me." I tossed him the laser saber. "I ended up in a gladiator fight. Got me a free weapon."

"Oh! I haven't seen one of these in ages!"

With a violent jerk, the laser saber came to life. The red beam cut a beautiful hole through Zander's eye and out the back of his head, but he was master of the one-eyeball eye roll.

"Splendid."

"Ha! I did the same thing!" I slapped my thigh. "And all this time, I thought Luke was an idiot for staring down the barrel of his father's saber. I guess it's a common trend in the universe."

There was something hauntingly beautiful about the rebuilding of his eye, his brain. The fabric of his body weaving itself together, small tendrils of skin and bone fusing to make room for the most gorgeous silver-green iris I had ever seen. His hair filling out in the back, giving me only a few minutes of bald Zander.

I ran my fingers through the sprig of blossoming hair. It was thick and soft in my hands, like it had been cleaned and conditioned on its way back to life. This close to his face, I could smell his breath, the gentle tang of tea he had been drinking before I had come home.

And then, I was tasting it, too, his lips soft on mine, my body relaxing against his, feeling the warmth of him against my chilled skin. I hadn't known how cold I had been until his touch woke me up, and then I couldn't be aware of anything else except his perfect body against me, his arms wrapped around me and holding me close.

We were home. We were safe. And he was mine. I pulled myself away to breathe a sigh of relief, of joy, and he pressed his forehead against mine, nuzzling his nose against my cheek. I fell into him like I was dust and he was the sun.

Which was when the screaming began. We pulled apart, turning to the closed door.

"I've got her this time," he said, which went without saying since it was him every time. He planted a soft kiss on my forehead before slipping into Blayde's room, turning on the lights, and reaching for her before she got any worse.

I felt like an ass. Here I was, trying to romance her brother as she was falling apart in the other room. Blayde hadn't slept a full night since our return; every time she managed to close her eyes, she woke up screaming, thrashing. The first night, she had torn down the bookshelf. We cleared the room immediately, stuffing my junk into any nooks and crannies my apartment had left. Not the right time to KonMari my crap, but I did try, just to keep my mind off things.

It wasn't like any of this mattered in the long run. I was immortal now. I would have to give up my life on Earth sooner or later.

And here I was, thinking about myself again. I am a garbage person.

"Is she okay?" I asked, as he shut the door behind him.

He shook his head. "I'll stay with her in case she wakes up again."

"We need a more long-term solution than you depriving yourself of sleep until she gets better."

"There isn't exactly a therapist trained to deal with immortality here," he said. "Since there aren't any immortals out there in the first place. It would be a terrible-paying job."

"Florida!"

I was on my feet, flying to my room before Zander could bridge the distance between us. He leaped over the sofa as I pulled down my suitcase, ripping open my closet and flinging all my summer clothes into the open luggage.

"Florida?" he asked.

"Florida!"

"Is that a resort?"

I shook my head. "It's a state. More precisely, it's the state my parents live in."

"Ah, Mars! It's a planet. It's very red!"

"What?"

"I don't know. I thought we were yelling out places with no discernible connection to current events."

"Oh. Right." I grabbed the drawer filled with Zander's shirts and upended it on top of mine. "It just hit me. We need a place to lay low from the not-FBI. Blayde needs somewhere to heal where it's not gloomy for months on end. We need sunshine. Ergo, Florida!"

Florida, Florida, Florida. A song ran through my mind, telling me everything would be better if we just went to Florida. To get away from people who recognized me here. To get away from a certain secret agent with undisclosed motives. To get away from myself.

Space was supposed to be my vacation. Instead, I had almost died until I reached the point where death was no longer an option. Time for a real break.

"By that logic, we should be going farther south. Australia?"

"Ah, but we have a place to stay in Florida. And local currency, which means we can get there by car and lay low off the government's radar. No credit card trail, you see?"

"Isn't this a bit hasty?"

"Oh, it'll be fine. My parents will love it. They keep telling me I need to come down for a visit."

"If you say so. I just think you're running away from something."

"So? I can do that sometimes, can't I?"

He held out my mug of tea. I still hadn't drunk any, and I was too busy to start now. "How much thought have you given this plan?"

"Exactly none." I closed the suitcase and then remembered I needed a toothbrush. Then I had a small meltdown when I remembered I didn't need to brush my teeth anymore. Only, I probably should, anyway, because of halitosis, or was that something invented in the 80s to sell more mouthwash?

"Sally, you need sleep." The hand on my shoulder

was reassuring, too much so. I couldn't focus on him right now. I had to get us all to safety. I had to get Blayde better again. I had to…

I nodded slowly. I was doing a lot of that lately. My hands shook as I zipped my suitcase shut, my trembling fingers barely responding to my commands. Was it true panic coursing through my veins? Or just the memory of how I should react?

How real was anything that I was feeling right now?

"I need to talk to my mom first," I said.

"Not at four in the morning, you don't."

"Fair point."

He handed me my tea. When he had gone to get it, I hadn't seen. But the mug was still warm, still comforting in my hands. Zander planted more kisses on my forehead in a row by the first, reaching behind me for the suitcase so he could wheel it out into the hallway. The place his lips had touched my skin warmed like my fingers against the mug. I drank it in.

This was going to work; I knew it. Florida will do me good, do us good. Nothing could go wrong there.

I mean, it's Florida. How bad could it be?

THREE

THE GREAT AMERICAN ROAD TRIP
AIN'T ALL IT'S CRACKED UP TO BE

BELIEVE IT OR NOT, BLAYDE WAS RELIEVED WHEN I told her we were driving all the way to Florida—something to do with hating public transport. Understandable, in her line of work.

I tried to lift everyone's spirits at the prospect of a bona fide road trip, a true Terran experience. Zander was over the moon. By the time I had everything packed, he had returned from CVS with bags upon bags of chips, cookies, and enough soda to propel ourselves into orbit.

"Took you long enough," I said, stuffing the bags into the trunk around our suitcases.

"Got into an impossibly deep conversation with the cashier. She asked how I was doing, and, well, it's a long answer. Put this on!" He tossed a sweatshirt to Blayde, who was sprawled across the back seat, one arm flung over her eyes to keep out the light and the duffel on her lap crushing her as I packed the car around her. Blayde didn't own many clothes, instead borrowing everything from me, and the items she didn't hate had been carefully folded into the my duffel. She had wrapped her arms so tightly around it we wouldn't have been able to pry it off her with a crowbar.

"I'm not cold," she said.

"It's to fit in with the general population," Zander replied. "We're trying to be covert, aren't we?"

"I'm not sure matching *'Virginia is for lovers'* sweatshirts are considered covert," I said, putting on the one he had gotten me. In our identical hoodies, we looked like a local improv group on tour or maybe an eclectic a Capella team from a Virginian liberal arts college. Come to think about it, the idea might have been genius.

We hit the road on that crisp February morning, Blayde falling asleep instantly cocooned in her oversized sweatshirt. I had to keep myself from staring at her dressed like that, sleeping so deeply I could barely see the terrifying warrior in her features anymore. It was like putting a Snuggie on a Doberman.

Just like that, she was out, and the silence belonged to Zander and me.

Alone—for the most part.

For twelve hours—just about.

Both avoiding the conversation we should have had the second we'd come back, but one neither of us could face because of the depressed immortal alien we were trying to care for.

Or maybe she was just an excuse.

"So," said Zander, almost like he was reading my mind. I drummed my fingers on the steering wheel.

"So?"

"You see, the downside to your road-trip plan is that you can't shut up our conversation by kissing me."

"I'm shutting you up?" I scoffed, feeling my shoulders tighten. What was wrong with me that I couldn't have a normal conversation anymore? "I thought you were the one instigating all the kissing."

"Some, I'll admit. I read an online listicle that said—"

"You read an *online listicle?*" I laughed then cringed, checking on Blayde to make sure I hadn't woken her up. "I never thought I would hear you say those words. And in this context, no less."

"You're trying to divert the question."

"You haven't actually asked a question!"

"What is our relationship?"

"So, we *are* in a relationship?"

"How should I know? What's Earth's policy on this? I might be pretty rusty on the mechanics of dating humans. I'm pretty sure there's something monumental in the fact I'm about to meet your parents."

"I don't know for sure. There are no handbooks for dating aliens. And trust me, don't look them up because the few that are out there are a little less than savory."

He let out a heavy sigh. "This is what I was talking about."

"Poorly written alien erotica? Sorry, I'm generalizing. I'm sure there's some wonderfully written alien erotica. I simply haven't read it."

"No, *this*. This lack of communication. I've been part of quite a few dating rituals—most involving feathers and a whole lot of choreography, some more in the spaceship-handstand category—and the ones that worked all had open communication."

"Can you please not bring up your past relationships? I'm not ready for that history lesson just yet."

"You see? This is something we should be talking about, yet there's been no real talking since we returned to Earth. Not like we used to. What happened to us?"

"You mean other than a library full of your hopes and dreams blowing up because of my creepy, manipulative ex? I think that's enough to make things… tense. We're different people now."

"No, we're really not. I left Earth last week, for me. And despite what you think, you're the same you who entered the library, just with a bit more time on your hands."

"Am I really?" It was hard to pay attention to the road now. My hands were shaking, and it took all my focus to keep the car straight. "It's just hard, you know. To realize from one day to the next you're not going to die."

"That feeling… it comes back from time to time. Eventually, though, you can't remember when it started."

"I'm afraid."

"Of what?"

"Of that. Of not remembering who I am. Of changing so much that I'm not myself anymore, but not caring because I have no recollection of who Sally Webber really is."

"You won't forget."

"You did."

"I think I wanted to, back then, anyway. Every time I struggle to find an old memory or if one pops up, I feel like there's something there telling me not to look. A warning from myself."

"Is that why Nimien remembered everything?" I shuddered. "He said he did, didn't he? He remembered, but he changed anyway."

"I don't think he truly wanted to forget. He has spent how many millennia planning his revenge? If you can't accept yourself, you can never forgive. As a result, he lost himself completely. You're not like that."

"So, what'll happen to me?"

"Whatever you want to happen."

"I want to stay myself. Already I'm different. Hell, Zander, I killed a man. And I know he's not really dead, but I did that. I wrung his neck until the life left his body. And on top of that, I traveled through time. I messed with time itself, Zander! There should be consequences for this. I'm being punished, and I can't—"

"You survived." His hand found mine on the steering wheel, and the trembling stopped, if only for an instant. "You are so strong, Sally Webber. And you're not going to be punished for being strong. You did what you had to do. You didn't need anyone else to help you with that. In fact, you saved my life. So, stop punishing yourself because you think you deserve it. Blayde needs to heal and so do you. Accept it."

"But I am healed. I'm always healing. Already, I can't feel pain. Am I even human anymore?"

"Human? How do you even define 'human?' Yes, you were born to the *Homo sapiens* species. But what does that matter in the scale of the universe? What matters more: who you were born to or who you are? And you are Sally Webber."

"Even though I wish it would matter—and I believe it matters—why, in the whole scale of things, does it?"

"Sally," he said, suddenly serious, "I've lived for so many years I've lost count. I've traveled from one end of the universe to the other. I've been to planets you've never imagined and galaxies beyond your wildest dreams. I've seen civilizations rise in an apogee of brilliance of genius and seen them fall in the blood of war. I've seen people come and go; I've seen them love and hate; I've seen loyalty and betrayal, hope, fear, rage, and serenity. Witnessed the death of a star, the birth of a world. And in all that time, there's only one thing of which I am entirely certain and can say with complete honesty. I am completely and irrevocably in love with Sally Webber." My eyes filled with tears now, rolling down my face in fat lumps. "Oh frash, I didn't mean to make you cry."

"It's not you." I sniffled, stopping the tears in their tracks. "Actually, yes, it is you, you sweet sonuvabitch. I also didn't know you were such a romantic." I let out an awkward laugh. Shit. Not a healthy reaction. I was a bit overwhelmed, after all. "I want to say all that back, but I don't have the words like you do."

"Let's keep it simple, then. Back at the library, you said you loved me. Did you mean it?"

"Of course, I meant it. I love you, and I should have been telling you that every minute of every day since we came back."

He let out a breath so deep I didn't think his lungs had the capacity for such relief. The sound sublimated my tears into laughter in an instant.

"What?" he asked.

"I found you outside of the universe and broke the

laws of physics for you, and you still thought I didn't really mean it when I said I love you?" I chided. "What do I have to do next? Conjure Derzan out of thin air?"

Now he was laughing too. "I love you too. By gods, I love you too," he said, the relief palpable. "I was so scared you'd tell me that all this changed that. That that was why you didn't want us to talk."

"The great and powerful Zander, scared?" I was shaking now, but not from fear anymore. "I love you. I want to say some grandiose thing because the words don't feel like enough, but I can't find anything bigger than them. And it's like a weight is lifted from my chest every time I get to tell you that I love you. It's not a secret anymore. It's not something I have to push down or drown out. I love you. And I love being free to love you, you know?"

"I take back what I said earlier." His hand dropped from the steering wheel to my knee. "The car is a terrible place for this kind of conversation."

I knew what he meant. At that moment, I wanted to leave the car to make its own way to Florida, to find his lips and speak to him with something deeper than words. His lips, that tongue, the warmth of Zander all around me, I could so easily dive into him and stay in his embrace.

"Forever is terrifying," he said, pulling away, "but I'm here for you, every step of the way. And that's a promise I intend to keep. Putting the 'F' in BFF, right?"

I almost swerved the car off the road as I caught Blayde in the rear-view mirror, awake and wide-eyed, munching on Chips Ahoy. Her gaze met mine, and she froze mid-bite.

"You're gross," she said. "But just so you know, I love you too."

My heart fluttered. "Thanks, Blayde, you know that—"

"I was talking to the cookies, but sure, whatever floats your goat."

I drove for another hour, stopped for snacks, then we switched. Zander took the wheel as Blayde nursed an extra-large strawberry milkshake in the backseat. We hit a diner for dinner, switched again, and I was now driving again, our games of *I Spy* getting less interesting as the day turned to night.

Despite never going to visit, I loved my parents' home. It was right off the water, the ocean breeze filling every room with fresh, salty air and the constant nuisance of sand, the one making up for the other. My mother decorated everything in an almost minimalist way, leaving everything to look airy and light, whites and blues with a hint of wood to balance everything out. It was always spotless, as if no one lived in this showroom at all.

They had moved here following John's death. None of us could stand our old home anymore: a family house had memories crammed into every crack of the floorboards, every chip in the paint. After I moved out, my parents decided on early retirement, and settled in Florida. I had hated them for it at first, and it had taken me years of therapy to realize that me running off to university wasn't just embracing a new chapter, but it was an escape as well.

It was late into the night when I pulled into the driveway. The second the car shut off, I gasped. I had forgotten how thick the air was down here, the sticky sweetness of it. For a second, I sat there, hands on the steering wheel, feeling my palms sweat into the plastic. None of this should have bothered me, not by Zander's account. My new and improved body should have ignored the heat and humidity. I shouldn't be wanting to claw my sweatshirt off.

"You all right?" Zander's hand at my wrist made me jump. He wasn't sweating. No, he looked quite at ease in the new air. Blayde was already slamming the car door shut behind her, not waiting on either of us.

"Yeah," I replied.

"Hard to be back?"

I nodded. That wasn't the whole story, but it was the only one I was able to tell. I slipped out of the car into the warm Saint Pete night, gagging on the humidity while simultaneously relishing the feeling of solid earth beneath my feet.

My mom was waiting on the porch, the light suddenly on, warm and red and welcoming. She opened her arms wide. And I, the terrible daughter I was, saw her in that instant cast in long shadows with all her wrinkles highlighted as if with a Sharpie and realized that one day I would be here and she wouldn't. I would outlive her, my planet, and who knew what else.

"Sally!" She stepped forward with arms outstretched. "It's been so long!"

I rushed to her and wound myself around her in the tightest hug I could muster. My mom was here, I was here, and everything was going to be all right. Mommy would kiss it better. I was going to make it through this. It took everything in my power not to break down on her shoulder. She wouldn't notice the tear that had already dried on her sweater. She hugged me back, harder than ever.

"My god," she said, and I pulled away, but her eyes were on Zander. "You look just like him."

He nodded. "Identical twins."

Mom reached over to shake his hand. "I never knew your brother, but he was a good friend to Sally. I'm so sorry for your loss."

Zander put on a good show of looking heartbroken, shaking her hand while wiping away a tear with the corner of his sleeve.

"And this is Blayde," I said. She stood farther back on the driveway, clutching my duffel to her chest. "Zander's sister. The one who connected us in the first place."

"Blayde." She smiled, extending her hand. "Curious name. Where are you from?"

Blayde's body remained frozen as a popsicle, looking to Zander for help, seemingly only two feet tall. She looked back to my mom. "London. Veen. I mean, Earth. I mean, no. Why do you ask? Where are you from?" She blurted out, one word tumbling out after the other.

Mom gave her the most mothering smile she could muster. I had seen the look before; she had given it to me so many times in the past few years. The one my therapist told her was best.

"It's such a pleasure to finally meet you, Blayde," she said. "I'm sorry for your loss as well."

Blayde turned her gaze to the ground and spoke no more. Mom shot me a glance, and I nodded, though I wasn't quite sure of the question. *Yes, this is why we are here* seemed the most reasonable answer.

"Pleasure to meet you, Mrs. Webber," Zander said, layering his voice with good-natured charm as he wrapped an arm around Blayde to usher her forward.

"Just call me Laurie, please. Need any help with your bags?"

Zander ended up grabbing both of our small suitcases from the back, while Blayde trudged in after my mother, duffel in a tight embrace. The house hadn't changed since my last visit, all perfectly clean and proper, uncluttered by heavy furniture or knickknacks. Good old reliable homestead. Blayde's eyes darted back and forth across the room, scoping out her new environment.

"What a lovely home!" exclaimed Zander as he shut the door behind him. "So much room for"—he read something small off his hand— "surfing!"

With a bark, a fluffy, brown comet barreled into his legs. He threw up his hands in terror as the tiny dog made circles around first his legs then Blayde's. She squeezed the duffel tighter, frozen in place.

"What the?" Blayde sputtered as the small creature sniffed her shoes, nose to the ground. The dog then proceeded to inspect Zander before coming to me, her whole back end wagging in excitement. I laughed, crouching down to greet her.

"What... exactly is this?" asked Zander through gritted teeth and a forced smile. I scratched the doggy behind the ears, and she closed her eyes, leaning into my fingers.

"It's a dog." They still didn't relax. "Come on, Zander. You've seen loads of dogs out and about in town."

"Never got this close to one." He gulped.

"What's gotten into you? Galli wouldn't hurt a fly." I picked up the small dog as she frantically licked my face.

"It has a name?"

"*She's* a pet, Zander. Get over it. She's a sweetie pie." I put her back down. Blayde shook her head, saying nothing. Galli gave her one of those trademarked puppy-dog stares but after finding no additional pets, took off toward the kitchen, long ears flapping behind her.

"You didn't tell me your parents had a dog," he said.

"You've dealt with much worse than a house pet before."

He said nothing, which made my gut twist for some reason. Before I could put my finger on why, my father had flown out of the kitchen and wrapped me into a hug so tight he almost squeezed me out of existence.

"You're back!" he exclaimed, his voice muffled by the hug. I pulled away with surprising strength.

"Hey, Dad." I was happy to see he was beaming as much as I was. "I want you to meet Zander and Blayde."

"And that's Xander with an 'X,' right?" he asked, reaching to shake Zander's hand. "That must have been confusing growing up."

"You have no idea." The two shared a quick laugh. "Lysander and Alexander, and we both wanted the same nickname. Ended up going by nearly the same thing. You get used to it."

"It's late, so I've got your beds all ready," said Mom, emerging from the library nook. "Zander, you'll be in here. Sally, you and Blayde have your room. I hope that's okay."

"That's perfect. Thanks, Mom."

The room upstairs wasn't exactly *my* room. I hadn't had a room in my parents' house since they moved out of my childhood home. They simply rearranged the den whenever I came down, setting up a cot in the corner like it had been waiting for me all along. A blow-up mattress had been placed against the opposite wall to make room for my extra guest, and, for a second, I felt like a kid walking into her first slumber party. Blayde followed me dutifully up the stairs, still clutching my duffel like her life depended on it.

"You go ahead and take the bed," I told her, wheeling my suitcase to the blow-up mattress. "You're the guest, after all."

She grumbled her thanks and flopped down on the mattress. She was out like a light, the bag still crushing her gut.

I slipped out of the den, switching off the light to give her space to rest. Downstairs, Zander had been shown to his makeshift room—the couch in front of the bookshelves in the little breakfast nook by the kitchen—but my father was so enamored by this sudden male presence that he couldn't seem to leave him alone.

"You a steak man?" he asked, and my mom held back a laugh, gliding past the two of them into the kitchen. Galli couldn't decide what to make of the stranger, so she sat next to the fridge, hoping someone would give her cheese. Seeing Zander surrounded by the normalcy that was my family suddenly made everything feel even less real than they were this morning.

"Your friends seem lovely," said Mom, snapping me out of my thoughts. She handed me a mug of hot chocolate I hadn't seen her prepare.

"They're wonderful people," I agreed. The chocolate was heavenly, sending warmth tingling down my spine. She pulled another mug from the microwave and brought it over to Zander, who was still engaged with my dad, though his wide eyes were more like a deer in headlights than a man in conversation.

"Adventure journalism," he said in answer to a question I hadn't heard, before taking a sip from his mug. "Sometimes photography. Does the term 'explorer' work for you?"

"You travel much?"

He laughed wholeheartedly. "More than I'm ready to admit."

"You seem rather young, though, aren't you?"

"Stop hassling him, Hal." Mom brandished another mug and pushed it into his hands before turning to me. "Where's your other friend?"

"She's zonked out," I replied. Zander's shoulders sagged, and he took a sip of cocoa to mask his frown.

"It is pretty late," said Mom, placing a hand on my shoulder. "I should let you all get to bed."

"Hold on, I want to know more about adventure photography."

"Hal, bed!" Galli followed them out of the room, throwing a quick glance at me before deciding the parents were definitely more interesting. Zander and I stared at each other over our piping hot mugs as my parents slipped away, and I felt the tension leave my body. We were here. We were safe. And, for once, I had been the one to take care of us three.

"I should go, too," I said, awkwardly.

"You don't have to. I meant what I said earlier. If you need to talk—"

"No, Zander, really, I'm fine," I said, punctuating my sentence with a genuine smile. "We're on vacation now! We can start on all the classic Florida hotspots. Cape Canaveral! Disney World! Universal Studios! I mean we have a bit of a drive, but nothing like today."

"Disney World?" He squinted. "Oh, right, time travel. You don't have the planet yet."

"You have to stop dropping all this future stuff on me, please?"

"Of course." He reached forward for a kiss, his hand settling on my mug instead. "Are you going to finish your cocoa?"

My face was still warm when I got into bed, staring up at the ceiling, Blayde's quiet breaths setting the rhythm of the room. No panic from her tonight, not yet. I closed my eyes, trying to will myself to sleep too.

I wanted to get up, sit by Zander's side, and tell him everything. Why I wanted to come to Florida when running from Felling. But it was unfair of me, so unfair, to ask him to sit and listen to my fears about my family when he had lost his own so many years ago. My decision at the hands of Nim had forced me to sacrifice a normal relationship with my parents, and I couldn't make him feel worse than he already did. He was the only one of us to make it out of the library mentally and physically unscathed, and he deserved all the peace he could get.

I would have to make peace with the fact that my time with my family was limited now. I had to make it count.

FOUR
MALL MADNESS
AND OTHER EXTREME SPORTS

THAT NEXT MORNING, I WOKE UP SMILING. TWO seconds later, I remembered that whole pesky immortality bit and the part where I was being stalked by an FBI agent, and it turned my smile upside down. I needed breakfast.

I pulled myself off the air mattress, stumbling out of my bedroom door and making my way down the stairs one foot at a time, gaining balance as I slowly woke up. Both Zander and my mother were sitting on the back porch, noses in newspapers. As if feeling my gaze, Zander looked up and beamed, his smile exploding at the sight of me.

"Laurie and I are having coffee," he said, pointing to the mug. "There's more in the kitchen if you want any."

I cringed. Zander and coffee didn't mix well. "You... you feeling all right this morning?"

He let out a small giggle. *Crap. I thought he knew better. Hold on, was I also supposed to stop my coffee habit now that I was like him? Did immortality mean no coffee?* "I'm wonderful, just wonderful. Here, you just have to read this."

He shuffled the paper around and shoved it into my hands, angling the article under my thumb, squished between the obituary of a famous rodeo clown and the breakup of the infamous power couple with an obscure name I couldn't for the life of me split into its compound units. He was right; this was much more important than coffee.

"The Mayans predicted the spaceship hoax?" I scoffed. But as ridiculous as the claim seemed, knowing that the jerkface emperor and golden pyramid had been on Earth, this story had a kernel of truth. And that was enough to send me into a panic.

"Do you need to sit down? You can take my seat. I need more coffee, anyway."

"No!" I shouted, a little too loudly. "Um, I'm good. But don't drink too much. You know what it does for your heartburn."

Mom let out a small laugh from her seat at the edge of the porch. "You two sound like an old married couple."

"We're neither old nor married, Mom." I pretended to ignore the look Zander was giving me—it was surely coffee induced anyway—as I skimmed the rest of the article.

"'Archeologist Joseph Malone believes he has managed to translate the pictograms on the wall of an ancient Mayan city in Mexico. Malone has been studying the pictures for most of his academic life, but his belief that the recent alien hoax was no hoax at all and was the key to finally understanding the story. According to his report, the Mayans had seen a goddess arrive, and she protected their world from an alien attack. After the victory, she ascended to the heavens, leaving an immortal to rule on earth as her representative.

"'The strange part of this story is the chronology," says Malone. "Has it already happened, or is it yet to happen? Or has it happened many times before? The Mayan symbol for 'cycle' is placed as an affix to the legend, a sign that history may repeat itself.'"

"Time is an ill-*uuuuu*-sion," Zander chanted. I shoved the newspaper back at him, retrieving his mug.

"Aliens. On the walls of Mayan temples?" I shuddered. If the goddess was meant to be me, I needed a makeover. This was getting out of hand. Serena should still be around, though, in one form or another. Maybe I could…

"Good morning, Blayde. Did you sleep well?" My mother rose to her feet as Blayde slipped out of the sliding door, still in the same clothing as yesterday. She sported a delicate frown this morning.

"Good morning, Mrs. Webber. Thank you for the comfortable accommodation. I slept very well."

"Laurie, please." My mother ushered Blayde to her seat. "I'm so glad you did. Would you like some breakfast?"

"I already ate. I'm sorry you're going to have to buy more oatmeal. I seem to have finished your box."

"You must have been really hungry," Mom exclaimed. "There was quite a bit left."

"I must have," she agreed. "But I recommend maybe choosing a different brand. next time. It was really dry."

"Really? I've been buying this one for years. How much water did you add?"

"Water?"

Mom slipped back inside, a bemused look on her face as she slid the glass door shut behind her, leaving the three of us alone on the sandy porch.

"So," I said, switching on the event planner in me, "I'll take Blayde to the mall this morning so she can get real clothing, not just hand-me-downs from me. Then we hit the beach when we get back."

"Aren't we going to talk about the article?" asked Zander.

"What is there to talk about? It's another academic trying for his fifteen minutes of fame in the wake of an international crisis. He's on page eight. Nobody cares anymore."

"But we know the truth," he said, dropping his

voice to a whisper. I followed his gaze to the kitchen where my parents were pouring each other cup of coffee. "And sooner or later, the rest of the world will too."

"No, they won't. Felling won't let them."

"I still don't understand what this Felling person does?"

"Me neither. But retail therapy should make us feel a little better about that."

A few minutes later, we were dressed and ready to go. I ran into Dad, who was lamenting the death of Vasquez, whose days were cut short by drugs, and how he seriously hoped I wasn't on 'em, and then we were out the door.

Alien shopping trips were full of judgment, and most of it was well deserved. The first time I took one shopping, I made it out relatively unscathed, though with a twinge of embarrassment for all of humanity. The second time was the same, except with a lot less smiling and a whole lot more snark.

And the unscathed part was challenged more than once.

Even without words, Blayde was master of snark. All it took was one glance at the dance of her fingers across the hangers, a delicate pinch of someone who didn't want to dirty herself with the best ready-to-wear clothing Terrans had to offer. Her face remained the blank slate it had been since the library, but her body told the whole story. At least she hadn't been this picky when it came to sharing my wardrobe. She was starting to look like one of those evil alternate-reality people, the kind who went around chanting about the wonders of imperialism in that parallel universe everyone avoided.

"Anything you like?" I asked, despite the obvious. I watched her fingers moving each item one by one down the rack, awed by how delicate they were. I had seen this woman destroy metal cyclops three times her size with those tiny hands, which seemed better suited for piano than murder.

"Not particularly. Let me reiterate: I am fine wearing what you loaned me."

"No offense, but I'm not." Already I was pulling jeans off the rack for her, slim fit in dark colors she couldn't say no to. "Your swashbuckling already cost me one of my favorite blouses, and I'm not ready to lose a new one."

"That's fair, but I could just go back to my clothes. I'm used to wearing them repeatedly."

"Yes," I said for the millionth time. "Metallic bell-bottoms are... not of this time period."

"But they're Infiniweave! Completely pliable. Like wearing nothing at all."

"Yup, I can tell, and so can most people on this planet." I handed her a nice collection of denim, making sure she took them out of my hands. "You go try it on in the dressing room right over there."

"They look good. We can go."

"Blayde, come on. When's the last time you went shopping? You know how this works."

"No," she grunted. "It's been more of a 'grab what you can get, pay quickly' lifestyle up to now."

"Even your brother was more compliant than you."

"Zander loves his costumes. Not as much as he loves you, but close."

"Oh no, you can't sweet talk your way out of this one. You need pants."

She trudged to the dressing room, muttering something under her breath even I couldn't decipher. When she returned, she pushed the entire bundle back at me.

"They all fit."

"Do you want them all?"

"I want my space pants, but I guess these will do."

At least we had her bottom half covered. Getting her to pick out shirts was going to be another story entirely. She trudged along beside me like a sullen teenager, hands stuffed deep in her sweatshirt pocket, eyes fixed straight ahead.

"We can stop in any one of these." I gestured to the window displays. "And, hey, if you behave, I'll get you some cinnamon pretzel bites."

"Don't patronize me," she snapped.

"I'm just saying. They're really good pretzels."

"If you say so."

"And besides, you act like a kid, I'll treat you like a kid."

I bit my tongue. I sounded like my mother. And in no way was I Blayde's mother. If anything, I was a glorified handler. Neither was a good look for me.

"I just don't understand why we have to buy clothing in a fairground," she muttered.

"What?"

She gestured at the merry-go-round before us. "I mean, this is not clothes."

"Oh, come on. I've been to Da-Duhui, remember? Having games and things inside a mall is not an outlandish premise."

"Then what do you call the children riding robots?"

"Obnoxious. Can you stop with the whole Earth meta-commentary, please?"

"Fine. What about here, then?" she said, coolly, waving at the Hot Topic. "They seem to have a lot of shirts."

"Are you trying to drag out the teenage thing?"

"Do I look like someone who knows the cultural habits of pubescent Terrans?"

"Good point."

I hadn't stepped in a Hot Topic since my uber-mild-emo phase, but the mere fact Blayde was taking initiative meant I couldn't turn her down. The store was deserted, but the vibe was still the same: a wall of band and pop-culture shirts, racks of clothes for all walks of life, some fun knickknacks, and accessories. Blayde stared at the wall while I looked through the new merch, trying to root myself in my time, my place, forcing my mind to focus on what was left of my Terran existence.

"You shouldn't be here," came a man's voice. I spun on my heels, but the only other person in the store besides me was Blayde, and she was too busy trying to make sense of band shirts than attempt to throw voices.

I turned back around and almost jumped out of existence. My heart gave a terrified leap, and I felt my atoms choosing to wing it in space rather than deal with this stranger before I reeled myself back in— quite successfully, I should add. Standing half an inch from my face was the only employee on staff, wearing, of all things, Kiss makeup. White grease paint was smeared down his cheeks, black diamonds on his eyes. It could have been impressive if it wasn't so startlingly close to my face.

"You shouldn't be here," the man repeated. He pulled his long, black hair up into a ponytail, flashing a glistening smile.

"Um, I'm sorry, do I know you?"

"You need to get out," he insisted, eyes staring right through me. I resisted the urge to shudder. Part of my mind kept insisting that phasing out into space was still an option, a part I had to keep telling to shut up.

"I'm pretty sure there isn't an age limit on this store, dude."

"I don't mean the store."

I could feel my forehead knot. "The mall?"

"Florida. This is our space. You can't just show up here and expect no one to notice."

"Is there a problem here?"

Blayde appeared at my shoulder, suddenly a whole foot taller than when we entered the store. For a second, I felt relieved that the Blayde I knew was back in action. A fraction of a second, before the meaning of the man's words hit home.

"You are," the man hissed. "You think we don't know you? *When the Iron and the Sand come to town, shit is going down,'* as the saying goes."

"Well," said Blayde, "that is an extremely lazy rhyme."

"I mean it. If we know you're here, you can bet your ass the Agency does. And we don't want the Alliance in Florida. Do you hear me?"

"The state seems big enough for all of us," said Blayde. "Besides, we're not doing anything except investing in the tourist industry. Aren't we, Sally?"

"Yeah," I said, as calmly as I could. I was beginning to see why the stranger was so highly made up. There was something in his features that wasn't quite right. "Wait. Is this a cover for alien residents?"

"Like you didn't know," he spat. "So like I said, will you kindly screw off or—"

Lightning fast, Blayde slapped him across the face. He slapped her back, the sound ringing through the empty store. She slapped him again. He returned the favor. *Slap, slap, slap, slap.* A facial game of ping-pong.

"Hey!" I reached between the two to push them apart. "Fine, dude, we'll leave your store. But you just lost paying customers."

"Get out of Florida. It belongs to us. We were here first!" he called out after us before Blayde shut him up with a handful of clothes she was no longer going to buy.

"Well, that was weird," I said as we returned to the mall's atrium, more confused than anything else. "Apparently, you have a fan."

She shrugged. "Apparently. But we're not on the Agency's radar, or they'd be after us already."

"The Agency?"

"You know how there are a few hundred aliens that visit Earth all nice and touristy? Like Mister Paint Face?"

"Uh-huh."

"Well, they have to get official papers to land here. The Alliance is making a pretty penny off your planet as a tourist attraction, and the Agency is how they manage their guests. If they catch you without a visa, they'll fine you until the inevitable heat death of the universe."

"Since when? I'm pretty sure the Youpaf didn't stop for papers. And Mr. Grisham loved the whole isolated vibe of the place. Wait, aren't the Killians their allies? Why didn't they help them?"

"Did you miss the part where they're called the Agency?" she asked. "I've never seen an agency actually do their job quickly. They probably have enough paperwork backed up to build you a second moon. Not to mention it's an Alliance outpost: no one who works for them actually wants to be here. Lazy as shit too. They've been using random name generators to come up with human aliases for their tourists. You can spot them miles away. Last time we tried to get a legal name here, Zander was given Sputnik Soda. And even I can tell that Paris Albatross is a terrible name for a Terran. "

"I'll name my next cat that."

"You don't want to do that. He was a terrible singer."

"So, why would that make you a danger to Florida exactly?"

"Who knows? I mean, we have a nice bounty on our heads. Can't remember why. But, however useless, capturing us means a lot of cash."

"That sounds more like a reason for the Florida aliens to want to keep you." A shiver ran down my spine as I became more aware of eyes on my neck. "Shit!"

I didn't know what the flash of light was, and I didn't want to waste time finding out. I grabbed Blayde around the shoulders and threw us both into the nearest storefront, just in time to see the floor where we had been standing turn a scorched black. From the safety of Spencer's Gifts, I gaped at the place I had almost been blown to smithereens, feeling my atoms reaching for safety outside of this planet. The air before my eyes flickered with spots of black, and I closed them, trying to force myself to stay.

Blayde was up on her feet in an instant, throwing herself into the clothing rack before our attacker had time to reload. Okay, not sure if super-silent laser beams needed reloading or not, but I threw myself into the rack with her just in case it didn't.

"What the hell was that?" I half sputtered. Half whispered.

"Either someone wants our heads or wants us out of Florida," she hissed in reply. "Probably time to call off our shopping trip."

"Is this some kind of ploy to avoid picking out shirts?"

"Sally, am I really the type of person to do that?" I didn't reply. "Okay, fine, but I'm not fooling around. Someone is after us."

The clothes parted in a flash. "Well, this is a surprise."

The man glaring down at us wore a store uniform, but I doubted he was a local. His blue Mohawk was an impressive feat of engineering, reaching for the sky like certain gala hairstyles I had seen, oh, I don't know, at a certain mayoral party halfway across the galaxy.

"You're not welcome here," he hissed. "Leave us the hell alone!"

He took a swipe at Blayde, who disappeared before his fist reached her, and collided with my jaw instead, sending a flash of heat through my face, the bones shattering.

Suddenly, Blayde was on his back, arm around his neck, choking him with a pink plastic tube, an impromptu bachelorette rodeo giving me the giveaway I needed. I flew from the rack, diving into an aisle of fluffy, pink Valentine's Day gimmicks as my jaw knit itself back together, filling my face with white fire.

Blayde pulled the tubing tighter, scowling. The blue-mohawked employee was desperately trying to buck her off, but she held fast. He folded himself in two, sending her flying off his shoulders and colliding with a stack of edible underwear on clearance.

He tossed the pink tube and the rest of the beer bong to the side as he threw himself at Blayde, who rolled out of the way just in time to avoid him. But now, Mister Kiss Face was here, flinging himself at her.

"This is exactly what I was saying!" he spat, and she jumped to the other side of the store. "You keep drawing attention!"

Blayde grabbed a lava lamp from its display behind

her and swung it by its cord over her head like a lasso. "I was trying to buy a shirt!"

Lava lamps are not supposed to be shaken like that, but it sure makes for the ideal projectile. It flew straight and true, crashing on the Mohawk guy and shattering into a mess of glass and hot goo. He screamed, grabbing the closest thing to him, which seemed to be some sort of plush phallus, flinging it at Blayde. It bounced off her confused face.

I spotted the gumball machine in the corner and flew at it, avoiding the two mall employees who were too focused on Blayde to pay attention to me anyway. I threw it on the floor, only for it to bounce back and roll, completely ruining my cartoon-inspired plan and pulling all eyes to me.

"And who the hell are you?" spat the Mohawk man, goopy former-lava running down his shirt. "You should be on our side!"

"And whose side would that be?" I spat right back, reaching behind me for a weapon and finding only hair extensions.

"Unofficial off-worlders," said the Kiss guy. "Isn't that what brings you to Florida?"

"We blend in well here," said the Mohawk man. "I mean, your skin wrap is good, but the face is wrong."

"There's nothing wrong with my face!" I shouted and pulled down the entire display. Which, of course, didn't do anything to distract the guys, only made the Mohawk man throw his hands up.

"Oh, come on!" he stammered, and I cringed, remembering my own days in retail. Then again, I'd never tried to kill customers, no matter how much they made me want to.

Lightning fast, the Kiss guy whipped out a blaster and took a shot at me. I threw myself back in the pink aisle to avoid it, stifling a scream at the sight of the hole in the wall behind me, a hole that had almost been me. I crawled down the aisle, hunting for anything I could use as a weapon, anything at all, but fluffy, pink handcuffs were probably not going to help.

"This is mall security!" a voice echoed through the store, sending my eyes rolling. Took him long enough. "Put down the weapon and come out with your hands up!"

I kept crawling. So much for staying incognito. We hadn't started this, and we weren't going to end it.

"Blayde," I hissed through gritted teeth, but she was nowhere to be seen. I crawled around the aisle into what seemed to be Bob Marley-inspired goodies, staring down and away at the scene unfolding in the front of the shop.

Then the security guard turned the corner and whipped out a blaster, which I was pretty sure isn't part of a mall cop's usual getup.

"Hands up, enabler!" he spat at me, and I scrambled back the way I'd come, hands and feet sliding on the cold tile.

"Sally!"

Blayde's voice came out of nowhere, and suddenly, there was a plastic dong smacking me in the face. The pink beer bong from earlier had been hiding a naughty secret, part of the bachelorette party fun. I tried not to think about it as I grabbed the end, pulling tight, our stretched rubber tube clotheslining the security guard, pulling his legs right out from under him. He fell flat on his face, brought down low by a willy bong.

Blayde leapt over him. "He's one of them. Jump!"

And she was gone. Outside the window, Blayde walked by, a confused onlooker clutching her shopping bag like she hadn't even set foot in the store to begin with.

Great. The only way out was through.

Or, quite literally, through. If I could jump along with her.

Then Blayde was back, throwing out her hand and grabbing my shoulder tight.

Now, I was outside the shop, watching it all go down, an onlooker like the rest of them, but annoyed at the three men—aliens—for ruining my girl time.

"You have your pants?" It was the only thing I could think of asking as Blayde marched up alongside me. My hands trembled against my sides.

"And shirts too," she replied, opening the bag slightly to show me her new finds.

"You robbed the store?"

"They tried to kill us. They owe us!"

I cringed inwardly. This was the Blayde I knew, bold and brave and furious, but this was my planet too. I thought I was a good person; I thought I was toeing the line. Instead, I was shoplifting with my bestie after trying to break a gumball machine.

The security guard made a good show of arresting his buddies. He took the Kiss guy's blaster, nodded, and discretely stuffed it under one of the displays. He glanced outside the store and was positively glaring at Blayde, who only looped her arm through mine and guided me away. And in an instant, it hit me that those men were not the only unofficial off-worlders in the mall that day.

There was a whole community of aliens in Florida, and we had walked right into it. Next time I decide on the holiday spots, have someone else please veto me.

FIVE

SECRET ALIEN BEACH HOLIDAY,
NOW WITH STALKERS

WHEN WE GOT HOME, DAD AND ZANDER WERE
bonding over some football,. By the look on Zander's
face, none of the rules made any sense, but Dad
didn't seem to care as long as Zander cheered for the
right team. How Dad had found a match to show him
that was running so early, I had no idea. Just seeing
Zander sitting there, shouting at the television from
the comfort of the sofa and waving his hands like his
owned the place, made my heart flip. It was all so
normal, so human.

Blayde pushed through with her bag of new
clothes, silent from the second we had left the mall. I
suppose that was to be expected. A single round of
head-bashing wasn't enough to solve her current
state.

"Success?" asked Zander, scooping some guac into his mouth with a chip.

"Super success," I said, but the look in Dad's eyes told me it wasn't the moment for any conversation not involving feet or balls. "Swim?"

Having a beach instead of a back yard was probably my favorite part of my parents' home. In a few minutes, we were all changed into our suits and rushing back out the door.

"Sunscreen! Sunscreen!" My mother yelled at us as we stepped outside, and we spent another few minutes rubbing cream all over our unbreakable bodies. And then we were out. On a beach, breathing the salty air, toes curling in the fine sand.

Two feet firmly planted on Earth. Breathe in, breathe out. You are home, Sally Webber. You are safe.

We set up our towels right out of reach of the waves, and I plopped myself down, happy to be able to relax, Blayde at my side, Zander rushing the waves.

"Do you like the beach?" I asked, hoping that our morning cardio had helped bring her back to a state of conversation. I could only guess at the turmoil inside her head, knowing from experience how difficult it was to speak when that black cloud guarded your tongue.

"I'm not exactly sure what I'm meant to be doing."

"Relax. Swim. Tan. Hey, is it possible for us to tan? I mean, with regenerative cells and all. Am I stuck with this color forever?"

"I honestly don't know." She shrugged, turning to the ocean, watching as Zander thrashed in the waves. He was fighting something, something that didn't want to be wrestled out of the water. Not sure who started it.

"You don't go to the beach?"

"Beaches have different customs over the universe," she explained, tracing sigils with her finger. "When we went to Llamar, beach etiquette was to bury yourself in the sand and let the nutrients soak into your skin. The sea was for lunatics."

"So, naturally, Zander."

"Naturally," she said. "And myself, once it was obvious he needed retrieving. You don't throw yourself at the mercy of whale cultists without backup."

"Wait. Was the cult worshipping whales, or were they—"

"They really appreciated human sacrifice: it meant their ad campaign was working. But I wasn't much of a believer in the sipping of the great straw to bring upon the end times. Catchy hymns, though. I was singing about the Great Sip-Sip for weeks afterwards."

As the distant thrashing ebbed into silence, Zander turned to face us, cradling in his arms a hammerhead shark, who wasn't all that happy to be out of the water.

"Put it back!" I shouted.

"What?"

"You heard me! Put. Down. The. Shark."

Zander dropped the beast into the water with a splash, and the terrified creature swam hastily away. He laughed, waving.

"Blayde!" he shouted, and suddenly, his antics made total sense. "Come on in. The water is fine!"

"No, thank you." She rolled over, dug a hole, and quite literally stuffed her head in the sand.

Zander's eyes closed for a second, but then he was back to his smiling self, waving at me instead. "You coming?"

"It depends. Is the shark still out there?"

His head bobbed in the ocean, farther out than I had expected him to be.

"Nah." Even from here, between the waves and the salt, I could see him break out in a smile. "What? You scared of a little shark?"

I dove into the waves, feeling the crisp water like soft, silky sheets against my skin. My muscles were powerful in the current, and I breached the surface whooping with joy. I threw my eyes open underwater, feeling the sting of salt but unperturbed by it. Life teemed under the waves. Little crabs and schools of fish swam by, avoiding me as I plunged through their domain, awed by the magnificence of the world under my feet. It was more alien to me than any other world I had set foot on.

Zander was waiting for me, now so far from the

shore that the house was nothing but a pinprick. His hair must have been impermeable. Even after swimming all this way, it still held its signature volume, each and every strand straining to reach the universe outside our atmosphere.

He swiped a hand through it. "Earth to Sally?"

"What?"

"You're staring," he said, removing his hand and letting the hair return to its usual takeoff position. "What's going on?"

"What do you mean?"

"Oh, come on. We're out of earshot of everyone and everything now. Except maybe that shark, if it likes eavesdropping. Something is obviously bothering you."

I shrugged, pushing myself a little deeper into the water. "Something happened at the mall, and I can't wrap my head around it. Actually, a lot of stuff happened."

I gave him the rundown—the unofficial off-worlders' threat and fear, all of Florida being some kind of weird haven, and Blayde's temporary transformation. He rubbed his hands on his face, letting out a breath of exasperation.

"I let you out of my sight for a few hours, and you almost get yourself killed?"

It was my turn to frown. "Zander, I can't die. And besides, I handled myself awesomely."

"But they attacked you because they saw you with Blayde. If we weren't in your life—"

"Stop that," I snapped. "You are, and this is a thing that happens. We're in this together. And somehow, having aliens to fight off is bringing the best out of Blayde, so we got a few outfits and made good progress on helping her heal. This morning sounds like a raging success to me."

He didn't look very happy about any of this.

"You need to stop worrying about me," I said. "And we need to stop worrying about Blayde. Because she is going to get better; we both know it. She just needs time."

"I'm not sure time is the best medicine with her."

"What do you propose? Stabbing her a few times to remind her how much she likes pointy things?"

"Well…"

"You can't be serious."

"I wouldn't be that direct," he said, his eyes fixed on his sister on the shore. "But if this morning proves anything, it's that Blayde isn't herself without a purpose. Trying to solve our past has driven us for so long, I don't quite know what to do with my eternity now that I have to put the search behind me."

"There has to be another way to get answers," I said. "Has to be. Nimien can't have been the only lead."

"But until we find the next direction, we're even more aimless than when I first met you. You see what it's done to Blayde. She needs a reason to get up in the morning."

"Then we'll find her one. But she's fragile right now, for lack of a better word. Unhinged, if you need a worse one. We can't stay in Florida, not with the off-worlders having an issue with us. But we also can't just pop into space and find her a cause."

"It's worked in the past. And besides, the universe is such a big mess, the odds of us stumbling on some good to do are in our favor. You saw that firsthand."

I wanted to remind him that Nimien had choreographed every one of those disasters but thought better of it. I was still trying to get a grip on my own guilt for bringing Blayde down here in the first place. I had been so sure she needed rest and calm to gather her thoughts and start to heal, but by the sounds of it, the opposite was true. She needed action and adventure, a quest to see her through until the end. What did Zander call it? Not a reason, a purpose. But finding someone a purpose was as probable as finding one's way through an infinite universe. How were we meant to find Blayde a reason to endure her eternity? And wasn't all this covering up the real problem with random distractions? My therapist would have a field day with this.

Speaking of distractions, Zander jutted his chin at the beach, making for a radical subject change. "That car's been there for a while, don't you think?"

I followed his gaze, to the black SUV parked at the

end of the development, three doors down from us, away from anybody's driveway. "What about it?"

"We're alone on the beach. Where are the drivers?"

I shrugged as the car drove off. "You see? It was just waiting there. Probably visiting a neighbor. Plus, don't you think if we were being spied on, they'd do it in a normal-looking car? Not a pitch-black, right-out-of-a-movie Ford Escalade?"

"Well, then, maybe it's that green one that's been following us," he said, pointing out another, just as it drove past my home. "I feel like I've seen it go by five times already."

"Or it's just a popular model this year." I shrugged. "It could be nothing."

"Or it could be anything. The off-worlders know we're here now. And we don't know how deep their network goes."

"I just need a little more time with my parents before we go anywhere," I said, reaching for his hand under the waves, pulling him close. "If they're going to be a distant memory for me one day, I want to make it a good one."

He nodded, and we swam back to the shore.

· · · · · · · · ● · ● · · · · · · · · · ·

Blayde went to bed early and was already asleep when I slipped into the room. I sat down on my mattress, sliding off sandy flip-flops I certainly should not have dragged through the house, swapping my clothes for comfy PJs. It was only when I silenced my phone and started to stretch out for my own sleep that I heard it.

A sob.

Blayde, actually crying. Not a heavy torrent of tears, but a slow, quiet drizzle. The kind where you pull into yourself but can't catch every overflowing drop. The kind when everything hurts, and you can't fully put your finger on why.

I didn't think. I got up and quietly crossed the room, wrapping an arm around her as I curled up against her back, letting her sob against my chest. She tensed, but if she wanted me gone, she could have snapped my body like a twig. I held on, offering her a life raft through the storm.

"What are you doing?" she asked, her voice so low I thought I had dreamed the words. This was the first time she had said anything unprompted since we came back from the library. I felt my heart lurch with pride.

"I can go," I said. "If you want to be alone, I can sleep on the couch."

"No, stay. Please stay."

I kept her hair out of her face as she sobbed into her pillow, every sob wracking through her body like she was a live wire. She clutched onto my wrist tight enough that the old me might have lost the entire hand. For hours, I held her like that, waiting for the storm to pass.

"Why does this hurt so damn much?" she said, her voice raw at this point.

"Do you want the scientific answer or a human one?"

"Why not both?"

"Because some words help you see clearer, and others make you feel better. The truth, more often than not, hurts even worse."

"Fine, give me the human answer."

"It hurts because it was important," I said, and she snorted. "Here, you want another one? It hurts because the universe has a plan, and something wonderful is coming your way."

"Whoopee," she grumbled. "Last time we thought the universe had a plan, it turned out you had a stalker."

My heart sank. "Thanks for reminding me."

"You want to come cry with me?"

"Gladly."

This time, we both cried, though being the bigger spoon made all of her hair stick to my wet face, which distracted me from the crying. But I had a right to cry, dammit. My life had changed way more than it was humanly allowed to, and that wasn't counting the stalker ex I murdered or the alien-hunting FBI gal. Everything was a mess.

"Now, can you give me the scientific reason?" asked Blayde, breaking my spiral of thoughts just when I needed her the most.

"Um, this is just a hypothesis," I replied, brushing her hair off my face. "But you know how this whole immortality thing means no pain?"

"My current predicaments would disagree with you." She nodded, pulling herself slightly away from me, tugging her sheets to wipe her eyes.

"No physical pain, I should say."

"This feels pretty physical."

"Stop interrupting." I sat up on the bed, and, for a second, I felt like I was twelve years old again, trading secrets with Marcy in the dead of night. But Marce was off on her honeymoon, and instead, I had my boyfriend's sister. "Right. So, this whole immortality thing means we don't need to worry about burns or cuts or even lightning strikes. Pain is a defense mechanism, alarm bells to stop our dumbass human selves from making a mess of our fragile bodies. Right?"

"Since we can't get permanently injured, no alarm bells."

"Exactly. That's how Zander explained it to me, but what kind of damage can we inflict on ourselves permanently?"

Blayde sat up straight. "Trauma. The things we see, the things we do. They mess us up for life, and since life, in our case, is eternal—"

"We're given an insanely loud alarm bell."

"So, why can't I remember anything being as bad as this before?" She tossed her pillow on the floor so she could scoot up to sit on the head of her bed. "Those kind of events would leave some kind of scars, no?"

"Maybe that's what reset you," I said, my fingers snapping despite myself. I grimaced at the sound.

"What?"

"Between the library visits. Every time you came and gave... the head librarian one of your journals. And then the next time, you didn't remember your last visit."

"I assumed I had just, I don't know, lived too long to remember anything else. Like going senile, but for immortals."

"Maybe. But someone was supplying you with all those identical red journals."

"Oh," she said. "I can't believe you're seeing the patterns, and I'm not."

"It's okay." I put my hand on her arm, giving it a squeeze. "You've been mind-stabbed. You need to recover a little."

"I can't stay here like this," she muttered. "What if my mind wipes itself clean? What if I forget all this, and the cycle begins all over again?"

"We broke the cycle. The library is gone."

"All those journals." Her gaze went blank, her frown stony and cold. "All those memories. Gone."

I looked down at my hands. Blayde may have been the one to have lit the match, but I was the reason Nimien had manipulated them. His obsession with me had cost them their entire past, their own history. The truth to their identities.

Blayde pulled the covers up and slipped her legs into the warmth, which I took as my cue to leave. I made a one-legged shuffle onto the end of the bed and stood, watching as she tucked herself in, her mind having returned to the stupor that had plagued her since our return.

What if we were right? What if her mind shuttered off the memories to protect her from permanent damage? Would she forget everything tomorrow morning?

But that didn't make sense. Zander wasn't shut off or experiencing the same trauma as Blayde. Whatever was resetting their memories must be simultaneous, some kind of reoccurring event that wiped everything, giving them both a clean slate.

Maybe the red journal was a freebie. A 'thanks for hiring us to wipe your brain' type of gift, like the toothbrush your dentist handed you as a kid after you had a particularly noxious cleaning.

Once Blayde was better, we'd go after the source of the journals. Until then, I'd help her through this. I had all the tools that kept my head above water during my depression. How hard could it be to keep a thousand-year-old alien afloat?

As if on cue, the quiet sobs began again. I said nothing as I slipped back into her bed, letting her brace herself against me as she fought not to drown in the night.

I wasn't even sure when I'd fallen asleep. Minutes or hours later, the room still echoed with the rush of rain against the roof, and a thunderous bang sent Blayde flying out of bed, throwing on her sweatshirt in the two strides it took her to barge out the door. There was someone out there in the storm, pummeling on the door like the call to adventure in an epic fantasy tale.

I slipped into the hallway, tripping over Blayde, who was crouched on the landing, her eyes fixed on the front door below.

"We're not alone," she hissed, and I nodded, though it went without saying. That was pretty normal of her, too, to think I was too daft to notice there was someone knocking on the door loud enough to wake the whole block. I went along with it.

A hand on my shoulder, and now there were three of us crouched on the landing, each peeking out over the other to get a better look at the door. Which wasn't altogether the most effective way of answering it.

"Someone's out there," said Zander softly.

"No duh," Blayde spat.

"What are we all doing?" Now, Mom was in a half-crouch behind us, clutching a squirming Galli to her chest, who took the proximity to Zander's face as an opportunity for kisses. Zander said nothing, letting the dog give him the full wash.

"Where's Dad?" I asked.

"He took an Ambien." She shrugged. "He's out like a light. What is happening out there? Sounds like they're trying to break down the door."

"Maybe if we actually went downstairs, we wouldn't be asking ourselves that," said Blayde. She extracted her laser pointer from the folds of her sweatshirt, clutching it in her fist as she dashed down the stairs.

"Should we let them in, whoever they are?" asked Mom. "They're probably soaked right now."

"I don't know, Mom. Do you want a wet stranger traipsing around your house in the middle of the night?"

"Don't give me attitude, missy," she said, shoving the dog at me. Galli squirmed, trying to get at my face, and then I was the one being showered with licks. Lovely.

Down at the door, Zander and Blayde were making things even more dramatic than they had to be. Each leaned against a side of the wall, their weapons drawn. In Zander's case, it was a butter knife, but I had no doubt whoever was on the receiving end wouldn't care to notice.

"Get away from the door, Laurie," Zander ordered. His free hand wrapped around the doorknob, poised, waiting for Blayde's signal.

"Is that… is that my silverware? I pull out my good cutlery, Sally, and your friends go swiping it?"

"The real question, Laurie, is why you would have such a thing as bad cutlery in your house," said Zander. "But I promise I'll return this one."

Zander flung open the door, hoping, perhaps, to spring the knocker unawares. Fat chance, seeing as how they had been pummeling the door for a good ten minutes now. And that diligent knocker was none other than a sopping wet James Felling, beaming as her eyes landed on her target, the man she had been hunting for years, the one and only Zander.

SIX

NO ONE WILL EVER GET A
FULL NIGHT'S SLEEP AROUND HERE

THERE'S SIMPLY NO FEELING QUITE LIKE SHOVING your mom into another room as your government-issued stalker barges inside in the middle of the night. Watching as the stalker hugs their victim like their life depended on it just makes things all the more confusing. But you learn to roll with these things and relish the silver linings, such as the fact that I hadn't disappeared and flown across the universe to a random planet out of pure panic.

Always nice to be mildly in control of the situation.

"It's you. It's really you!" Felling exclaimed, clutching Zander's face in both hands, inhaling his breath. Zander was too shocked to react and simply stood there, eyes zipping back and forth so fast it was like he was watching an interdimensional tennis match.

"I am me," he said, his eyes landing on me and begging for me to take over, which was definitely a turn of tables I was not expecting today.

Blayde, eyes wide and full of terror, took a hesitant step back, only to squash Galli's tail in the process. Galli yapped, drawing attention exactly where it shouldn't have gone.

"What are you doing here?" I asked. "Have you been following us?"

"Blayde!" Felling cried, as if seeing a long-lost friend. "It's really you! In person! Here!"

She dropped Zander and flung herself at Blayde, who was caught between preparing an attack and simultaneously apologizing to the poor, disgruntled doggy.

Too slow. Blayde got a hug too.

"Is this another one of your little friends?" asked Mom, yawning. "Should I be charging for turning my home into an all-hours Airbnb?"

"Sally, so good to see you." Felling turned to me as an afterthought, ripping her gaze from the siblings, as if turning her back meant that they would turn to smoke. Which, admittedly, I didn't blame her for doing, as that had happened to me before.

Galli sniffed at Felling's legs and, after being thoroughly ignored, turned back to Blayde to beg for pats. She picked up the dog, her pointer holstered behind her ear. She almost looked like a local art student, black rings around her eyes included.

Meanwhile, Felling looked smart in her navy-blue pantsuit, even if said pantsuit was soaked through to her bones. Her hair, dripping onto the carpet, was otherwise free, framing her face in a dark halo. She turned to my mother finally.

"So sorry to intrude at such a late hour, Mrs. Webber. It's a matter of national security."

"Of course it is." Mom rolled her eyes. "I'm going back to bed. You all mop up that mess, or that'll be a matter of national security next."

She grumbled as she made her way back up the stairs, and I half-expected Galli to follow, but the little cocker was too snuggled in Blayde's neck to ever want to move again.

"So," said Felling, breaking the short silence, "I bet Sally's told you everything about me."

"Um, not really," said Zander.

"Not anything," said Blayde. "Who are you again?"

"She's the one who's stalking me," I clarified. "Shall we all have some tea?"

Zander folded up his bed, returning the little nook back into its original state as I put the kettle on. Blayde stared at Felling like she might have telekinetic powers and if she stared just enough, maybe Felling's head might explode.

"You look so familiar," said Blayde, her voice barely above a whisper, no hint of the earlier confidence left.

"You remember me?" Felling's face lit up, and I

tried to center myself as I brought the tray of mugs back into the room. It was surreal seeing these two in the same room, two different worlds of mine clashing together. Zander came back with a box of Cheez-Its, plunking them down on the table as his contribution to the gathering.

"So, we *have* met?" he said, jutting his chin at the agent. "Let me guess, did we save your life or something?"

"You don't have to be so passive-aggressive about it," said Felling. "But, yes, you did. Shanghai, 1999."

"Shanghai," said Zander. "Is that the place with the community of elderly robot giraffes?"

"No."

"Then refresh my memory." He took a long sip of his tea, watching Felling intently. Blayde distracted herself with the dog, who had somehow managed to fall asleep in her arms.

"I grew up all over the place," said Felling. "My father's job brought him all over the world, working for the big banks and such. Well, after mom died, he fell off the deep end. Tale as old as time. He gambled away money we didn't have and fell in with the wrong crowds, and I was the only thing of value worth taking—so, hello, kidnapping!"

"Hold up, you were a kidnapping victim?" I sputtered. Felling nodded.

"So, these total assholes are about to cut off my finger because, hey, nothing says *I'm a serious kidnapper'* like a teenager's finger, when suddenly out of the blue there are these two… supersonic space ninjas. They come out of nowhere, knock out everyone in sight, free me, tell me to steal every canned good in the building—which I did because who's going to say no to supersonic space ninjas? And it turned out all the cans were illegally imported American chili. My kidnappers get busted by the customs and border control officers, and my dad and I get home free."

"And you're sure these… supersonic space ninjas—" I started.

"I was fifteen. I was terrible with names."

"You're sure they were Zander and Blayde?"

"Hello?" She waved a sopping wet arm at my guests. "Have you see them with swords and lasers?"

"Fair enough," said Zander. "But I don't think that counts as a proper introduction."

"You kept yelling about bringing space justice. It definitely made enough of an impression. After we were settled back in the States, I looked you up. Turns out, you went through a catchphrase phase, and people all over the world were writing about the Space Justice guy on a forum. You even have a subreddit now."

"Is that the place where they sell essential oils?" he asked.

"No, you're getting that mixed up with Facebook. How long did you live on Earth, exactly?"

"You know, I think I do remember you," said Zander. "It's funny to recognize someone from how many years ago, someone now fully grown. I've never been around to watch someone grow up. It's like seeing two snapshots side by side daring you to spot the differences. At first glance, they're so different you wonder how this could be a challenge in the first place. But the harder you look, the more you realize nothing had changed at all."

Felling blushed a deep shade of scarlet.

"We're getting off topic," I said, wishing Galli would sit on my lap to stop my own jitters. Blayde probably needed her more than me, though. For a woman who was terrified of dogs just yesterday, she sure was giving this spaniel a whole lot of puppy kisses. "So, you used the internet to track down Zander and Blayde, entered the FBI—or whatever Men in Black agency—used government funding—my taxes!—to hunt down your space-justice people, yada yada yada. If you followed us all the way to Florida, couldn't you have waited until morning to say hi? And hold on, didn't I tell you not to follow us?"

She threw her hands up in the air, shaking her head. "I know, I know. But I couldn't be patient and wait for you to come to me. Not when there are lives on the line. Not when the most recent attack was only half an hour from here."

You could have heard a pin drop were it not for Galli's happy panting. I didn't know which part to pick up on first, so I focused on the stalking part and stuck with that.

"You followed us," I snapped, "all the way to Florida?"

"Sally, you didn't tell me this was life or death," said Zander, rather sharply.

"Felling deals with creepy *X-File* murders all the time," I said. "This is just an excuse to get up and close to her supersonic space ninjas."

"I swear this is more serious than that," said Felling, so defensive she still hadn't dropped her hands from earlier. Down between her blazer and her trench coat—full-on *MIB* stereotype, through and through, except in navy—I could see her holster, and the thing was empty, just to make some kind of silent point. I gritted my teeth.

"Are you accusing *us?*"

All eyes turned to Blayde, whose voice was so light it could have belonged to a child. She stared at Felling with a dazed look in her eyes, as if she were looking at her but not quite seeing her.

"Excuse me?" sputtered Felling.

"You said the last attack was half an hour from here. I suppose none of the others were in Florida, or else you wouldn't have been stalking us in Virginia."

"I wasn't stalking," Felling muttered into her tea, one hand still airborne.

"Semantics." Blayde raised her voice. "In any case, people are in danger. What happened?"

"I can't divulge any more information unless you agree to take the case," said Felling. "All I can say is that the attacker most certainly is not human."

"I've gathered, otherwise you wouldn't have stalked the only non-humans you know." Zander was obviously trying to hide his smile. "I assume you don't have any other off-worlders you could go to. Unless Sally is right, and this is just an excuse to say hello to your heroes. In which case, color me flattered."

"Don't call it an excuse. Call it an opportunity."

"Ah, so you *do* have other alien friends?"

"Eh, no."

"Whatever. And there have been four deaths so far?"

"Three. The local attack was stopped partway through," said Felling. "Not too far away from here. The 911 call came in about two hours ago. She was found by one of her colleagues – according to the call, she was driving home but the storm was too much, so she went to see if she could stay with her friend. She found the door unlocked, let herself in and found the victim. It matched the killer's usual M.O. I was called in soon after. I spent the rest of the time trying to wake you."

"Oh, exciting. The walls are closing in on this mysterious murderer!" Blayde clapped, dropping Galli, who slid off her legs with a yelp, rushing to me instead. Poor baby. Another victim of Blayde's whims.

"Blayde," I hissed, "we're not getting involved."

"Oh? Why not?" She crossed her arms like a sullen toddler. "This sounds interesting."

"Because people are dead, and we're not equipped to handle this." And because Felling was still a wild card, but I wasn't going to say that to her face.

"Correction, *you* are not equipped. I've been involved in murders on thousands of different worlds."

"Which end of the investigation were you on?"

"Sally," Zander interjected, "why don't you help me sweep up this mess?"

"What mess?"

He stood up, swiping his hand across the table, sending the box of Cheez-Its flying. "I made a mess, but I don't know where the Robo-tronic-vacu-suck is in this house. Sally, this being your home—"

"Fine, whatever." I crushed crackers underfoot as I followed him to the kitchen, knowing full well Galli would have the mess cleaned up before either of us could find a broom.

"I don't like this," I stammered as soon as we were alone. "It could be a trap. You realize this could be a ploy to get at you?"

"What in the stars could they do to us?"

"You're telling me that in all your years traipsing around the galaxies, no government agency has conducted alien experiments on you?"

Zander rolled his eyes. "Yeah, it's unpleasant, but

you get over it. And sometimes they make you nice snacks."

"Not all the time, I suppose."

He frowned. "No."

"All this time, I've been trying to protect you," I snapped. "I've been keeping a low profile, protecting your image. I'm the one who came up with all those cover stories when the plant blew up and you were gone. Now you're telling me you don't mind if the government not only knows about you, but uses you for their own ends too?"

Zander was silent at first. Pensive. It was odd to see him without an automatic response at his lips. He leaned back against the kitchen counter, arms folded, face slack.

"But what if she is telling the truth?" he asked, eyes sparkling. "What if people are dying, and the only thing standing between justice and more deaths is, well, us? I mean, have you seen Blayde this engaged since she got back? Look at her. Listen. She's asking questions. She's alert, eager. This could be good for her."

"Solving an *X-File* as therapy?"

"If you put it that way." He shrugged. "Yes?"

He was right. Putting it that way did make it seem like a win-win. Except for the part where we'd become government contractors, which was not a good place to be as an alien. If we were working a case, did that mean we'd get a paycheck? Maybe Felling should have led with that.

Back in the living room, Galli had indeed vacuumed the floor and taken off with the rest of the box to boot. Mom would not be hearing about this in the morning. Even being an adult with teleportation, her grounding was the kind that stuck.

"Sorry, I have no idea who this Mulder is," said Blayde, "and I'm aware how government agents work, thank you. I don't need pop culture references. I hate pop culture references."

"You're literally wearing an *X-Files* shirt right now."

"Well, I didn't know that when I swiped it. And that doesn't help me know who he is."

"We are going to get paid for this, right?" I asked.

Felling rolled her eyes. "Does this mean you're done trying to be incognito? Because you realize if you want a paycheck, I'm going to have to put names on a whole lot of government files."

"So, that's why you want to hire us. Free labor, huh? I thought the government frowned on that."

"Need I remind you I pay my taxes like the rest of you?" said Zander.

"And I told you that you can't put cash in an envelope and write the word "TAX MAN" on it. That's not how it works."

"Well, excuse me if I didn't get an education on your planet," he scoffed.

"Actually, I'm pretty sure I didn't learn that until I

was well out of public education," said Felling. "Anyway, does this mean you're in? You'll help us?"

"If it will get you off our backs, sure," I said. "But we do expect compensation. I'm tired of government drones promising one thing and never delivering."

"Is this about the robot that destroyed your bathroom door?" she asked.

"This is exactly about the robot that destroyed my bathroom door."

I found myself smiling. For all her rough edges, Felling was the same person who had been by my side throughout the whole return-of-the-Sky-People ordeal. The whole planet would still believe in the failed alien invasion if it hadn't been for her work with the press. The woman was a powerhouse and a damn good agent.

What bothered me was not knowing to what end her skills were being used.

"Shall we be off, then?" she said, sliding off the banquette.

"What? Right now?"

"Better to interrogate the witness while the memories are still fresh." She scanned me up and down, eyes squinting. I was still in my PJs, and a professional look this was not. "But we can wait another ten minutes."

"You don't happen to have another magic lockbox, do you?" I asked. "I don't know if I have a good change of clothes. I packed for Florida, not a crime scene."

"Isn't it kind of the same thing?" Felling laughed.

"I don't get it," said Blayde. "Is this another pop culture thing? What did I tell you about pop culture references?"

"It's... will somebody give this woman access to the internet already?" said Felling. "Now hurry. It's like shepherding toddlers. I'll be out in the car."

I meant it when I said I had no appropriate clothing. Jeans and a plain t-shirt were the best I could do, and the shirt was only plain because the TARDIS had washed off. I dressed quickly, taking the extra five minutes to hunt down my dog and toss the cracker box into the recycling and Galli into my parents' room, where she'd either sleep soundly or keep them up all night with cheese farts. I was going to be super grounded in the morning.

Felling sure didn't nope out of the spy stereotypes. Her black SUV screamed government stipend and reeked of chicken wings. I slipped into the back, having to heave myself up into the seat.

"You drove this monstrosity when you were tailing me?" I asked. "Should I ask about the mileage on this beast?"

"The better question might be how you didn't spot us," said the driver, beaming as he turned back to shake my hand. "Hey, happy to see you again. Dustin. Dustin Cross. We met at the café. The night you—"

"You mean two nights ago? Yes, I remember all that." It wasn't every day you meet a fan. And some days, the distinction between "fan" and "stalker" could be particularly flimsy, especially considering this stalker was government funded. "So, I take it you know Zander and Blayde?"

"By reputation alone. Y'all ready to save the world?"

I found myself squished in the middle seat of the oversized car, which was much less spacious when stuffed with immortals at peak physical prowess. The roads were empty at this time of night, and we followed the moon down the highway in silence. Cross would occasionally try to start a conversation—he made it very clear this was the first time he'd met aliens—but the tension in the car was too high to take it any further.

"So, this case, elaborate," asked Zander, peeling himself away from the window. Felling nodded idly from the passenger seat.

"The victim is in critical condition but able to speak," she said. "The doctors have her under sedation and are treating the pain, but she's touch and go. Even so, she could be our only lead."

"But we have a problem," added Cross. "No one knows the right questions to ask since no one has ever dealt with this kind of situation before. We need you."

With the two in the front and our little trio in the back, it felt like Mom and Dad driving us to football practice or some kind of disappointing family vacation where no one realizes the aunt they never knew they had was secretly the family therapist. Even so, when Felling handed back the case file, we dutifully spread it open across my lap so we could all see, making me feel even more like a child.

"Three murders along the east coast alone. All spread out. No motive, no leads. No one would have connected them if it weren't for the way they died."

I thoroughly regretted laying eyes on the pictures. The base of the neck of each of the victims had deep, red holes bored into the flesh. A disgusting shade of green radiated from their skin. One gaping wound in the center; four smaller marks around the edge.

These people died in terrible agony. My stomach rolled, disgust bubbling deep in my body. If I could have thrown up, I would have.

"So, what killed them? Apart from the obvious," asked Blayde, bright-eyed and giddy. I pressed myself closer to Zander's thigh. "Are we talking blood loss or trauma? Was the spine severed, or was it something else entirely?"

"The spine was severed first, from what we could tell," said Cross, "but the baffling part is that it was drained."

"What was drained? The spine?"

"I wasn't finished, but yes. The autopsy of the other corpses revealed there wasn't a drop of cerebrospinal fluid left in their bodies afterward. The spinal cord itself seemed ripped from the bone by an incredible force."

It was a good thing immortality had some perks because Felling would probably have had to call a cleaning service after I was done with this car if my mortality let me do what I was wanting to do. So glad my guts were staying down.

"How did she survive?" I stammered. "His latest would-be victim. How could she have lived through something that could do... that?"

Felling reached back and scooped up the photos. I was thankful they were out of sight. "The report is being filed. Apparently, the assailant never finished the job."

"All women?" asked Blayde.

"So far, yes."

"Any other connection?"

"None. But we hope you would be able to make them."

SEVEN

LOW BUDGET DOCTOR PROCEDURALS
HAVE NOTHING ON US
AND WE DON'T EVEN HAVE A BUDGET

I TRIED TO AVOID HOSPITALS AS MUCH AS POSSIBLE since the GrishamCorp incident, but life doesn't always give you a free pass, especially once it has already let you survive the impossible. And I had used up all my free passes. I took deep breaths as we pulled up, though there was no racing heart to still, just tight nerves in its place.

"I'll go find parking," said Cross. Felling shot him a questioning look but said nothing, and the agent drove away.

We made our way through the maze of hospital corridors until we reached one sectioned off by an exhausted-looking policeman, who nodded when Felling approached and ushered us to the room. I caught my breath as we stepped inside. The darkened room was too familiar, the woman passed out in the bed too much like myself in those first days since the powerplant incident. Zander's hand brushed against mine, so subtly anyone could have missed it. But in that moment, I knew he saw what I was seeing. He had, after all, come to my bedside in exactly this way.

The woman was lying on her back, eyes closed, hair fanned out on the pillow. If I hadn't seen those horrible photos, I would have thought she was fine, except for how drained she looked in the face. White bandages peeked out from around her neck, but other than that, there was no obvious sign of her recent attack.

"Meet Samantha Greene," Felling whispered. "The 911 call came in a little past two thirty. She was treated immediately, but there was nothing they could do. Her spine was already irreparably damaged. All they can do now is attempt to stop the infection."

"I'll need to see the crime scene holograms," said Blayde, her eyes darting around the dim. "And playback from the nanos."

"What nanos?"

"*Veesh,* how far behind is your police work?"

"Forensics is combing her residence right now. You'll get them as soon as I do."

"No, I mean in the general scheme of things. If you don't have her nanos, at least give me her cam."

"She was a teacher. She didn't... oh. You mean some other futuristic technology you're going to rub our noses in."

"Not my fault your planet is lagging," she scoffed. "I'll do with what we have."

It seemed she didn't need us at all. Blayde was already examining the woman, staring at her from every possible angle, so intently her gaze could have prodded the girl awake. She fiddled with the settings of her laser pointer, shining it at a tip of her own finger before aiming it at the woman in the bed.

"Hold up. Your pointer does X-ray scans?" I stammered. "That's not how lasers work!"

"Who told you this was a laser?"

"You did. Does 'hand me my laser pointer' ring any bells?"

"I'm pretty sure I never said that."

She scanned the beam over the girl's body, though what it told her I couldn't make heads or tails of because I was certain the pointer didn't have a screen. Even so, when she was done, she nodded as if she had made an incredible discovery.

"Can we turn her on her side?" she asked Felling, who jutted her chin at the door. The pointer was gone before the doctor strode in, tapping his clipboard against his hip in annoyance.

"Ah, agent, I see you've brought a crowd." He scanned us in a sweeping glance. His lip curled in disdain. "I told you she wasn't ready for family."

"They're part of the investigation," said Felling. "Plainclothes."

The doctor dropped the twisted lip then picked it right back up again. "I see."

"Can you please turn her on her side?" asked Blayde, slipping into a familiar persona. I could imagine her with glasses poised on the tip of her nose, despite none actually being there. "I would like to examine the wound, Doctor..."

"Clarence. And you are?"

"Linda Cartwright, medical examiner for the NSTA."

"I don't know that branch."

"It's a subdivision of the FBI," said Felling, butting in with her own authority. "They deal with, um, serial medical attacks."

"National security of transdermal abrasions," added Zander for effect.

Dr. Clarence rolled his eyes, slapping his clipboard against his hip. "Well, what am I here for?"

"You can fetch me her medical records. That's a good man." Blayde waved him away, her nose practically roommates with the victim's neck. "All of them. Not just the notes on this event."

"We don't have them."

"What do you mean you don't have them?" Blayde scoffed. I could swear I felt her frustration at planet Earth raising the temperature a few degrees.

"This is the first time she's ever been hospitalized. Or received any kind of treatment, actually. She has never seen a doctor. I mean, other than for vaccines and such."

"And that's rare?" asked Blayde.

"Not for the price of a hospital stay in this country, no," I said.

"According to her mother, she's never even had the common cold," said Felling. "So it may be that she was just extremely lucky when it came to her health."

"Until now," Zander muttered under his breath.

Dr. Clarence strode to the woman's bedside, standing over her almost protectively. He studied Blayde's examination, saying nothing, but the squint in his eyes was judgy to the extreme.

"If there's any silver lining to this incident, it's this," he said, pointing at her forehead with the butt of his pen. "If she hadn't come into the hospital sooner, she wouldn't have known about the tumor in her brain."

"A tumor?" asked Blayde, straightening. She didn't seem all that surprised, so maybe her X-ray had worked after all. "Can you remove it?"

"It's in the early stages, so, yes, we can treat it, but if she had waited any longer, we wouldn't have known. But the wound in her neck? Nasty. It'll heal, but because of how much of her spinal cord is missing, she will never move anything below her neck again."

"Felling mentioned a bacterial infection, too."

The doctor nodded. "It's the darnedest thing.

We've never seen anything like it, and the way it spreads... it's far outside of this hospital's expertise."

"How would you explain the missing spinal cord?" Zander stepped in. "Your thoughts."

"It's strange," said Dr. Clarence, crossing his arms. "Though everything about this case is strange. From what we saw on the MRI, it was as if it was—I do hate to say this—sucked out. Like with a vacuum cleaner, but stronger. But why anyone would do such a thing..." He glanced down at his beeper, which was beeping urgently. "I'm sorry, I need to go. Take your time, but do not touch the patient."

As soon as he left, Blayde plopped down on the bed beside Samantha, grabbing her journal from inside her breast pocket and flipping through the pages at an alarming rate. The gears in her head were turning so loudly they muted all other sounds in the room.

"So," she said, licking her lips, "never-been-sick-a-day-in-her-life girl is attacked, her spinal cord is damaged for life." She turned to Felling, meeting her gaze. "I need the files of all the other victims. Can you get your hands on them?"

"On it," she said, striding out of the room with her phone pressed to her ear. "Cross and I have to run press to avoid this getting out. I trust you not to touch the patient, you hear me?"

Blayde shot finger guns at the door, which could have meant a whole lot of things and probably none of them what she intended. With Felling gone, I deflated, collapsing into the chair by the victim's side, trying to center myself as my head spun. Zander reached for my hand, and I grabbed his to steady myself.

"I'm sorry," he said softly.

"For what?" I gave him a smile, though it was a weak one at best. "I could have stayed home."

"You wanted a break," he said. "You deserve one. But here I am, dragging you into drama again."

"This isn't drama," I snapped. "As much as I hate being on Felling's speed dial, you're right. People are dying, and we can do something about it. We *should* do something about it."

"Well said!" Blayde didn't look up from her scan of Samantha's head, journal in one hand, pointer in the other.

I let go of Zander's hand. I didn't need his pity; I wanted his support. But this wasn't the time or the place to come out and ask for it. "So, thoughts?" I asked, turning to Blayde, part of me hoping for a quick and easy solution so we could return home.

"Hundreds," Blayde replied, putting her pointer between her teeth so she could flip through her journal more easily. She held a page, used her free hand to extract the pointer, slipped it behind her ear, and continued. "Life-sucking creatures, Terran legends from years ago, though it's most likely off-world tourists stopping for a treat. We would always consider a messed-up human being, but I'd rather give your people the benefit of the doubt this time."

"Thanks, Blayde."

"I just doubt they have the tech to kill someone this way. In any case, we won't get anywhere unless they let me autopsy the other bodies."

"You're certified?"

"I've performed hundreds of autopsies before, but I don't think the authorities here will let me work with a card from the Pyrinian University of Health and Science. Which I stole. To break into a morgue. To get Zander out."

"Ah." I sighed. "The eternal problem."

Blayde nodded but didn't have much time to say anything else, as Samantha was stirring. The woman squirmed, knocking Blayde's journal to the floor and forcing her to her feet.

"Who..." Samantha muttered, but Blayde was already flashing FBI credentials, too fast for the semi-conscious woman to notice the discrepancy between the face in the picture and the face of the woman holding it.

"Please, try to stay still, Miss Greene," said Blayde, her voice suddenly soothing. It was a voice I had heard only once before, after the death of the boy we had called Nim.

I had to get out of this room, but the room wasn't the problem; it was the patient before me. Everything she did reminded me of something, someone, of all the little steps that put me here.

Deep breaths. The only reason you're immortal is because of the choices you made.

But they weren't, not really. Not when they were forced on me like this.

"Are you all right?" asked Zander. I opened my mouth to answer, only to realize he wasn't talking to me. "Have they told you what happened?"

Samantha let out a heavy breath. "Oh god. I thought that was all a bad dream."

"Unfortunately, not," said Blayde. "Please, don't strain yourself. We're here to help. If this is too much, we can come back another time."

Samantha started crying, and I reached out a hand for her, then remembered she wouldn't be able to feel my touch anyway. I slunk back into the shadows.

I really shouldn't be here. I felt like I was intruding on Samantha's life, on Blayde and Zander's investigation. This wasn't my place. I was supposed to be home, to be...

No. Stop. I had to calm my mind, but there were too many thoughts in there, and they were getting louder. I started counting my breaths, focusing instead on Samantha, playing the spectator I was.

"Who are you again?" she asked Blayde, who was striking a pose at her bedside.

"I'm Agent Felling. I'm with the FBI," she said, flashing the ID yet again, so quickly that anyone would have missed the mismatched skin tones. "We've got a few questions for you."

"I want to sleep," she murmured. "It burns. It burns so bad."

"You need to remember what happened, Miss Greene," Zander added. "Focus. It's important. You're lucky to be alive. You're the only person to survive this type of attack, and your insight is invaluable."

She softened a little, the muscles in her face relaxing as she tried to remember. "I was coming home." Her face slackened even more, and the pause turned uncomfortable. She was slipping.

"From where?" asked Blayde, a sharp but gentle prod.

"I… was staying late. Correcting tests. I teach high school biology." She took a few deep breaths. "It took me forever to get home because of the storm."

"What happened when you got home? Anything out of the ordinary?"

"Nothing. I unlocked the door. Walked in. I think I put down my stuff, and then I got hit on the head. I woke up here."

"Any details between the time you put down your stuff and the moment you blacked out?"

"Ticking."

"Pardon?"

"Two large clicks. No, three? Like my clock got

really loud." She paused, the panic returning to her face. "Oh god. What if that was him?"

Blayde softly put a hand on her shoulder. "Do I have your permission to check the wound?"

She tried to nod, though it was obviously painful for her. I admired that strength. Even through all the pain, she was putting on the bravest face I had ever seen.

So much for not touching the patient. Together, they gently slid her onto her side, and with careful hands, they removed the thick bandage from the back of her neck. Instantly, we were hit by the smell. The flesh around the wound was slightly green, a putrid odor wafting from the cuts.

"You see this?" Zander commented, his sister nudging him in his ribs in response.

"I'm standing right here. Of course I see this. Sally, come have a look."

I approached, looking upon rotting green flesh at the back of her neck. It was disgusting. Even more so to think that it was attached to a living, breathing human being.

"Tell me what you see," Blayde ordered.

"Uh..." I scanned the wound quickly. "Five marks. Four like what you'd see from one of those crane games, but with one hole in the middle. Green skin? Blackish, petrol-like liquid."

"Black liquid?" Samantha spat. "Are you kidding me?"

"Sally, what do you think?"

"I heard of the Komodo dragon biting its prey and just waiting for the creature to fall from the bacteria it placed in the wound." I tried not to gag. "Could it be that? Wouldn't the hospital have disinfected it?"

"Obviously, their disinfectant isn't strong enough," she said, touching the side wound gingerly. Samantha made no indication of feeling this. "The bacteria is extraterrestrial."

"Aliens did this to me?" Samantha shrieked. "Oh, come on. Who the hell are you?"

"No, don't worry. There is no such thing." Felling had returned, partner in tow. "My colleagues just have a strange way of dealing with this type of issue."

"I've got another call to make," Cross said with a gag, spinning on his heels before even making it through the door. "I'll be outside." And with that, he made his escape.

Felling snapped on latex gloves, joining all three of us by the woman's side. "The infection was smaller when we found her. It spread by fifty percent by the time we got her to the hospital, but thanks to the quick reaction of the medical team, it is contained." She lifted a sterile metal rod from a tray. With one end, she prodded the central hole. "It connects directly into the vertebrae, into to the spinal cord."

"Like spinal fluid on tap."

"Exactly." She dropped the instrument onto a tray. "Any ideas?"

"She'll survive," said Zander, scowling at the others.

Out of sight of Samantha, Blayde plucked a sterile container from the tray and slipped a tiny sample of the black-green goo inside, sealing it tight and stashing it into her pocket.

I followed Cross out into the corridor as the siblings helped Samantha get comfortable. I was so out of place here, like a human partying on the goo planet. I wasn't a space detective. I was a girl who couldn't die, and that gave me no authority whatsoever.

I wish I could have said something to Samantha. Anything to help her feel better. But I got to walk away from my accident; she would never walk again. It was a terrible situation to be in.

I hadn't even thought about the monster who had done this to her. I balled my hands into fists. It had to be stopped, whatever it was. And maybe that's how I could make myself useful: be part of the group who beat the monster into a pulp afterward.

"You look as green as I feel," said Cross, handing me bottled water from the vending machine. "Hope you don't mind I already took a swig from this one."

"It's reassuring to know that you don't deal with cases like these every day," I said, accepting the bottle wholeheartedly. It's not like I had to worry about common germs anymore, anyway. The cool liquid was fresh against my throat, grounding me. Cross gave me a weak smile.

"And you do?"

I shook my head. "Nah. I'm new to the team. It's every *other* day for me."

He chuckled a little, just as the trio emerged from the ward. They were in deep conversation together, Felling squished between the siblings like a detective sandwich.

"You were right," Zander said. "Definitely not terrestrial. The bacteria that's causing her infection will never fully go away. No alcohol on Earth is powerful enough to sterilize it. The black liquid is a natural secretion. Her blood is trying to cleanse itself."

"We'll track down some kind of counteragent," said Blayde, holding up the tiny sample jar. "We can't allow this to spread. For the time being, clean the wound as frequently as you can. I've got to give them credit: the Terran doctors seem to have stemmed the bacteria's advance, even with their primitive tech, so have them keep doing what they're doing."

"On it," said Felling, tapping away diligently on her phone.

"And I'll need to perform autopsies on the other corpses," she insisted. "Make sure your doctors didn't miss anything in their examinations. We need to be sure what we've taken in order to consider motive."

"Motive?" Cross scoffed. "What kind of motive would an alien have to eat someone's spinal juices?"

"I can think of a few," said Blayde. "And, no, that doesn't make me a suspect, pal. Anything from a drug to a midnight snack and everything in between. It's entirely possible these women weren't all Terran either."

"Did you check Miss Greene?" asked Felling. "She *is* from this world, isn't she?"

"Problem is that human and Terran aren't entirely interchangeable. Case in point," said Zander, waving a hand over the length of his body. "Samantha looks entirely human and she's not in a skin wrap, but that doesn't mean she might not have been born off-world."

"Shit, so there's no way of knowing?" scoffed Cross. "Anyone can be an alien?"

"Trust me, you get used to it," I muttered.

"Pardon?"

"I went through a few months where everyone in my life turned out to be an alien. But you learn to live with it, really."

Cross laughed, though it was an awkward, disjointed laugh. I probably shouldn't have sprung that on him after only knowing him for such a short time.

"Can you help her?" Felling turned to Blayde with a pleading look in her eyes.

"No more than what we're already doing, no."

"But what about... what you did for Sally. Can you do it for her too?"

A chill fell on the hospital like a cartoon anvil. I felt it crushing me, just as I saw it hit the siblings at once.

"Felling," I hissed, but Blayde was already scowling.

"Sally warned me about you," she said, making Felling frown. "She mentioned how you saw us as walking dispensers of immortality."

"What? No!" Felling turned to me. "Really?"

"I never said that," I sputtered. *Wait, why was I trying to defend her?* "But you yourself warned me what would happen if I remained on the US's radar."

"Look, I'm not asking you to give your bodies over to the government, jeez," she said. "All I'm asking is that you do to her what you did to Sally after the power plant went *kaboom*. You helped her survive. Samantha will never walk again, all because an alien tried to kill her. Please, can you do anything for her?"

"What, because we're extra-terrestrial too?" Blayde sneered. "I said I would track down a counteragent, and I will. But we can't do any more than that."

"What's the worst that could happen? If you had such a gift, why not share it?"

"Because the consequences outweigh the benefits. Sally here is the perfect example. Immortal is forever. She's as cursed as we are."

"Well, thanks for that," I muttered. "Life's forever, and then you don't die. Can we go home now?"

The whole ordeal had gone by so quickly that the

121

sun still hadn't risen by the time we got back. With my parents still asleep upstairs, coming home felt like sneaking in, the three of us reduced to teenagers again as we let ourselves quietly into the living room.

Felling had handed us a heavy laptop as we slipped out of her car, the thing as black as the night around us.

"Here," she had said. "This will give you access to all the information we have so far on the victims. Every photo ever taken pertaining to the case is in there. Just don't post any of it to Instagram, understood?"

"What do weights have to do with this?" Blayde scoffed, taking the laptop from Felling. "We're not going to mail anything. We know better than that."

"Have you really not shown her the internet?" Felling asked, turning to me.

"Oh, god, no," I said.

"The internet is your version of interconnected servers, right?" asked Blayde. Our voices were low as we stepped into the house, and I was impressed with how low I could whisper now.

"Yeah," I replied. "I'm surprised you haven't found it on your own. Didn't you do all this crazy research on the power plant before you blew it up?"

"Yeah, but it was all word of mouth." She shrugged. "Every terminal I tried to converse with stayed silent, but then the text asked me what I was looking for and I didn't want to deal with AI anyway."

She flipped open the black laptop, and I pointed her to a browser, cringing as I did. She grunted her thanks before bouldering up the stairs, leaving me alone in the dark living room.

"Well, good night, Felling," I said. "I guess your stalking got you what you wanted. You've got your space ninjas back."

"Can we not do this now?" she replied, pinching the bridge of her nose. "I'm heading back to the hotel. If I get two hours of sleep, I'll call that a win."

I closed the door and collapsed on the couch, resting my head on an already zonked-out Zander's shoulder.

EIGHT

IF YOU DON'T GET A PER DIEM, THEN WHAT'S THE POINT?

"YOUR MOM THINKS YOU'RE CUTE," SAID BLAYDE, flicking me in the cheek. "But I think you two should find a room and leave the sofa to the professionals."

I tried to force my eyes open but to no avail. The beam of light fell right on my face. I lifted a hand up to block it, letting my vision return, and sat up on the couch gingerly as I yawned the sleep away.

Blayde was there, of course, glaring down at me. I was expecting the heat to rise to my face instead feeling it all over. My whole body must have been turning red as Blayde unceremoniously plopped down between Zander and me, laptop open on her lap, crushing our arms in a single instant and splitting me from the short, warm moment I had alone with Zander. And I had been asleep for all of it, waking up cuddle-less.

"Good morning to you too," Zander muttered. "Did Laurie seriously call me cute? That's weird."

"I think she means the two of you and your relationship. It was unclear. She might have been talking about the dog. But that is neither here nor there. We have lives to save, so sleeping isn't worth wasting time on. We need to go to Nigeria."

"Wait, what?" I blinked again, unsure if the sleep had fully left my eyes. It made no sense that this immortality stuff still left me as vulnerable to sleep deprivation as anybody else. "You already have a lead?"

"Well, actually, this is to help out my new friend. He's a prince, and he's having some banking issues," she said, shrugging, her shoulders digging into mine. "I'm worried about him and a possible coup in his country. He's such a sweetheart, and—"

"It's a scam, Blayde." I yawned as I reached for the laptop, which she slammed shut on my fingers. Maybe it was better if I just got up and stepped away from this mess.

"You must be pretty daft to think the prince of Nigeria has time to waste scamming random people like me," she scoffed.

"He's not the actual prince of Nigeria, though!"

"And how would you know?"

"Because I'm friends with him too," said Zander, hanging his head. "And I couldn't get the money transferred to him in time."

"Oh, not you too!" I needed coffee for this. "I'm going to have to sit down and give you both a serious introduction to the internet."

"I think I can handle myself fine, thank you," said Zander, making a point of standing up. "I'll have you know I was trying to find what you might call a 'side hustle.' I need to earn money somehow, don't I?"

"And when did the prince contact you?"

"The day we got back," he muttered.

"Exactly. You may be acquainted with the internet, but I was molded by it, shaped by it." And I could throw out random, badass quotes without either of them having any idea they were from a movie. Smooth move, Sally Webber.

"Well, internet aside, I did make some progress trying to identify a possible attacker," said Blayde. "The incidents were mostly in residential areas, so I think we're looking for a wolf in sheep's clothing. Since he somehow got access to their medical files— or lack thereof—it means he must have some sort of clearance. To create hacking technology for something alien to what you know is pretty extreme. Human costume? Easier."

"Changeling?" asked Zander. I shuddered at the thought. I kept forgetting that there were infinite possibilities in such an infinite universe.

"Or maybe just a plain skin wrap."

"Could it be multiple people?" I suggested, still halfway to the kitchen and probably not actually going to make it there, ever. "If there's a race that feeds like that, it could be the connection we're looking for."

"I doubt it," said Zander. "The marks on the necks are identical. The bacterial makeup is identical. I'm thinking a single murderer."

"That's if the local authorities ran their tests right," said Blayde. "Which they wouldn't have since they don't know what to look for. I need to autopsy the other victims."

"Haven't they already been autopsied?" I asked.

"I looked at their reports," said Blayde. "As Felling said, they weren't asking themselves the right questions. The best we can hope for is a fresh victim."

"You don't mean that."

"Sally? Your friend is back," my mother called from the living room. I hadn't heard the doorbell or even a knock, but Felling was suddenly waltzing through the living room, holding a box of donuts ajar.

"I come bearing donuts and terrible news, but the donuts should help."

"Let me guess," said Blayde. "The creature attacked again?"

"How did you know?" She blinked a few times, handing out the box gingerly. I grabbed a jelly donut, realizing quickly I was the only one who had even reached. *Oh, come on.*

"If these attacks are meant to feed the off-worlder, then him having been interrupted mid-meal wouldn't bode well for his health," she said. "It was more than likely that he was finishing his kill before we even met Samantha Greene."

Felling nodded, putting the box down on the coffee table, which was getting rather full of gadgets and food. "The victim is Greene's coworker, the one who placed the 911 call. An officer went to check on her this morning. Found her sucked dry."

Blayde was on her feet in an instant, pulling on her red leather jacket. "What are we waiting for? Agent, can I do the autopsy?"

"Have you ever...?"

"More than I can count." She reached into her wallet—which, for once, was in her pocket—and pulled out a laminated card with her photo on it. "I have a card. Not exactly valid on Earth, but, hey, it's still a card."

"I'd love to make this work, but there's no actual words on this," Felling said, handing the card back to Blayde. "I assume those things are letters, but they look like ants performing semaphores to me."

"Well, find someone who can read it."

"Blayde, I'm pretty sure no one can," she said. "I'm not even sure it's a language to begin with."

Blayde shrugged and tossed the card back over her shoulder. "So, where are we headed?"

I was glad I hadn't gotten into my PJs the night before since I wouldn't have had time to get dressed today. Already we were back in the car, donuts balanced precariously on Felling's lap as Cross drove us through the sunny roads along the Florida coast. Now that he wasn't cringing from Blayde's sight, he looked taller. A healthy glow radiated from him that wasn't there previously. A good night's sleep and a heaping does of confidence could do wonders to the complexion.

"Who was the last person to see her alive?" Blayde asked.

"I was, ma'am," Cross replied. "She was fine when I drove her home last night and fine when I left her by herself. I checked the house, of course, before leaving her alone, and nothing seemed out of place."

"And none of you thought to place guards for her protection?"

"None of us saw any danger, so no."

Blayde took charge, much to her brother's annoyance. She snapped on latex gloves, waltzing into the victim's home as if she owned the place. Felling followed her closely, grabbing a clipboard from a table.

The young woman's body was propped up on a chair, head lolling forward and wounds exposed. I took a deep breath then regretted it. The smell hit my nose like a train in the night. What a horrible thing to happen to someone. I stared at the floor rather than the corpse, avoiding the truth of the situation. All eyes were mainly on Blayde as she searched the room, her eyes more alert than an entire investigative team.

"Less residual bacteria on this one," Blayde remarked, stepping in as the photographer finished their job. "An almost clean wound. Not sloppy like the last."

"The door was unlocked this morning," said Cross. "No sign of forced entry."

"None of our suspects have anything to connect them to this girl, except the fact that they tried to murder her friend."

"You can't just waltz in here and take my case!" A cop appeared at her side seemingly out of nowhere, ripping the clipboard from Felling's grasp. I glanced over at Cross, who shrugged, as if to say this happened a lot. He smiled in my direction, a kind smile. I turned back to watch Blayde, now examining the girl herself. She reached over to the cut and dipped her finger into the wound, making us all collectively cringe. She lifted her finger to her nose, sniffing deeply, and shrugged.

"See?" she said, her voice steady, no matter the crudity of the situation. "The bacteria's inside the hollowed-out bone as well."

"Which means?" asked Zander.

"The spinal fluid wasn't sucked out. It was licked out. Do you have reptiles on this planet? The kind with very long tongues?"

"That's gross," I muttered.

"No kidding." She pointed at the disposition of the wound. "The four marks at the cardinal points are where the teeth probably latched on, and the central hole is where the item the creature used to clean out the spine entered the body."

"Any idea what could have caused this?"

"No. But I know where to look," she said, making a beeline for the door.

"Hey! Where do you think you're going?" Felling stepped in front of her, casting a glare at the cop she had just abandoned.

"We're done here," she said casually. "And I've got a lead on a lead."

Felling stepped aside without a word, but the look on her face was as stern as my mother's. Zander and I followed her out, walking past the agent, trying to look a little bit apologetic.

The little green car was only parked half a block up from us, though by the frantic look of the two men inside it, it was far enough that they hadn't expected to be spotted. Blayde was knocking on the driver's window before they had time to buckle their seat belts for a safe getaway. They were polite enough to roll it down.

"How do I put this?" said Blayde, leaning casually on the car. "Take me to your leader."

"Get lost," said the driver. He looked remarkably like the Mohawk guy from the day before, sans blue hairstyle. His ears had the kind of spreaders you could have looped a finger through. "We're just minding our own business here."

"Yeah, no idea what you're talking about, lady," said the man next to him. But before either of them could move, Blayde was already slipping into the backseat of their car, sending them into a tizzy.

"What the hell, lady?" spat the driver. "Get out of here! Who do you think you are?"

"Who do you think I am?" she asked, gesturing us to join her. "Seeing as how you've been following us since the mall yesterday, I should ask you the same question."

"What? No, we haven't!" he stammered, but it was too late. We had already piled in the back seat, leaving Felling to watch us from afar, overly confused and maybe a little hurt.

"There's no point in denying it," said Zander, strapping himself in. "We need to talk to the head of your organization. And carpooling is so much better for the environment, don't you agree?"

I wasn't quite sure I was following any of this. I could hear my mother's voice in the back of my head telling me to get out of here, that climbing into a stranger's car was the dumbest idea on the planet. Especially if said strangers were aliens who had it out for us. But the driver took us right back to the mall without incident, past the shoppers and around back to one of the more remote employee entrances. He parked as close as he could get, letting out a heavy sigh when he pulled the hand break.

"He's not going to be happy," he said, more to himself than any of us crammed in the back.

"Who? Your boss?" asked Blayde. The driver nodded.

"Just promise you won't kill him. Or any of us. It would be really nice to not die today."

"Kill him?" It was Zander's turn to sputter. "We have absolutely no reason to kill any of you. Why do you think that?"

"You're the freaking Iron and the Sand," said the other alien. "It's what you do."

"Our reputation proceeds us," said Blayde.

"A false one, it seems," said Zander. "Who told you that? The Alliance?"

The off-worlders didn't answer, instead stepping out of the car as smoothly as two men running away from an explosion. We followed suit, letting them lead us through the back of the mall and into the labyrinthine confines within.

"Look, we don't kill people," said Zander awkwardly. "I mean, not people who don't deserve it. And then we enter into the whole philosophical question about morality—"

"You won't kill me if I ask you to shut up, will you?"

The hallways were as bright as an Alliance ship and just as confusing. Our guides brought us around in such a way I couldn't possibly tell which store we were behind. They knocked on an innocuous office door and let themselves in, visibly cringing as they stepped past the threshold.

"What the duck?" The man at the desk was as sedate as the rest of his office, a game of solitaire hastily closed on his computer to reveal a detailed spreadsheet, which he scrutinized, furrowing his thick brows in concentration. That brow rose as his eyes landed on the three of us—well, Zander and Blayde mostly; I didn't think I added much to his surprise—sending his expression skyward. "Oh, duck me. I told you to trail them, not lead them right to me!"

"They wanted to talk," said the driver. "I was—"

"We were afraid of saying no, Lenzini," the other one interjected. "They saw us. They knew our faces."

"Just to be clear, none of us actually threatened anyone," said Zander.

"It was implied," muttered the driver.

"You have no ducking right to threaten my people," Lenzini spat. "Let alone come here to see me. I thought we made it abundantly clear. You are not welcome."

"May I sit?" asked Blayde, not waiting for an answer as she took a seat across from Lenzini. It was hard to tell what kind of alien he was, if he even was alien. His skin wrap was incredibly believable, if only a little stereotypical of an Italian pizza chef, which he could well have been. The bristling mustache under his nose was magnificent in its own right. Between the brows and the 'stache, I was sure a passing cat could easily scare those busy caterpillars off his face.

"Well, make yourself at ducking home. Seems like you already have," he muttered. "Have you come to threaten me too?"

"We're not threatening anyone," said Zander. "We're on holiday."

"Oh, taking a break from terrorism?" said Lenzini. "Seems fair. It must be exhausting not getting any sleep at night. Murder tends to do that to you."

"Why does everyone think we're terrorists?" asked Blayde. Zander and I remained standing, though I wasn't sure it helped the situation. I wasn't planning on looking intimidating today. "Look, you don't want the Alliance to know you're here, and neither do we. Seems like you're not on the best terms with them, and we're not either. But as for the terrorism thing, you know the Alliance as well as we do. Don't you think we make for great scapegoats?"

"Get the surf out of my office," the man spat. "I don't want anything to ducking do with you. Any of you."

I started to turn toward the door, feeling defeated, but my gut tugged me back. Zander and Blayde might have been pariahs, but I was relatively new. Not that I liked having to talk with an alien mob lord, though I had done it before, and the last one was much creepier.

"How about with just me, then?" I asked, stepping forward.

"And who the duck are you?"

"Exactly," I said. "You don't know me. The Alliance doesn't know me. I'm a neutral party. I'm a local, actually, and I need your help."

"And yet you threw in your lot with these ducks?"

"I'll tell you why, if we can talk." I shot a glance at Zander, who seemed as shocked as I was. But something deep inside me was taking control, and I wasn't going to turn it down now. "They don't even need to be here."

"Fine," said Lenzini. "I'll talk to you. But these duck-holes need to get the duck away from me. Far ducking away."

Blayde said nothing as she got up, clapping me on the shoulder as she stepped around me. I took her seat, keeping my eyes fixed on Lenzini, trying not to show my fear.

I had dealt with mobsters before. Alien mobsters, in fact. It wasn't my first rodeo, and between him, Maakuna, and Grisham, I was pretty sure I could hold my own. Especially since we had common ground.

But first things first.

"What's the story with all the ducking?" I asked as the door behind me clapped shut. Both our off-world stalkers had exited, too, probably to keep an eye on the so-called terrorists, leaving me alone with the previously unknown Mario brother.

The brows furrowed together, caterpillars giving each other a little smooch. "Not everyone can afford top-of-the-line translators. Mine's secondhand, and the parental controls glitch a little."

"I like it," I said, leaning back in my chair. Did it make me look confident? I sure hoped so. "There's definitely some language I don't want translated."

"My pod agrees," he said, smiling a bristly smile. "Though, sometimes, I miss being able to really express myself, you know? There are some words that aren't translatable for a reason, and they're too perfect for a situation to pass up."

"Like when two terrorists show up in your office?"

"Precisely," he said with a curt nod. "And you are not the third?"

"I'm the intern. To the whole planet-saving bit, not to the terrorism bit. And from what I can tell, the Alliance isn't too happy about Zander and Blayde saving planets, especially when it's usually from the Alliance itself. I'm sure you understand, seeing as how you're hiding out here yourself"

Lenzini smiled—actually smiled! —and let out a single, thunderous guffaw. It brightened up the whole room.

"You can't ducking expect to come in here and tell me that thousands of years of history books are wrong just because the Alliance wrote them," he said. "You're right, though. We don't care much for them, but we tolerate them. They certainly tolerate us. We know they're aware of our presence, but so long as we don't stick out, they have no reason to come down here and put us back in line. Florida is the perfect cloak. The Terrans here tend to be much stranger than we are. Aligning ourselves with you puts us right back in their ducking sights."

"We're not asking to work with you," I said. "Heck, we don't want anything to do with you. We don't want to make waves either. But someone else is, and they're doing enough to draw attention right here, right now. Neither of us want that. So, any help figuring out who this off-worlder murderer is would benefit the both of us."

"Sounds like a ducking alliance if I ever heard one," he said.

"Trust me. We talk today then never again. I won't even set foot in your mall from today onward. You have my word."

"And Florida?"

"Well, my parents live here, so it's going to be hard, but we can refrain from the planet-saving while we're in the state. Keep all Agency attention where it should be: on the actual dangers to the status quo. Like that spaceship they should have dealt with last week. Oh, I should mention, I'm the one who stopped them from incinerating all of us."

He leaned back away from the desk as his screensaver popped up, starting a slideshow of sweet family pics. Lenzini surrounded by half a dozen people dressed in matching Christmas sweaters, laughing children at their feet. A new photo showed, this one of a child with his dog. The classic American family, though a little larger than life. People worth protecting. His entire stance in a single image.

"If this will get you the duck off my back, then fine," he said, throwing his hands up in the air. "What can I do for you?"

I tried not to show the wave of relief that washed over me. "Well, you know the off-worlder community around here. Have you ever encountered a race that feeds off the spinal fluid of young women? You might have heard of the string of murders along the east coast."

"Spinal fluid?" His eyes went wide. "A Tallagan. Ducking smufetty duck. There can't be a Tallagan lose on Earth!"

"So, you've heard of them? Any idea how we could recognize one if they were in a skin wrap?"

"Girl, if there as is Tallagan lose on Earth, let alone Florida, then we're all royally ducked," he said, shuddering. "You said it's already fed?"

"Murdered four," I said. "Attempted five."

"Duck," he hissed. "And the Agency hasn't come down on it? They don't issue permits to races that feed off Terrans, so it shouldn't even be here in the first place. Which means they're going to come down on this *hard*. This is ducking fantastic. Florida is ducked."

"We have to stop it," I insisted. "If the Agency isn't going to do anything about it, then someone has to."

"I see what you mean," said Lenzini. "If this Tallagan continues to feed, then the Agency will have no choice but to bring out the big guns. We need to stop it before it can feed again."

"Zander, Blayde, and I are on it," I said. "And we'll deviate the attention away from your people. But we need help to find it."

Lenzini looked terrified. Already, the tension in the room was brimming so high I could almost feel his heart racing. I wanted to reach for him, reassure him somehow, but I was the last person who could.

"How?" he asked. "How the duck can we help?"

"Well, how do we recognize a Tallagan in a skin wrap? There has to be a way, isn't there?"

"Skin wraps are made to be undetectable. That's the whole point! I suppose if you get too much pure salt on one, it might cause a rash, but there are millions of people here. There's no ducking way you can test through them all. Not to mention, some Terrans would break out in hives, with or without a wrap."

"Okay, then what about the feeding? There has to be a way to know where or how he'll strike next."

"All I know of their race, and I don't know much, only hearsay, is that they need the pure spinal fluid of a healthy human," he said. "The human-like creatures they feed on on their planet are the prey sort, not like here. The equivalent of cattle. The Agency shouldn't have let through any visitors from the Tallagan system. They're banned since one of them rekindled old human myths."

"Vampires?" I asked. "With the whole life-sucking thing?"

"I thought those were honey badgers."

"You sure they don't have any tourists from that system?" I stammered. "Or someone high ranking who can evade these regulations?"

"No, the Agency doesn't offer priority resettlement packages. Plus, no high-ranking official ever comes to Earth. No offense, I really mean no offense, but to them, compared to planets like Pyrina or Da-Duhui, Earth is insignificant. Why do you think we started a new life here?"

"I've heard that before," I mumbled. "You're sure there's no other way you can track it down?"

"If you want to find its next target, I suppose you need to find a human healthy enough to appeal to it."

"So, a needle in a haystack."

Lenzini inclined his head. "I'm sorry I can't help more. And I can't ducking believe I'm throwing my lot in with the Iron and the Sand. But if we can do anything to help, let me know. If the Alliance comes down on Florida, we're all ducked in the duckhole."

NINE

I ALWAYS HATE THE DOUBLE-CROSS

"AND YOU'RE ABSOLUTELY CERTAIN HE SAID Tallagan?"

I caught up with Blayde in Lenzini's storefront, which turned out to be a blacklight putt-putt mini-golf course. She didn't seem too impressed by the interstellar putt-putt course in front of her, instead glaring at the children failing quite dramatically to finish even a single green. Though I wasn't sure we could even call it a green, seeing as how they were all glowing purple.

"Certain, though Lenzini's in the dark with the rest of us about how to apprehend it. Good thing he wants the murderer gone as much as we do."

"How is it even finding his prey?" asked Blayde, pursing her lips. "Stalking them? Tracking them?

There must be a way for the Tallagan to know who the ideal meal will be."

"I hate this line of reasoning," I said, "but you're right. Figuring out who has access to the medical files across state lines is the only lead we have right now."

"Felling should be able to help with that," she said. "That or her magnificent computer. Or maybe Svetlana."

"Svetlana?" I asked. "Is that some kind of alien expert?"

"No, she's my fiancé," Blayde replied. "I met her on the internet. She needs something called a green card."

"But you're… never mind. Where's Zander?"

As if on cue, Zander appeared from behind the glowing neon windmill in the very center of the course. "Try it now!" he shouted at a kid down the way. The child smacked his putter as hard as he could against the orange ball, sending it flying into the spinning wings of the mill—only for them to stop right when the ball approached, letting it through unscathed.

"Hey! Get that man off there!" shouted an employee, and Zander flew out of the store into the main concourse. Blayde slapped me across the back.

"And that's our cue to leave," she said, peeling off toward her brother.

The off-worlder carpool meant that we were left at the mall without transport, but rather than hiring an

Uber, we had our own chauffeur on call. Not that Felling would like it if we called her that to her face, but she responded immediately to my call, picking the three of us up like preteens after a school trip.

"This had better be good," she said from the passenger side. Cross was quietly doing all the actual driving, leaving her to turn around and scold us. I wasn't much of a fan of this power dynamic.

"Well, we know the race that's behind the attacks," said Blayde. "Tallagan. This one is feeding off the spinal fluid of humans. The only lead we have is that they somehow know how to go after only the healthiest Terrans, so they have access to Earth medical records."

"I was going to say all that," I said. "I did all the investigating, so why do you get to show off?"

"Children, please," said Felling, and I found myself scowling. It was all ridiculously childish. "Right. So, that's definitely progress. We now have a species to tie to the deaths."

"And it's a bit of a relief to know we're not stark raving mad about the alien thing," added Cross.

"What? We don't count for anything?" asked Blayde. "In any case, we finally have a lead. But we need to act before the Tallagan strikes again."

"Is it worth asking how you came by this information?" asked Cross.

"We went to talk to the local extraterrestrial

community," I explained. "They don't want this murderer around either. Draws too much unwanted attention."

"From whom?" asked Felling, raising an eyebrow.

"Alliance," I said. "And their tourism industry, apparently."

"Makes sense," said Cross, nodding slowly. "The Alliance is notorious for coming down hard on anyone who doesn't toe the line. It's why our job has been fruitless for so long. Most of our cases, our leads, reach a dead end after the Agency interferes."

"The Agency?" asked Felling. "Is that the tourism thing you mentioned?"

Blayde nodded. "They filter those who get to visit Earth, try to maintain order, and keep their interference incognito. Stick to the shadows, manage from inside of most governments. It makes sense you've never heard of them before, Felling. The question is, Cross, how have you?"

A spontaneous blizzard wrapped around the whole car, dropping the temperature to ten below. The conversation went so cold I could have caught frostbite.

"Some of my CIs have come through them," he replied, breath steaming before him.

"I thought you said we were your first?" said Blayde. "You know very well you don't have to flatter me. So, tell me, Agent Cross, which agency are you actually with? The one you claim along with your partner or the one with the great, big 'A' that gets in her way?"

Cross said nothing, and the minute of silence felt like it stretched to infinity. Felling's hand slid to the weapon under her blazer, her eyes fixed on him, driving holes right through his face. Finally, he shrugged and shouted, "I'm out," before throwing himself out the door of the moving car.

"No!" shouted Felling, flinging herself across the seat, but she was just short of reaching the open door. The car swung wildly off the road, causing the cars behind us let out a volley of honks, and she grabbed the steering wheel and ripped it back, sending us speeding into a Target parking lot.

"Shit!" I swore, but Zander and Blayde were already gone, jumping into the chase, leaving me alone with Felling to deal with the out-of-control car. Her legs shot across the midline, and she slammed on the brakes, bringing the careening car to a stop in front of a cart return.

"What the hell?" she spat, unbuckling her belt and tumbling out of the car, one hand still on the butt of her gun. "What the absolute hell?"

I was still trying to figure all that out too. Cross had never seemed the undercover type nor was Felling the kind to be duped. But how had none of us noticed? An Alliance operative, here, with us this whole time, right under our noses, and with the resources of Felling's whole department behind them.

"I'm so sorry," she said, her entire body trembling. I had no idea, I thought—"

"None of us did." I put a hand on her shoulder. "Now, let's go catch your partner."

"Do you have a weapon?" she asked. "Oh god, where is he? What is he?"

"We have to catch him first," I said, kicking myself internally for having forgotten the laser saber at home. "Have you seen Zander?"

The road we had just left was now in chaos. Those who had seen the man fling himself onto the road or saw our car spinning out of control into the lot had pulled off to the side, staring at us. But there was no sign of the literal double agent or the two aliens chasing him.

"He works for the Alliance," said Felling, face blanched. "He works for the Alliance, and I put Zander and Blayde right in front of him."

My hands curled into fists. All this time I had been afraid of Felling turning us in to the American government, but I never considered the Alliance. I had been right to think this partnership was a terrible idea.

I caught myself: this wasn't on her. This was on the Alliance, with its fingers in every one of Earth's pies, having eyes everywhere, pulling strings behind the stage, enjoying the thrill of using all our English idioms. The Agency thought they could make Earth a tourist trap, no matter the cost to the locals.

The off-worlder community had been right to fear them. We all should be afraid, very afraid.

"I'm going after him," I said. "I'll meet you back at my parents' house."

"Wait, Sally."

One thing I had learned from the siblings was how to make a dramatic exit. All this time, I had been holding back the urge to leave, and it was so easy to let it go, as easy as an exhale. Before Felling could say another word, I flung my atoms into the universe. I wasn't directionless this time; I knew exactly where I was going—after Cross—and nothing or no one, not even the universe, could stand in my way.

Though in a very real sense, I had no idea what I was doing. I felt the panic set in, the stretch and pull of the million pieces of me splitting and picking a star at random, a place I could simply be. I had dissolved myself into chaos and now had no way of controlling it.

How had I done it the last time? I had locked in on one thing and one thing only, on the man I would follow to the ends of the universe and back again.

I came into being half a foot in the air above Zander, and gravity did the rest. I fell on top of him hard, knocking him down into the earthy soil of the Florida wetlands. I didn't stop to process how easy he had been to find. I didn't think about his far-flung warnings of how easy it was to get lost in the infinite universe. I just knew. I knew where Zander would be and how to get to him.

What I didn't know was how I knew, but that didn't matter when we had an alien to catch.

"Sally?" Zander sputtered, rolling me off him.

"Sorry! Keep running!" I said, pushing myself up on my feet. "I'm not that good at this yet!"

"You—right."

And he was off, throwing a terrified glance my way before speeding after Cross between palms and ferns.

I heard Cross shout as Blayde knocked him down, somewhere so close I reached them in just a few seconds. Blayde had Cross on his belly, pressing her knee into the small of his back, and he struggled beneath her, stronger than he looked. Her face contorted as she struggled to keep him down. Zander watched over the scene, giving her room to contain him.

"It's too late; it's too late," hissed Cross, the smile on his face stretched beyond the point of creepy and reaching the level of positively unnerving. "There's no point in holding me. The bounty is mine."

"The bounty?" said Zander, glancing up as I approached, dropping his eyes back to Cross just as fast. "I hate to break it to you, but you're the one who's trapped, asswipe."

"Oh, but I don't need to catch you." He flung himself onto his back. He grinned up at Blayde, who stood and pressed her foot against his torso. "I planted the seeds. The Agency will see you now, if they haven't already. It's not me they'll be looking for."

"Not you...?" I said, pushing forward. Blayde looked up at me, confused. "You're not working for the Agency?"

"Working for them? No, they've been hunting me for years," he said, laughing harder. "And you know what gets them off my back? Turning in the terrorists they're been looking for all this time!"

"Oh frash," said Zander. "You set us up."

"He can't have," I sputtered. "He's been working for the...um, still not sure, but let's stick with FBI. He's not supposed to know who we are."

"He's been drawing the Agency's eye," said Blayde, pressing her heel even deeper into his chest. "He's leading them right to us. He's the Tallagan."

"He's the... he's the murderer?" I said. None of this made any sense. But the agent's sorry state last night... his healthy glow this morning... it wasn't due to a good night's sleep and an impressive skincare routine. "Well, shit. This is a bit worse than being a double agent, isn't it?"

The air exploded in an instant, red filling my eyes and my lungs before I could think. And just like that he was gone, faster than before. A murderer on the run.

"Frash," said Zander, brushing the smoke from his eyes. "Well, we're the worst investigators this planet has ever seen, aren't we?"

Felling was waiting for us back home, trembling as she sipped a cup of tea from Mom. The rest of us joined her, drinking the fresh pot with varying degrees of tremors.

"So, let me get this straight," said Felling, putting down her drink. "Dustin wasn't a double agent. He was the murderer we've been tracking? I don't know what's worse: not having noticed he was working for aliens intent on keeping us in the dark or not noticing he was a cold-blooded killer who feasts on young women. Should I mention we've been partnered for two friggin' years?"

"Oh, you're back into LARPing?" asked Dad, stopping on his way to the kitchen with his empty coffee cup in hand. "Is it too late for me to join?"

"Dad, I love you, but this is a really bad time."

"Right, right. Carry on, enjoy, and all that," he said, muttering under his breath as he left for the beach, feelings obviously hurt.

"You had no way of knowing, Felling," said Zander. "I suppose he weaseled into your department specifically to elude the Agency's eyes. If anything, the murders are our fault, seeing as how he was trying to draw us out."

"Only now, we need the Agency to catch him before they realize we're here too," said Blayde, slamming her fist down on the table so hard it made the teacups rattle. "Which means we have to reach *them* before he does."

"No, Blayde," Zander spat. "We don't need to announce ourselves. We'll probably get arrested."

"How else are we going to throw him into their sights?" She inclined her head. "If they haven't come for him after four-and-a-half murders, they probably won't come for him at all. We have to make them take charge of him. Make it so they have no other option than to arrest him."

"We're not going to the Agency," said Zander.

"We have to," she insisted. "And we have to make them believe their entire relationship with Earth is on the line."

"You're kidding me," I stammered. "All this time we were talking about avoiding the Agency, trying to keep as far away from them as possible, and now you want us to go up there? And where exactly are they?"

"Oh, the dark side of your moon." Blayde shrugged.

"What?" I said. "Oh hell no."

"It's the perfect place for it," said Zander. "Your moon is tidally locked with Earth, so it's always showing the same face. Popping a space station on the side you never see is easy. Avoiding your probes is child's play for them."

"Thanks for the science lesson," said Felling. "I've stopped questioning their logic at this point. You tell me they invented a spaceship that travels with star spit, I'd believe you."

"Evidently, Felling can't go up there," Blayde continued. "Sorry, but you're inexperienced. I know you think you know how to handle yourself with off-worlders, but once you get up there, you'll be overwhelmed."

"Does my training count for nothing?" Felling retorted. "I know how to work undercover, Blayde."

"I'm sure you're an excellent field agent," said Zander. "But you've never been off your planet before. You will be overwhelmed. And those extra seconds of distraction just to get your bearings when everything is backwards might cost people their lives." He paused. "It's not an insult. You wouldn't bring a new recruit on an important overseas undercover mission when he'd never left his own country and you had never worked with them before, would you?"

"Not around aliens, you don't," Blayde said coolly. "Sally, same issue, but at least you have a little more experience than she does, and I guess trust isn't too much of an issue with you. Not to mention, you already have a translator. And now I remembered why I never wanted to meet a fan: for all the composed demeanor on the outside, Felling is practically a child trying to get the answers to the universe."

"Thanks?" I said, trying to ignore the aghast look Felling was shooting each of us. I had no say in any of this.

"We'll have to risk it with you"—she looked at me—"but you'd never be able to fly the ship on your own. Zander and I would have to go along; there's no question about it. Even if there's a chance of us getting caught, it's better we be your backup than have you fly up there alone."

"But can I just say it?" I asked. "We don't have a ship, and the moon isn't exactly that close."

"We'll find a way to get there," said Blayde. "We have too."

"Area 51 has some ships, right?" said Zander.

"Oh, come on," I said, shocked once again by the casualness of it all. "You want to break into Area 51, steal a ship, infiltrate the Agency, and stop a spine-sucking murderer all without getting arrested by one government or the other?"

"Yes," said Blayde.

"And how do you expect to do that?"

"We'll figure it out as we go along. We always do, don't we? Accidentally awesome."

At this, Felling let out a guffaw, practically falling to the floor in laughter.

"What?" said Blayde. "Did I offend your Terran sensibilities or something?"

"Area 51 doesn't have spaceships," she replied, wiping a tear from the corner of her eye. "That's just a myth propagated by the fringe media."

"How do you know?" Blayde asked, crossing her arms over her chest. "Have you ever been?"

"Well..."

"Have you?"

"No."

"If they don't have ships, no harm, no foul," said Zander. "There are other ways to get off-world, but I'm not dragging the Floridians into this. There's just no easy way of saying that you need a ship because you fancy a joyride right into enemy territory."

"So, what about me, then?" asked Felling, more tense than the past, present, and future walking into a bar. "I'm just supposed to stay on Earth and pretend everything is hunky-dory?"

"If you have any hunks on hand, it could release some stress," said Zander.

"What? No! My former partner is running around snacking on women, and I'm just supposed to let him continue until you catch him? I have to go after him!"

"You can try," said Zander. "You do know him better than any of us."

"Not well enough," she croaked.

"In any case, you can definitely try to track his location," said Blayde. "But you've seen firsthand how dangerous he is. So, I would recommend focusing your efforts on keeping your own agency from panicking once we steal one of their ships. Cross will probably try to draw us out again, but if he can't, he'll try to make a break for it too."

"You can't be serious."

"Deadly," Blayde insisted. "I have dealt with

monsters like him before, and I know the type inside and out."

"Because it's exactly something you would do?"

"Precisely, though I don't appreciate how you framed that as an insult. In any case, no one ever wants to stay long on Earth unless they're up to no good. Or have unhealthy priorities," she added, and I could almost feel her sideways glance slip over to me.

"Fine," said Felling. "I'll get my coat. Time for me to see how well connected I really am."

TEN

ALIEN STORES SELL ALIEN PRODUCTS, DON'T ACTUALLY CATER TO ALIENS, THIS REPORTER FINDS

I THOUGHT RIDING DOWN THE COAST WITH BLAYDE in a car was bad, but airplanes were a whole other story. Despite Felling ushering us past security and avoiding all lines—which made me feel like the celebrity I never wanted to be but could easily get used to—there was no avoiding the hour-long flights in tight quarters with a woman who was gearing up to bash some heads. I could only take so many hours of listening to her slamming her fist repeatedly into her palm.

How many lifetimes would *that* last? I shuddered, sinking into my seat, making myself small, pushing my feet into my duffel bag. Before long, I was so focused on being mad at Blayde that I had completely forgotten why we were flying at all.

Oh, right. We were going to break into the most secretive military base on the planet. Groovy.

"You scared?" asked Zander, midway through our second flight.

"Um, yeah," I stammered. "I'm freaking terrified. You know what the government is said to do to aliens, right? I'm taking a wild guess here and saying neither of us is a big fan of butt stuff."

"Are you guessing or asking?"

"We are not having this conversation here, come on."

He lifted his hands defensively. "You're not being at all subtle, you know."

"And neither are you."

"You two are idiots, and if you don't shut up right now, so help me, you're walking from here." Blayde's fist stopped the self-mutilation long enough for her reprimand, but then she was right back at it, hitting her palm repeatedly.

And there was the core of the problem: Zander and I could never have a real discussion about our relationship while she was around. But she would always be around, in the end.

And always was a long, long time.

Another black SUV was there to pick us up at the airport. Felling got the keys from the driver and took over the vehicle at once. Cityscape soon gave way to desert and then more desert as we drove under the arid sun. Even in February, the air wanted to kill you out here. I couldn't imagine wanting to live inside an oven for a lifetime, especially one that randomly decided to turn up the heat from time to time.

Now free of airplane onlookers, Zander cleared his throat, his energy rising, lifting the excitement in the car. My hands trembled with the slow realization that we were about to do something highly illegal. Only this time, it was on my home planet, where a permanent record was a thing that actually mattered.

I never thought in a single minute in any of my adventures with Zander how saving the world would affect my credit score. Now, I couldn't get mutual funds out of my head. Would immortality affect my insurance rates? Where should I put my long-term investments?

"So, what's the security like, exactly?" he asked Felling, who snorted into the steering wheel, pulling me out of my financial spiral. I fiddled with the handles of my duffel bag to keep them steady.

"Like I have that kind of clearance?" She laughed. "Nuh-uh. I get you guys to the gate, or wherever you want to go outside the fence, and then I'm out of there. There's only so much I can get away with."

"So, we're our own recon?"

"Yup," she said. "Look, I might have gained some brownie points with the whole saving-the-Earth thing, but I traded in a lot of favors that night, and even my newfound street cred is not enough to just waltz into Area-friggin'-51, so this is as far as I can get your. If you get caught, you keep my name out of it, you understand?"

Blayde scoffed. "Like we'd ever be that negligent. I'm walking immortality juice. I don't let myself be caught by just anyone."

"You don't have to keep reminding me," said Felling. "All I'm saying is that I trust you all with my entire career, so don't screw this up."

"You can leave us here," said Zander. "I think this is the right place."

"Um, you sure?" said Felling. "This isn't the actual—"

"It'll do just fine."

I had never seen siding so green before. Or letters so vibrantly red. Zander was out of the car before it even stopped, dashing across the parking lot to a painted picture of a Roswell Gray, where he stuffed his head through the face hole.

"Take a picture!" he shouted. "Sekai would love this!"

"I'm not sure she'd like the bikini, Zander," I said, slipping out of the car after him. The Area 51 Alien Center loomed above me, casting a cool shadow over my back. Blayde spat on the ground behind me.

"This is a frashing disgrace," she muttered. "Killians deserve so much better."

"Should I just wait here, then?" asked Felling, watching Blayde with wide eyes. "Or do you—"

"Go home. Nothing to see here," she replied,

deliberately turning her back on Zander, who was doing his best to make his eyes large and Killian-like in the photo stand. I snapped a picture, if only to keep my nerves under control.

"Don't make me regret bringing you all out here," she said. "Screw this, it's just too absurd. My partner's in the wind and my entire career—let alone life—is in the hands of the space ninjas who saved me when I was fifteen."

"And me," I said. "I'm in this too."

"Not that you even like me all that much right now." She let out a deep breath. "And here I go, sounding like a child again."

"Felling," I said, as earnestly as I could muster, "I like you just fine. I just don't trust you as far as I could throw you."

"And none of that has changed?" She cocked her head to the side like a puppy. It was astounding how fast she could slip off her agent's cap and into real emotion. But that could have been an entirely new level as well. "Even after Cross?"

"I trust *you* fine, Felling. I just don't trust the people you work for. I didn't back in D.C., and I trust them even less now knowing what I know about the Alliance and the Agency and shit. When it comes down to it, you'll always have orders to follow."

"Then trust that everything I do, I do because I think it's right," she insisted. "And if you have a modicum of trust in me, that has to count for something. I'm putting a lot of faith in you, Zander, and Blayde right now. I should be stopping you from this mad dash of a plan. It goes against everything my employers stand for. But I trust you to do what's right." She tapped her breast pocket, and despite the fabric in the way, I could see the outline of her badge through it all. "This is an oath I took. To protect the people of this planet, even if it's from people I thought were my friends. Even if it means putting my life on the line."

She didn't wait for my response, instead peeling down the highway fast enough to leave a plume of dust in her wake, along with a very confused Sally Webber, who was starting to realize she had been totally and entirely unfair to one of her closest friends.

Shit.

"So, now that she's gone," I said to the wind, "have you two got an actual plan?"

Which is the moment when I realized they weren't with me at all. I was alone in the dusty parking lot, every hair on my body going erect.

They had left me.

Again.

They had taken the opportunity to spring off into the universe again, leaving me alone on Earth, leaving me to—

"Sally? Hurry up, will you? You have to see this shirt!"

Oh, they had gone inside the shop, just a few feet away. My body crumpled with relief.

Not the healthiest reaction, Sally Webber.

Inside, the Alien Center was just a store. A store with a lot of alien paraphernalia, but a store all the same. Zander was running back and forth with a handful of tie-dye t-shirts, happy as a clam.

"Oh my gosh, this is so perfect for you," he exclaimed, holding up a hot-pink mess to Blayde's chest. *Keep Calm, I'm Just An Alien In Disguise* was scrawled on the front.

"Sally, could you please explain to me why any Terran would want this abomination on them?" she muttered, looking up as I walked by.

"I wish I could."

"That's because they're not for Terrans," said Zander. "It's the perfect way for off-worlders to signal their existence to each other."

"Um, Zander, I hate to break it to you, but locals *do* actually wear them."

"Oh shit," he replied. "That explains why that Temovar tried to bite me when I gave him the alk'rik greeting."

"He wasn't actually from Temovar?"

"No," Zander shuddered. "I suppose he was just a duck."

Despite my insistence to the contrary, we each ended up with more alien shirts and hats than anyone should possibly own. By the time we left the store, we must have owned half of it.

"This has been a terrible waste of an afternoon," I said. "Do you two plan on storming Area 51 by night?"

"Nah, this is all part of the plan," said Zander, stripping out of his shirt and replacing it with the alien tie-dye.

"Ah, so you do have a plan?"

"Always."

"What Zander means is that we have a loosely connected set of goals and some idea of how to meet them," Blayde interjected. "All you have to do is stay behind us and run when we tell you to run. And keep up with the unscripted costume changes."

"Fair enough, but—"

"Let the pros do their job, honeybun," she said.

"Honeybun?"

"What? Zander can have pet names for you, and I can't?"

"Blayde," he hissed, "not here, not now."

We dressed in our tie-dye best, stuffed our normal clothes into my duffel, and strode out into the desert, past the billboards for burgers and lawyers until there was nothing but sand and brush. Apparently, step one of Zander's plan was literally just to wander the wastes until we found something. Which we did, eventually. After what must have been hours, the sun feeling low on the horizon, we stumbled upon barbed wire, which gave us a moment's pause.

Blayde raised her hand to shield her eyes, muttering mostly to herself. "We're too far out for security cameras. Sentry post?"

"I'd rather not appear on tape." Zander bit his lip. "Assuming you all still use tape?"

I threw my hands up into the air. "I think we're all digital, but this is Area 51. They could be using laser crystals or something."

"Crystals? How third century," Blayde scoffed. "Right, shall we do the cocky hitchhiker meets the undying girl? Seems like a good combo, at least to get us inside."

"Don't see why not." Zander turned back and grinned at me, just waiting, daring me to ask.

Well, my ego was sufficiently bashed. "Is anyone going to tell me what's going to happen?"

"No. Now drop down and roll in the dirt."

"What the hell?"

"Do it—and do it now!"

This must have been a test of faith. Or a power grab. I melted gingerly to the ground, watching as Zander did the same. Soon, the three of us were writhing in the desert sand.

"Don't we look great?" she exclaimed. "Now come on, we don't have all day."

Blayde had transformed. She was neither of the two Blaydes I knew. The depressed husk was gone, replaced by a pantomime of her usual self, replaced now by a happy-go-lucky valley college girl who was so damn tired of wandering through the desert. She stumbled; she panted; she was practically an alarm calling everyone and everything to our location.

It wasn't long until a lone, green truck found us— three lost college students wandering the desert after getting separated from our alien tour group. The man inside didn't look much older than us either. Lanky, with crew cut hair and camouflage fatigues, he was obviously with the military but wasn't exactly top brass. Not that any of them would station themselves in the middle of the desert sun for hours on end.

"Don't shoot!" Zander shouted, hands raised high, voice carrying over the dry air. "We're so lost, it's not even funny."

"Who the hell are you?" The soldier barked, parking the vehicle and taking a tentative step toward us. "This is a restricted zone."

"Oh my god, I'm so sorry! We were visiting the alien landmarks when we lost our group. Kinda puts a damper on our plans, let me tell you. We were hoping for a shortcut back."

The soldier sighed, pinching the bridge of his nose. "Sir, I can't do much to help you. You can't cross the base, if that's what you're asking."

"No, no, I can definitely see that." He scratched the back of his head awkwardly. "I just need pointin' in the right direction. Which way to the nearest town?"

"Back down that road," he said, indicating the path that followed the barbed wire fence and the markers. "But it's too long on foot to get there before sundown."

"Can't you—"

"No, sorry. Government property. I'm not permitted to drive civilians anywhere unless they're criminals."

"So, what's the most minor crime to commit for us to get a ride through your base?"

The sentry grinned, seeing where we were going with this. He was young, inexperienced, and relentlessly bored. "Well, the sun is pretty low. I'd be trading posts with someone eventually. I can pin you for stealing my hat."

"How close will that get us to town?"

"A few miles."

"So, what happens if I do... this?" In one swift move, Zander swiped the soldier's gun.

My muscles tensed. The shock on my face was real, the fear doubly so. No wonder they didn't want to tell me their plan. It was dumb as hell.

"Sir," the soldier snapped, keeping his voice steady despite the obvious annoyance, "what you have just done is many different shades of illegal."

"But how far is this worth?" Zander asked.

The soldier gritted teeth his teeth. "You'd be seeing a lieutenant for that. A few minutes walking distance to the closest diner, and they'll have phones you can use. But, gotta warn you, you'll probably end up in jail first."

Instead of handing it over, Zander tossed the weapon in the air, catching it and twirling it like a baton high above his head, far out of reach of any of us. Even Blayde seemed uncomfortable from his antics, cringing like me.

"What happens if I don't want to give it back?" Zander chided.

"That's going too far, sir."

"What are you gonna do about it?"

"I'm gonna... I'm gonna take you in for questioning."

"Are you now?" Zander's voice dropped an octave lower, a macho man stereotype if I had ever heard one.

"Sir, I am authorized to use physical force on you at this point. I must warn you I am trained in hand-to-hand combat."

"Bring it. I do CrossFit!"

It wasn't even a fight. Zander dodged the man's lunge, sidestepping in slow motion, practically handing the gun back to him. The soldier grabbed it, giving it a tug, only to slam the butt end into Zander's gut.

Accidentally shooting Blayde in the process. She collapsed, blood oozing from the gaping wound in her stomach, staining the desert beneath her.

"No!" I screamed, rushing to her. Despite knowing

she would be fine, there was that instinct that came when your sometimes-bestie just got killed. I threw myself to the ground beside her, reaching for her body, my hands shaking as I tried to turn her on her side.

She was definitely, irrevocably, dead.

There's something unnerving about looking into lifeless eyes. It's like walking around someone's home when they're not home, the knowledge that everything about them is here while they are not. I clutched Blayde in my arms, the tears streaming down my face only partially fake, as the two men stared in equal shock.

"You... you," Zander stammered, bringing his hands to his head, the gun dropping to the desert sand. "Dude, I'm so sorry. I didn't think it was actually loaded."

"Didn't think...?" the soldier spat. "This is not a game, civilian. You realize that, don't you?"

He was doing a surprising job of keeping it together. I probably wouldn't have, in his position. He picked up his weapon gingerly, then took aim at Zander.

"I'm placing you under arrest," he said, his voice steady, though I could see his hands trembling ever-so-slightly. He was as scared as I was. "Put your hands behind your head and follow me."

"Oh god!" I screamed, juicing it a little too much, surely. "What are we going to do?"

Zander was sobbing violently now, even as the

soldier shakily tried to place him in handcuffs. The soldier didn't come for me, not while I was cradling the corpse. I rocked her gently back and forth, not wanting to let her go. I knew what was coming next.

Blayde woke up screaming.

The soldier screamed.

I screamed.

We were all screaming, and let me tell you, it was hella cathartic.

"Holy shit!" she cried. "What the hell just happened?"

"You died, um, Suzanne," I said gently. "You got shot, and you died."

She flew to her feet, waving her hands in front of her face. "But I'm not dead. Why didn't I die?"

"Mark shot you!" I pointed a shaky finger at Zander, who stepped back in shock. "He killed you! I saw the bullet. You stopped breathing. I thought you were—"

"Is this my blood?" she stammered, drawing her hands to her abdomen. "Oh god, there's so much of it!"

"How…?" The soldier's eyes were wide as dinner plates, as if he had just seen a ghost. Which, by most accounts, he just had. Unless you'd rather call her a zombie.

She lifted a bloody finger, pointing directly at her brother, murder on her lips. Zander's own eyes were pushing the limits of human expression, ready to pop from his skull at any minute.

"You," she hissed. "You did this to me!"

"No! This is all wrong!" With one fell swoop, Zander grabbed the gun from the soldier's grasp and shot her again. You'd think the guy would keep better hold of his weapon this time around, but no.

"Seriously?" she scoffed. "Not again, come on." Her stomach exploded into shrapnel of skin and guts. Too late. She had died for the second time today, and she was getting pretty bored of it.

"What the absolute hell, man?" the soldier screamed. "What the hell is wrong with you?"

"She was a zombie!" Zander sobbed. "My sister was a zombie! You know what zombies eat, don't you?"

"Oh god, oh god," the man stammered, throwing his hands up to his scalp, dragging his hands back across the fuzz of hair. "Give me that!"

He grabbed the gun from Zander's hands, disassembling it in three swift movements. Zander let him, the picture of shock plastered on his face. I had to remember to thank him for having us change into the awful tie-dye because I was covered in far more blood than would ever wash out.

This time, the soldier didn't hesitate to put the Zander in handcuffs and stuff him in the passenger side of the truck before running to Blayde's side. He checked her pulse, and, still in shock, lifted her over his shoulder and threw her dead body into the back of the truck. He then turned to me.

"You. Get back there," he ordered, ripping my duffel from my hands in tossing it in the truck on top of the corpse.

"You saw that, right?" I asked, doing my best to sound afraid, though I was over the moon with excitement to see where this was going. "I had nothing to do with this. Oh my god, this is—"

"You're telling me. Get in the truck."

"Where are you taking us?"

"You and your friend have a lot of explaining to do," he stammered. "I have no choice. I have to bring you to the authorities."

"Am I going to be in trouble? You saw, I didn't do anything."

Sitting in the back of the truck, riding side by side with Blayde's corpse, I wondered oddly why we had to traumatize this guy for life when we could have just jumped to get past the chain link fence. Only then did it hit me that the only person holding us back was, in fact, me.

ELEVEN

YOU WOULDN'T STEAL A CAR.
YOU WOULDN'T STEAL A MOVIE.
PIRATING SPACESHIPS IS ILLEGAL.

IT'S HARD TO ADMIT, BUT AT THIS POINT IN MY LIFE, I was more concerned with Blayde's death than her revival. There had been a lot of panic over seeing her body ripped apart by bullets, but the minute she sat back up, groggy and gasping for air, the only reaction I had was a casual, 'Yo.'

"Did it work?" she asked.

"Did we get on base?" I shrugged, clutching the side of the truck as we bounced over the potholed road. "Yup. Did you traumatize a guy for life? Also, yup."

"Oh, he'll get over it." She pushed herself back up and stripped off her soiled shirt. "Not every day you see an impossible girl."

"That sounds like it should be trademarked," I pointed out. "*Impossible Girl*. Makes for a terrible perfume."

173

"It was also my stage name when I was a cage fighter, but that's neither here nor there," she said, wiping her skin down with a clean corner of her shirt. She glanced out the canvas of the back of the truck, muttered a few words, and threw her clothes onto the road behind us.

"Uh, Blayde? What's going on?" I asked, suddenly rather self-conscious. "I don't have to strip, too, do I?"

"Nah, you do you." She reached for the duffel bag. "No jumping, right? I'm not running across the base in those bloody things, and we can't let the soldier's story have any credibility. Don't worry. The clothes will make the vultures happy. If they look back here, they'll think he's crazy. I mean, a girl coming back to life just to die again? How insane is that?"

"Very."

She didn't give a rat's ass as to whose clothes she pulled out of the bag. One of Zander's casual tees thrown over my own pair of jeans, and she looked runway ready.

"He drives us on base, and we make a run for it." A bigger grin. "Aren't we lucky to have fallen on a rookie?"

"They probably have rather good defenses. Guns, weapons."

"Oh, we'll be smart. Just run when I tell you to run."

"And Zan? How will he know when to start running? I mean, he can't see us back here."

"Oh, he'll know. Wait, did you just call him Zan?"

The truck ground to a halt. In the front seat, the soldier was explaining to someone in muffled tones what had happened by the fence while Zander protested loudly, alternating between "This is a terrible misunderstanding" and "I demand to speak to the overlord!" Finally, we were let through, my nerves growing with every passing second.

"Any idea where the ships will be?"

"Biggest hangar doors are usually our best bet. Some crashed ships can be enormous."

"So, we're just going to wander aimlessly until we find a space-worthy ship?" I slung my duffel bag over my shoulder and put my sunglasses on, if only to hide how absolutely terrified I was. "I'm trusting you with this."

"As you well should." She peeked under the canvas curtain. "Okay, now."

Casually, she hopped out the back of the moving truck. I followed, duffel on my shoulder, hitting the ground with a loud thump, and sped after her as she disappeared behind the corner of one of the tall, white buildings. The truck continued without us.

What she did wasn't running: it made running want to lock itself in its room and cry. In seconds, she was navigating the labyrinth between the buildings, her feet blurring as she sped through the alleys at inhuman speed. Speed I probably should have unlocked somehow but still hadn't figured out, so I was stuck at my usual human pace, out of breath from suddenly forgetting how to breathe.

When we flew out onto the road again, it was somehow, impossibly, in front of the very same truck we had just left.

"Teeth!" Blayde intoned, raising her arms high. "I'm hungry for teeth, and I need them now!"

The soldier slammed on the brakes hard. Blayde moaned loudly, taking a stiff step forward, knees locked, one of her hands outstretched as she kept her eyes fixed on the sky.

"I want them white and shiny. I want them yellow and pointy! Teeth!"

The tires screeched as the truck came to a halt, the motor still running as our soldier friend took a hesitant step out of his vehicle, trying not to look directly at the twice-risen woman. She groaned heavily, an inhuman sound so deep and resonant it sent shivers down my spine.

It was the split-second distraction Zander needed to get free. As the soldier watched Blayde ramble about teeth, he twisted off his cuffs, slipped out of the truck, and darted into the shadows at my side.

"What is she going on about?" I grumbled. Per usual, there were a million other questions I would rather ask, but none seemed to capture the weirdness of this moment.

"Teeth?" he said, staring blankly ahead. "The undead *love* teeth."

"Let me guess. You know this from experience?"

"It's because of all the calcium."

Blayde was drawing too much attention to herself, but she didn't mind. She waved the soldier a quick goodbye and peeled off, breezing past us as if carried by the wind.

"Shall we?" I asked Zander.

"After you, ma'am," he replied, and we were running yet again.

Here's some fun running facts for all of you keeping notes at home. First of all, running is a lot easier when you've had a full meal and lots of water, so remember to stay hydrated. And second, and probably most important, your mind will want to give up way before your body. And when you have an immortal bod but a mortal mentality, every step feels like death.

Though it was kind of reassuring to know I could still feel.

Somehow, I was keeping up, despite the fire in my feet. The sweltering heat in my shoes and the friction from running wore down the plastic soles with each step. My knees resonated like gongs every time my feet slammed the asphalt, sending shivers up my bones. I was flying, and it was exhausting. I couldn't breathe fast enough, I couldn't keep my thighs from chafing, and I couldn't push the thought of where I was out of my mind.

Oh crap. We had just broken into Area 51. With no plan other than to run for it. No map, no inside help. Just three idiots and their stupid feet.

Hurry up, stupid feet.

Somehow, the siblings found their way around, arriving back in the open tarmac in front of the hangars. Blayde was right. It was obvious where the ships were being kept. The doors were twice the size as the other hangars, and the markings on the ground were completely different. The siblings pressed themselves against one of the metal walls, blending into the shadows and checking the road on each side before dashing across at top speed.

Guards stood at the small back entrance, but they were dealt with quietly. A strong, well-placed conk on the head was enough to give us a minute of privacy. Blayde whipped out her laser pointer, easily breaking the lock on the door, and we slipped into the facility.

One step into the place, and it felt like being on another planet. The lack of light was eerie enough, making the gigantic structures in dusty sunbeams even more surreal and otherworldly. It seemed all in all like a badly assembled jigsaw puzzle, each piece from a different era, epoch, and solar system. I froze in place, my eyes riveted on the massive constructs.

Holy shit. You heard it here first, people. There *are*

alien ships at Area 51. Although, you've probably already guessed as much.

"Broken, broken, missing wings, missing the motor, laundry ship, this is a septic tank," said Zander, marching down the hangar and pointing to each ship in turn. "No propulsion method, collectible... Ah, here we go." He pointed to one of the better pieces of the collection. "Can you believe this? It's a 614-A Angel. Not the best on the market, far from it, but it's reliable."

It was, for sure, one of the smaller ships of the set, only the size of a school bus. A little larger than the hoppers on the *Traveler,* but smaller than Dave if you counted his warp engine and larger if you didn't. The silver paint was chipped in areas, but the whole thing was intact and, hopefully, worthy of space travel.

Zander touched the hull of the ship, breathing deeply, his eyes closing as he fell into sync with the machine. Which, of course, set off more alarms than I could count.

"Do you hear something?" asked Blayde, nose in the air as she ripped off one of the panels on the door. She snipped a wire or two with her laser, letting the entrance ramp descend from the ship. Stale air wafted toward us, a clear sign that no one had managed to dismantle the ship before Blayde came along.

"You mean the entire base going into high alert?" I asked.

"No, more like... cheap elevator music."

"I hear it too," said Zander, before rushing into the ship.

"I think your coms are ringing," said Blayde, lifting an eyebrow. "Though it goes without saying that you're *supposed* to silence these things when you're about to storm a secret military base."

"I thought I had," I said, admittedly a little flustered by being lectured mid-raid. And I had silenced my phone, leaving it on only for...

"Shit. It's my parents," I stammered, but the siblings were too busy getting the ship up and running to pay any attention to me. I followed them inside, bringing the phone up to my ear.

"Hello?" I asked, the door closing behind me with a hiss. Inside, the layout was simple. The cockpit was much bigger than Dave's spaceship, most probably because this ship was more space-worthy than a simple interstellar shuttle. The chairs even had much better upholstery, like those in a luxury RV. Heck, the room was altogether rather cozy. I wondered idly how long it had been here on this base. Either the US military had just acquired this one or modern RVs looked unnervingly like out-of-date spaceships.

"Sally?" I had been so distracted by the ship I hadn't heard my dad's voice. And boy, was he terrified.

I dropped the duffel bag on the couch. Shit. I leave for a few hours and suddenly he's in danger? This was no coincidence. It must have been the government or the Floridians. Or maybe the Alliance had already found us…

"Dad, are you okay? Did someone hurt you?"

"Zander, doors," Blayde barked, indicating the front of the hangar where an absolute lack of exit was obvious. "Come on, brother of mine, do I need to separate you two until you can focus again?"

"Something tells me the doors will be taken care of," he said as he took the pilot's seat. His sister gave him a shove, but he didn't budge. Annoying and short on time, she sat down with a *humph* in the passenger side, leaving me in one of the couches in the back that had an absolutely terrible view. I clutched the phone to my ear, blocking the other so I could hear my dad better.

"Is that an alarm?" he asked. "What's going on? Where are you?"

"I'm, um, at Disney World," I said, regretting the lie instantly. Though it did fit when, a second later, the guns of our tiny ship made utterly satisfactory *pew pew* noises, blasting through the hangar doors as if they were butter.

I cringed. It was one thing to break into a military base, quite another to destroy government property. My taxes went into this place, after all.

"You need to get back here," said Dad, his voice dropping to a whisper. "There's… a woman."

"A what, now?"

"What do you think? Is she in good shape?" Blayde asked Zander, running her hand over the dash.

"They obviously had no idea how this baby works." He flicked a switch, and the whole ship lit up, the motors sputtering slightly but staying on. "The fuel tank is almost full. More than enough for a short jaunt to the moon and back. Oh, and even better, we have grav'!"

I stuffed a finger in my ear again. It was hard enough trying to understand what Dad was going on about without a spaceship rumbling to life in the background. I heard my dad breathe out in exasperation on the other end of the line.

"She showed up here half an hour ago," he said, voice quaking.

"Who? What does she want?" I asked, shoving my finger deeper in my ear, but it did nothing to quiet the whine of the engines.

"She wants to marry Blayde," he said. "Only, she seems to think Blayde is a man. Her name is Svetlana, and she just came in here from Russia. Apparently, Blayde met her online and promised her a green card?"

"Can you give me a sec?" I said, holding the microphone to my chest. "Blayde?"

"A little busy right now, hon," she replied. "You may want to put on a seat belt. We have company."

"I don't have a seat belt!" I sputtered.

She could have just said that she had seen dozens

of soldiers in formation by the hangar doors that were slowly opening, their rifles pointed at our small ship through the hole Zander had blown away. But Blayde was not known for her lack of theatricality or Zander for his lack of serious eye rolling, which he *was* doing at the moment, as he waved a bored arm at the assembled team.

"Seriously? Up against a spaceship with rifles?" Blayde scoffed.

"I don't think they were expecting us to actually fly this thing," I said, crushing my thumb over the phone mic. Dad did not need to hear any of this.

"What else would they expect?"

"I dunno. For us to snap a few blurry pictures for conspiracy websites?" I said. "That kind of stuff?"

"If they expected so little, why put so many soldiers outside?"

"Well, there goes that line of thought," I replied. "You were right, Blayde. Yes, they believe they can use rifles to shoot down a spaceship."

"Sally?" Dad's muffled voice rose from out of my phone. "Are you still there?"

"Yeah, sorry, Blayde's a little hard to reach right now. We're on a ride."

"Then tell her to get off. This isn't a joke," he spat. "This woman waltzed into our home and is eating all the Cheerios straight out of the box. With no milk, Sally. No milk at all!"

One problem at a time, Dad. Maybe this Svetlana

was better suited for Blayde than we gave her credit for.

"You could tell her to find a hotel," I suggested.

"I tried that," he said. "But Svetlana is madly in love, she says."

"Love at first email!" came a voice from the background, presumably the Russian bride herself.

All the while, our little ship was diligently rolling toward the massive hoard of soldiers, all armed to the teeth and in a surprisingly complex formation. Almost as if they had trained for this eventuality, despite how fruitless it was. The soldiers started to shoot, a low rumble of noise muffled by the strong hull of our ship. *Ping-ping-ping* replaced pew-pew-pew as the bullets ricocheted off the metal frame.

"Shit, Dad, I have to call you back," I stammered.

"Sally, no, don't—"

But it was too late. I had to focus on the fact that the US Armed Forces were shooting at me, which made me seriously rethink my patriotism.

"Do we have shields?" I asked, gripping the tattered RV seats.

"Against bullets?" Blayde scoffed. "No need, Sally. We're a flying tank."

"Not flying yet," I pointed out.

"Working on that," said Zander.

With a sudden burst of energy, the ship shot forward, pushing us back against our chairs. I flew backwards, tripping over my stupid couch. Flush with the wall, it made the perfect slide as the engines kicked. With a jolt of acceleration, I slid down the length of it, ramming into the armrest.

Blayde screamed in furious joy as we left the ground, soaring into the sky as we escaped the base. Poof. There went the clouds, little wisps of cotton by the windshield. The sky dimmed until it was pure dark. We had broken out of the atmosphere in a matter of seconds. No time for me to react or scream.

"Shit, that felt good," she said, slapping her brother playfully on the arm. "Didn't that feel good?"

"I miss Dave," he said, patting the dashboard sadly. "He might have been stubborn as a Darnubian, but at least he had character."

"Come on, this ship is fine," she replied. "Got us off Earth without reciting poetry, and that's what counts."

"Speaking of," I said. "Blayde, what did you do on the internet last night?"

"What do you mean?"

"That was my dad on the phone," I said, unable to restrain the rise in my voice. "Apparently, you bought a Russian bride."

"You did what?" Zander's glare was sharper than any of his swords, and I sure was glad he hadn't brought any of those along.

"She said she was looking for a better life, and you both are on my back about being a nicer person, so there."

"You're telling me you brought this woman over under false pretenses just because you're feeling guilty about all the shit you say about Earth?"

"Guilt? No, I just wanted the two of you off my back," she snapped. "And what do you mean 'false pretenses?' I paid for her ticket over here. She got what she asked for."

The thing about losing all sense of physical pain meant that everything else was heightened a million times over. Embarrassment and guilt were part of that party pack.

"Blayde, I don't even know where to start," said Zander, "so I'm just going to let Sally handle it."

"Me?" I said. "No. If I get started, I might not stop."

"Oh, yes!" Blayde squealed. "I do like this new, intense Sally! Give it to me straight, darling. How bad was I?"

"Well, for starters, I'm pretty sure that wasn't your money you used to pay for those tickets, though I'm not sure whose it was." I gripped my hands into tight, little fists. "Then, there's the whole thing about the Russian-bride premise I'm not sure you're fully aware of. Namely, the bride part."

"So, I marry her." Blayde shrugged. "I've been married countless times before."

I took a breath. My face was becoming hot now. "I'll dissect that another time. But she wants to marry you for your citizenship, which, may I remind you, you don't actually have."

"Oh, that makes much more sense," she replied, oh-so-casually.

"And we haven't even gotten to *how* you landed on a website for Russian brides to begin with," I stammered. "I certainly hope you weren't using my laptop because I'm pretty sure you let in every virus imaginable."

"So, I buy Svetlana a ticket back," she said, turning back to the console. "Plain and simple."

"So much for helping the poor girl."

"Well, what do you want me to do? Turn back time?"

"Apparently, you can, so why don't you?"

Maybe I had been too harsh, but she didn't say. In fact, she didn't utter another word. Blayde got up from the chair, walked briskly past me, and started to rummage through the duffel bag, grabbing a dress I did not recognize. She strode off to the back of the ship without another word, presumably to find a bathroom or simply a place to get changed, but she offered no explanation.

It was the first time I was worried that she wasn't stripping in front of my face.

TWELVE

NOTHING LIKE BEING TRAPPED IN A SPACESHIP WITH YOUR FEELINGS

THERE'S PROBABLY NOTHING MORE ROMANTIC than gliding through the stars at the helm of your very own spaceship, your man by your side, adrenaline rushing through your veins from goals well accomplished. It would be slightly more romantic if your boyfriend's sister wasn't sulking in the bathroom, but we make do where we can.

"Was I too harsh?" I asked, if only to break the silence. Zander hadn't said anything since she had left, his eyes focused on the dash. Not that he needed to do anything. Even the seat belt sign overhead was off.

"What?"

"Should I have held back?" I asked again. "With Blayde?"

He didn't look up. All my muscles tensed. "Talk to me, goose."

Again, nothing.

I scanned the console. Flashing lights and knobs and buttons, just like in any space movie worth its salt. But the steering wheel was pretty self-explanatory.

In one swift move, I pulled back hard on it, ripping it around, hoping for a brain-wrenching 360, letting the Earth flash over the windshield for half a second. Even the immortal among us still had terrible bouts of vertigo.

"What the hell, Sally?" said Zander as he finally, *finally*, looked up from his console.

"Stop shutting me out," I said, ignoring the fact that I was now flushing with embarrassment. "You keep going on about me not talking, but you never fill me in on these stupid plans of yours."

"It's not stupid," he said. "We're on our way to the moon. I'd call that a success, don't you?"

"A success?" I scoffed. "Sure, we succeeded. But the entirety of the plan was to run through an open military installation in the hopes of finding what we were looking for before they caught us. What were we supposed to do if they did catch us, hmm?"

"But they didn't."

"Not this time, but what about next time? What if we get separated? What then?"

Zander shrugged as he returned his focus to the dash. "You know plans. You start with something, then go through plans B, C, D, E so quickly there's no time to fill in the gaps. Blayde and I have worked together for so long that we just go with whatever."

"That's not the real reason."

"Yes, it is."

"Come on, Zander."

"I swear!"

I had been paying attention. This time, I flicked the control switch in front of my wheel before I yanked it. The ship did a satisfying barrel roll, the planet turning swiftly in the rear-view mirror, beautiful and twisty.

"Pirates?" came a shout from the bathroom.

"Sally's trying to teach me a lesson," Zander shouted back.

"Ah."

"No, I'm not," I retorted. "And this is exactly what I was saying. Just yesterday, you were all about listening and talking and keeping me in the loop. But no matter all your talk about us, well, talking, you're not doing any of it. We have all the time in the universe, but we're not making time for each other."

"How many times do I need to tell you I love you for it to stick?"

"Oh, don't worry. You've been very communicative on that front, but everything else? Radio silence."

He said nothing, which was probably more infuriating than if he had said anything at all. He pulled his hands through his hair, taking a deep inhale, exhale. One quick course correction—not that I had deviated us at all—and he was back to looking at me, his piercing gaze staring right though me.

"What do you want me to say?" he asked, finally. "Do you want me to admit that I'm terrible at making plans? Because Blayde has been saying that for years, and I already know it."

"That's really it?" I said. "Your plans are really a... collected sets of goals?"

He let out a laugh. "Way to make me feel any better about it."

"Oh shit," I said, relief washing over me in a torrent. "We just broke into Area 51 and stole a spaceship. Which I am now flying. To the dark side of the moon."

"Correct."

"I really stole a ship from Area 51?" It sounded absurd. It felt absurd.

"Team effort." He pulled out a tin of Pringles from my duffel bag. "Hey, can I eat these?"

It was my turn to roll my eyes. The duffel bag was becoming a real Room of Requirement here. He started to eat the chips in content silence until I spoke up.

"You promise you won't keep me out of things anymore?" I said, anxiously.

"Of course. Where is this coming from?"

"I don't know." I took some deep, calming breaths. "It's just when we were at that tacky gift shop and you and Blayde went inside, I didn't see you go. So, my first instinct was—"

"No." Zander's gaze became twice as intense. "You know that will never happen again, right?"

"I do, I do," I said, but I couldn't stop the shudder from rolling under my skin. "But part of me doesn't. Part of me remembers what it was like when you two left me, and it's still raw."

Zander dropped the Pringles. I didn't know why my eyes were riveted on the spilled can when he had his arms around me instead. I leaned my head onto his shoulder, breathing in the smell of him, reveling in the warmth that was just for me.

"I'm not going anywhere," he said. "Ever again."

"You swear?"

"On my life," his voice dropped to a whisper. "We'll never lose each other. I can promise you that."

The was a moment of silence. A sweet, warm silence where we let each other just be. The wonderful weirdness of having my ear pressed against a man's chest and not hearing a heart beating made the quiet even more intense.

"How did you jump where you did?" he asked, and the warm moment was gone.

"What do you mean?" I said, though I knew very well what he was talking about. Zander had made it very clear that you could either jump randomly or to a place you could see—never to a person, like I had.

"Back when we were chasing Cross. You didn't

jump to catch up; I would have seen you running with us. You jumped from the car. You jumped blind."

I nodded slowly. "I just… I thought of you. I knew that if it worked when I found you in the library outside of time, finding you on Earth would be much easier."

"But how did you know how to do it?"

He sounded oddly… jealous. It wasn't the happy tone of an uplifting friend, proud of your accomplishments. It was the terse tone of someone who wanted to know how you had what he wanted. And I hated being on that side of his voice.

"Instinct?" I said, biting my lip. "I just knew where you were. In my gut."

"That doesn't explain how you knew how to reach me. I knew you were on Earth when I lost you. I knew the when, I knew the where, but I couldn't get anywhere near you."

I didn't say what I wanted to say—that he hadn't even tried, not really. Not that I knew every detail of our time apart when Blayde took him away from me, because I didn't, but from what I could tell, he had given up the second she had made the situation seem impossible.

Why was I still enabling her?

"Bathroom is free, brother-mine," said Blayde. "And I'm in charge of the plans from here on out, and I'm going to have to borrow Sally for most of them, thank you very much."

EARTHSTUCK

A stranger appeared on my left, her raven-black hair falling to her shoulders in a cascade of curls, framing the face of the pale beauty before me. Dark sunglasses hid her eyes. She was dressed in a light and loose flowery blouse and a jean skirt that went all the way to her ankles, giving her an overall professional lawyer hippie look. "Oh, don't look so surprised."

"Where on earth...?"

She rolled her eyes. Was that a perk of immortality—eyes constantly rolling around in our heads like loose marbles? "You pack a duffel bag; I fill it with things that will be useful. I got you a costume as well," she added as an afterthought, either to Zander or me, or maybe both of us. It was hard to tell with her obscenely dark glasses.

I snatched the bag from her hands, frowning as I took in the mess stuffed inside. Did everyone here think my bag was free storage space? Not only was there an assortment of tangled wigs and clothes, but there was the occasional snack bar swimming around and a self-help book entitled *Advertising and You.*

"What the hell is this?" I stammered, pulling out the book.

"Some light reading for the plane," Blayde scoffed. "Don't blame me for your parents having a ridiculously dreary library."

"I meant the mess. Since when have you been using my duffel?"

"Since forever," she replied, reaching in and pulling

out an orange, which she bit into, skin and all. She spat it out. "Gods, this is wretched. Anyway, it's not my fault you never paid any attention to your bag. You left it in my care when we were in Da-Duhui, and it hit me just how roomy it was. How do you think we got those costumes when we saved you from the mob?"

"You've been using my bag this whole time?"

"You never said anything." She shrugged. "Now, go get changed. Time's a-wasting."

I wanted to scream a whole slew of obscenities at her. I mean, come on. She used to go on for hours about how I had no place amongst them, yet, apparently, my bag was allowed to stay. My beloved duffel was more useful to her than I was.

And then it hit me. This was the most Blayde thing she had done in days. Stepping all over me? Abusing the internet? Talk about the long and winding road to recovery. As strange as she looked with her black hair, pale skin, and dark glasses, I felt like I was looking right at the Blayde I had always known.

"Why are you smiling?" She took the bag back and tossed it at Zander. "Here. You go first since your Sally-Wally is having a nervous breakdown. Bathroom is straight in the back; you can't miss it."

"I'm not having a nervous breakdown," I said, as Zander rose, kissing me quickly on the forehead on his way out of the cockpit. Blayde threw herself into his chair the second his butt left it, propping her feet on the dashboard with a sigh.

"I might have been a bit preemptive," she said, "considering what I'm about to tell you."

I wasn't sure if I should be worried or just prepared. Responding to all her jabs about Zander's and my relationship was an active sport, a bit like tennis, except you never knew when the other was going to serve—or if they were using a ball or maybe a grenade instead.

"Dear god, if this is another bit of unsolicited relationship advice, I swear—"

"Um, no," she said. "Stay focused, Sally. We're on a mission here."

Well, that was a bit of a relief. "Then what are you worried about telling me?"

"Well, I've been giving this a lot of thought," she said. And apparently, she had because she was coming at it with more tact than she usually gave. "Seeing as how we can't put Zander in charge of any planning, I've been trying to work out what we're going to do when we arrive at the Agency."

"I assume his plan would have us do a few high-speed laps through the place and hopefully walk out with Cross topping their most wanted list. Maybe with some explosions on the way."

She laughed. "Precisely. You know him better than I give you credit for, Sally-Wally."

"Don't call me that," I spat, but inside, I was

beaming. Coming from her, that was a high compliment.

"I've been muddling this over in my head," she continued. "The only way for us to go through the Agency uncaught, however good our costumes are, is to stay away from knowing eyes."

"So, what's the point of having great costumes if they're not going to work?"

"A few extra minutes of anonymity can be the difference between the success and failure of a mission, but it won't be enough against the Agency. They make what Felling does look like child's play. If that child was a recently divided single-cell organism and the adult was one of the higher dimensional space unicorns who watch our every move."

"Wait, what?"

"What I'm meaning to say is that it's the Agency's job to see through disguises. The entire point of their existence is to manage and maintain off-world visitors to Earth, after all, so they're a master of disguises on every level."

"So, you're saying our costumes are no match for them." I licked my lips, which had suddenly gone dry. "Even if you were to wear an entire skin wrap, they'd see right through it."

"Precisely. They know our faces. *Veesh,* they have every guise we've ever used on record. And worse, they have LifePrint, patent pending."

"Let me guess. It can read your aura?" I scoffed.

"You're joking, but yes," she said. "It's all that but a whole lot less New Agey. A collection of biometric recordings that knows exactly who you are, no matter what you're wearing, even if you've turned your skin purple, grown an extra leg, and became a master of the jig. The Agency is set up with a few, especially in the administration department, so you'll be by yourself there. Zander and I are probably recorded in there as criminals already, so going through them is out of the question."

"Then why bother dressing up in the first place?"

"Getting revealed by a LifePrint scanner is one thing. Getting spotted by a kid who's seen your mug shot on TV is entirely different. We did just steal a shuttle from the suspended islands, what, last week? Not to mention hacking into their computer and stealing the address for the reclusive library and then blowing it up. Our trail is hot again, and there's a bounty on our heads, as you well know. Just as a precaution, we'll wait for you in the lobby."

I felt the emptiness in my chest return. Shit. "So, the plan is no longer to run around causing a mess. It's for me to do all the running by myself."

"Except with a fair bit more sitting, nodding, and filling out forms," said Blayde. "But, as I said, Zander and I will be in the lobby if you need either of us."

Easy for her to say. They have lifetimes of training and a habit of running on the wrong side of the law. I had been tip-toeing the line on worlds I didn't know, but this was Earth we were talking about. My planet, my home. One misstep, and my life there, let alone my family, would be in jeopardy.

"I should have waited at home," I muttered.

"I literally just told you we can't do this without you," said Blayde, throwing her hands into the air. "You're immortal. Learn to live like it."

"I'm immortal, but my family isn't," I said sternly. "What happens to them if things go south?"

"Sally, do you think I'd let anything happen to Hal and Laurie?"

I didn't know how to answer that. Blayde hadn't cared much for me when I was mortal, so I doubted my connected family would have a pass. "Yes?"

"Well, I promise you this time that if anything does happen to you—and nothing will; dare I remind you that you literally can't die—then we'll make sure they're both all right. All right?"

"But... what am I supposed to do?"

"Protect your planet." She smirked. "You walk up to the head of security and ask, as sternly as you can manage, to do something about the extraterrestrial serial killer they've been ignoring."

"Right, easy-peasy," I replied. "But what if they came to Earth without going through the Agency? I'm pretty sure most criminals don't, I don't know, just waltz into the local border patrol and announce they're coming to do shady business."

"Oh, trust me, the Agency will have their eyes on

them, no matter who they are. Anyone who goes around chomping on women's necks is bound to draw Agency attention, and they will have their eyes on him, dare he expose the planet to the existence of aliens. This was Cross's intention since the very beginning. Speaking of, you probably shouldn't mention that you already know he's Tallagan. Take this sample of bacteria I swiped from the last victim and have them do the heavy lifting. And here's Felling's ID too. You need something from a legitimate Earth agency, and it was quicker than getting one made up for you."

I ripped it from her hands. "You stole from Felling? What the hell, Blayde? She's helping us!"

"Hey, if things get too hot, your real identity cannot be connected here. This saves both your asses. Not to mention the Agency will be trying to keep all this under wraps anyway."

"Well, it's nice they care enough to stop a panic," I said, and those marble eyes of mine went on a whole roll. They must be unhinged. I slipped the ID and the goo sample into my pocket, gritting my teeth. The little leather bifold felt heavy there.

"Oh, they don't care about your people's wellbeing, trust me," she replied. "The tourists wouldn't keep coming if this planet was contaminated. They want a virgin world."

"That's hella creepy."

"It's part of the fun of space tourism. Oh, look, speaking of."

I had been staring at her so intently I had entirely missed the moon looming before me. The space rock I had spent so much of my lifetime gazing up at was now right in front of me, slowly filling the entire window with its stunning, grey gleam. Never before had I seen its mountains and craters in such detail. Pictures just couldn't do it justice—the depth before me, the sharp contrast between sun and shade.

I gripped the arms of my seat, fingernails digging into the duct tape that held the antique together. I was here. I was at the freaking moon. My moon.

"Are you… are you crying?" said Blayde, her head suddenly breaking my fantastic view of the moon beyond.

"I'm gone for ten minutes, and now you're making Sally cry?" said Zander, arms instantly around me. I put my chin on his shoulder, keeping my teary eyes riveted on the grey light. I realized I really was sobbing now, a torrent of emotions spilling through my rattling eyeballs.

"I didn't say anything," she pouted. "Sally got emotional at the sight of that space rock."

I hugged Zander tighter. His broad chest was a warm wall around me, the embrace a sweet relief. With the dash hidden behind him, I almost felt like he was cradling me in the space above the moon, the dusty surface for my eyes alone.

"I don't get it," Blayde said. "We take you to so many different places, and this is the one that brings you to tears? Not impossible cities or long-lost colonies, but a little rock only an hour from where you grew up? Next time I get you a present, you'd probably spend more time with the wrapping paper than the actual gift."

I wanted to say something deep and profound. I wanted to tell her how it felt to be, just be, above the surface of a moon I had seen every day of my life. This sturdy, reliable rock that connected my entire world. Only two dozen other Terrans had ever made it this far before. Half that had ever landed and taken a few steps on its surface. And it took them days to get here, not hours.

I wanted to tell her how the other planets had been so alien, but this moon wasn't at all. It was Earth's back yard. So close, yet just out of reach.

"It's the freaking moon, Blayde," I said instead.

"Zander, take note," she said. "Sally's bar for visiting planets is... this high."

I pointed out the window, and he turned his head away for a split second, false hair brushing my cheek and tickling my nose. I hadn't even paid attention to his costume until now. I extracted myself from his hug and gazed upon his bespectacled eyes. The small hexagon glasses Zander wore gave him the same hippie look as his sister, a loose-fitting, flowery, off-green blouse and pair of bell-bottom pants completing the entire outfit. Somehow, he had acquired hair a wig, and his light brown hair was no longer short and reaching for the stars, but now long and smooth, his shoulders covered completely by the mop of dirty brown.

"Who are you meant to be?" I asked, trying to control my laughter. My nose was still sniffly from the sudden outburst of sobs, making me sound like a donkey. He fell back against the floor, leaning his head back against the console, groovy as can be.

"I thought we would dress as ordinary Terrans," said Blayde. "Fool the Agency into thinking we're blithering idiots."

"Who somehow got a ship and managed to fly through space, knowing exactly where to find their base of operations?"

"Hey, we're effective, blithering idiots," she said. "And speaking of the base of operations..."

We had flown clear past the side of the moon that was so engraved on my eyes. From here on out, it was new territory for me—the far side of the moon, one I had only seen in photographs.

But I wasn't interested in the surface anymore, not when there was an entire alien space station casually chilling in the shadow. Massive metallic spires extended upward and down, away from a large central ring, tiny windows specking the body enough to give me the astronomical scale of the complex. If someone had roped together four guise liners and tossed them very hard into space, they might have made for a terrible discount version of the Agency.

"All this for a tourist trap?" I gaped.

Zander pushed himself up a little, glancing over the console, shrugging slightly.

"It's not much," he said. "Even you've seen bigger."

"I could make a phrasing joke right now, but I'm not going to," said Blayde. "I've matured. In any case, don't be offended, Sally. It's not that Earth isn't interesting. It's just, I don't know, a little dull for most tastes."

"I'm not offended," I said. "I'm terrified."

We drifted closer to the massive station, leaving the moon to hide us from the Earth. The structure really was shielding itself from view in the most natural way possible, by putting an actual moon in its way. Though how it stayed in orbit without moving was a complete mystery to me.

"And we're incoming," said Blayde. "Drop your identities and get into character because it's Agency or bust right about now."

THIRTEEN

IT'S NOT TERMINAL; YOU'VE GOT ALIENS

FUZZY WIGS ASIDE, THIS WAS BASICALLY FIRST contact. At least as far as the aliens were concerned when it came to me, and I was determined to make it as uncomfortable as possible. Because, hey, when you set out to make something terrible in the first place, then everything going wrong means everything is going right. And knowing how frequently everything in my life went terribly, utterly wrong, I was going to jump the gun on this one and just make it so.

The doors hissed open, old gears groaning from their brief jaunt through space. The Agency's parking bay was as dull as it gets, except for the fact that there were spaceships instead of cars, but this wasn't my first hangar bay at this point. Even so, I put on a good show of being wowed by my surroundings. No point ruining my cover by letting the Agency know I already had some alien experience.

I was flanked by two strangers, absolutely foreign-looking wearing costumes so intricate that it was impossible to tell that they were, in fact, Zander and Blayde. I had joined them in the flowy, hippie garb, the hair of my wig wavy and long. I was already missing my tie-dye apparel, even as mucked up by Blayde's murder as it was.

The huge shuttle docking lot was connected directly to the terminal by a small elevator, a link from space to the central hub of the Agency, a sudden transition from grey darkness to a large shopping mall with duty-free shops lining every side of the stingily shaped hall. Dull, grey metal gave way to sleek, white walls, and for a second, I thought the *Traveler* had thrown up all over this place. I guess the Alliance had a single architect they hired for everything.

Zander led the way along one of the raised walkways, above the swell of happy, duty-free shoppers. Leafy greens hung from above, giving the impression that the artificial lights were just filtered sunlight through glass roofs of a conservatory. Music pumped through the speakers, surrounding us in gentle sway, making the entire place feel a little like a mall and spa had a dysfunctional space child.

"We're not seriously getting answers here?" I asked, unable to hide my awe of this place. How all this was hiding just a few hundred thousand miles from Earth beneath our very noses boggled my mind. It was like picking up a rock and finding that worm-kind had a terrifyingly advanced society just inches from the surface.

"Once we get out of the terminal? Sure," said Zander. "Just keep an eye out for security as we go."

Blayde pointed her long finger at a sign on the wall. "Spaceport security. Follow the signs. Be clear, concise. We'll meet you back here." She paused, her eyes falling on something far in the distance. "I have some important shopping to do. Good luck."

Zander and I watched her go, her hippie dress quickly disappearing in the crowd. The terminal really was packed, and it vaguely reminded me of my time on Da-Duhui, the massive port perched on the top of one of the highest buildings on the city planet. Only here, there were actually humans.

Not that they were all that human under their skin.

"I'll be right here," said Zander, ripping my attention from the maddening crowd.

"Like, right here in this spot or somewhere in this massive terminal?" I asked, shifting from foot to foot. "Because I'm not sure what to do if anything goes wrong."

"Just be creative. Adapt. And if I'm not standing right here when you come back, you make your way to the ship and you leave. Understood?"

If my heart were still beating, it would have

stopped right then and there. "I can't leave without you."

"It'll be fine, I promise," he said, reaching gently for my hand. His touch sent shivers up my spine, and in that minute, greedily, I wanted to rip off his disguise just to see his real face, the wordless reassurance that came from knowing he was there.

"I really can't leave. I have no idea how to start the ship," I said. He grinned that broad smile of his, and my stomach did a happy somersault. Then the nerves came again. "And I won't. Things tend to go horribly wrong whenever we're separated."

"Sally, you found me across the universe as you were *dying*. I'm pretty sure you'll find me in here. You can find me anywhere."

I pushed myself up on my tiptoes, pressing my lips against his for the gentlest of kisses. I could feel him holding back, wanting, as I did, to fully embrace in this moment. The danger reminded us that any minute could be our last together, and an eternity apart was a fate worse than death, since that was off the table now.

"I'll be back before you know it," I said. With a deep, agonizing breath, I filled myself with the smell of him before turning around, marching toward another big Sally moment.

There was a huge difference between using a fake name and fake identity to infiltrate a spaceship or a gala on an alien world and doing the same in orbit around your own home planet's moon. While everything out there had felt like a terrible fever dream, here, reality was amped up to a thousand. I could feel the air from the recyclers bursting against my skin, not cold, but raising the hair of my arms and neck.

As I walked deeper into the terminal, the humanoid aliens became fewer and fewer. A family of nine-foot tall cockroaches that stood on their hind legs were bickering loudly about where they would eat, and a man with his skin made of embers asked me for directions, followed by a woman whose ear burst into flames as she stood in place, asking where the man had gone. Everywhere I looked, a new form of life unknown to man went about planning their vacation on such a primitive world, their faces blazing with excitement.

"Look, Ma, I have a soda can!" said one, holding up an empty bottle of root beer.

"Yeah, but I have the diet version," said another, who I could only assume was a sibling. "It's a collector's edition!"

"Ma!"

The mother, the largest of the three, promptly ate both cans in one go.

I turned my head away from the now-sobbing kids, following the signs to the administrative wing. Each step took me farther away from the bustling terminal and deeper into the station itself, stores giving way to bare, white walls with gleaming polish.

I could feel my nerves rising, though, at first, I didn't know why. Well, meeting with the head of an alien security agency might do it. The people treated my planet like a zoo, something to be explored as a primitive land. That just made my blood boil. It didn't make my skin writhe like this did. No, the walls themselves set me on edge - because they were the same white corridors that Nimien had chased me down, begging for the pleasure of keeping me captive.

I didn't realize I had stopped until I felt a gentle hand on my shoulder. I had pressed a palm against one of the walls, catching myself from stumbling, a stumble I had somehow skipped. That was worrying. I squeezed my brows together, trying to keep myself grounded. No matter how scared I was, I couldn't let my panic send me to the other side of the universe.

Now, to deal with the hand. I took a step away from it, the metal appendage staying fixed in the air where my shoulder had been. It was attached to a small, hovering globe, the little, white body affixed with an oversized eye and not much else. Two long, spindly arms extended from both sides, stiff at the elbow like it was in the process of shrugging and had somehow gotten stuck.

"Are you all right, miss?" it asked, and I nodded. There were no tears to wipe, no panic attack to dispel.

I really was fine for all intents and purposes, except for the worry eating away inside.

But the robot did not go. It hovered there, five feet above the ground, staring at me with its large, buggy eye.

"Well, thanks, I guess," I said, turning to go. I made it a good ten steps before I realized the robot had drifted along to follow me. I turned, and it was still there, as if waiting for me to give him a tip. Did robots have a need for currency? Was I supposed to give him a bolt? Or was that speciest?

"Can I... can I help you?" I asked, suddenly feeling deeply observed. Which, admittedly, was a bit late of a reaction on my part, seeing as how he was all eyeball and not much else. Even those arms barely counted.

"Oh, right, yes," it said. If it could clear its throat, it probably would have done so now. Instead, it just bobbed an inch up and down. "Sorry, first day on the job. I'm supposed to confirm your identity before you access this portion of the station. Security, you see."

"Um, I'm not quite sure what you're looking for," I said. "Sorry, I left everything of mine on the planet."

"Oh, right, not every organic knows what I am," the robot said, and with a large, exaggerated swing of the arm, he brought his metal hand swinging at his face. The hand flung away at the last second, the elbow hinge unable to bring it any closer. It recoiled backward.

"Are you okay?"

"Fine, fine," it said, and I could swear it was grumbling. "My maker had a sense of humor. Apparently, my predecessors had the flaw of hitting themselves when they had majorly screwed up, but instead of debugging the system, they just started making us with short forearms. Thus, we swing, and we miss."

"But wouldn't you know better than trying to slap yourselves if you're sure you will miss?"

"Then what's the harm in trying?" it said, doing another one of its small bobs. "Now, I apologize again. It's my first day here. I need you to put your hands in the air and turn around three times."

"Um, okay," I said, and did as I was told, putting my hands up and turning around once, twice, thrice. The white hallway was so featureless that I lost my bearings halfway through. "Good? Can I go?"

"Oh, no. I didn't start the scan yet. It's just the first time I've ever seen a biped. And you manage to stay balanced on those two twigs? That's unlikely."

"You're literally floating in the air. I'd like to say you're less likely to stay balanced than me."

"I've got anti-grav technology." It drifted up five inches or so, making it so I had to look up to meet the one gleaming eye. "I physically cannot fall."

"Oh, yes, this makes it even more likely than basic bipedal motion. I don't suppose you evolved to be this glitchy." This was such a waste of time. Just trying to reason with the little bugger was tedious. I had places to be and people to save. "Natural selection wouldn't give you the urge to slap yourselves without the ability to ever do so."

"Ah, but isn't that the purpose of life? To strive for impossible things?"

Why people programmed bots to have philosophical quandaries, I would never know. Maybe they just wanted to waste everyone's time. Either way, I had to get away from the little droid. It had seen way too much of me anyway. Would Zander take the bot and break it? Smash it against the wall to destroy its data? Only what if the droid was connected to a cloud, with my face already swimming through their records?

"Now, tell me which ocean scares you the most," it said, breaking me out of planning its demise.

"What?"

"It's part of the LifePrint procedure," it said. "Now please, hold still. I'm trying to scan you. And tell me, clearly, which ocean scares you the most?"

"Do you mean in terms of creatures that live there? Or like depth? Or based on a movie—"

The bot made a negative sound. "I cannot elaborate the question. Tell me which ocean scares you the most."

"I'd say the Pacific Ocean. Now can I go?"

"We're not done yet. How many pancakes cover the roof of a doghouse?"

"What does this have to do with my identity?"

"I will ask the questions. How many pancakes cover the roof of a doghouse?"

"I don't know—eighty-eight? How is this helping you read my soul or whatever?"

"I'm getting to know you deeply," it said. "And we do not have time for a dinner and a movie, so please, let me ask you the required questions. If you could be any kind of bear, which would you be?"

"Polar. How many of these do we have to go through?"

"Look, this only works if you put in some effort," it said, mildly exasperated. "These things can't be one-sided. Now, have you ever thought about having children?"

"I beg your pardon?" I spat. "What kind of question is that?"

"An essential one, if we want to see where this thing goes."

"What thing? You're a robot; I'm a human. You're interrogating me in a hallway, and I don't even know your name. Kids! What the hell kind of question is that?"

"I sense that this is deeper than just me asking the question." It took a hesitant drift toward me. "Why does the question make you angry?"

"Because it's rude," I stammered. The nerve. Whoever programmed this bot was a monster. "Because it's not something you ask someone you don't know. You don't know my life! You don't know who I am, what I've been through, I just…"

I slid down the side of the wall. Oh, *Veesh*. The stupid bot was right. This was about more than just the question. In less than five minutes of knowing me, the LifePrint had found a way to wound me to my core.

"You do not match anyone on file," it said calmly, as if it hadn't just shattered the little bubble of happy and calm I had been trying to live in ever since we came back from the library. Ever since I had been turned into something else.

Someone who no longer was mortal.

Who may not entirely be human either.

Who hadn't taken the time to assess her future beyond the fact that it was long and she was in love.

The bot began to drift away without another apology, despite being so full of them earlier, leaving me alone on the hallway floor, shattered across the— surprisingly—shag rug. I had half a mind to rip off one of the strands and fling it at the thing for all the good it would do me.

"Hey, LifePrint thingy," I shouted, my voice cracking somehow. "What even am I?"

"What do you mean?" it replied, rushing to my side quicker than a puppy to a bone. "Why are you on the floor?"

"Wasn't that the purpose of your little scan?" I

sputtered. "To get to the bottom of me, of who and what I am?"

"Yes, it was. But rarely does one ask to see the results of the scan."

"It's your first day, LifePrint. Admit it, things aren't going the way they told you they would."

The bot attempted to scratch its head, the little metal hand swinging aimlessly over the sphere of its body, never quite reaching. "Well, no, not exactly."

"So, what does your scan say about me?" I asked, no, insisted. My fingers twirled into the shag, aiming to pull. "Who am I? What am I?"

"I wouldn't know any better than you," it said. "I only read what you gave me."

"Which was? I want to be a polar bear, and I break down crying when you ask intimately personal questions?"

"In effect."

"So, your kind doesn't read souls. You just get a sense of people."

"Correct."

"And that works for positive identification? You can actually match people based on this?"

"We are very, very good at our jobs."

"So, what's your sense of me?"

"That you want to be a polar bear, and you break down crying when you ask intimately personal questions."

I snorted. "At least they programmed you with a sense of humor."

"As I said, no one asks to see what we find," it said, and gently rotated one of its arms down to the floor, making a leg for me to brace against as I stood up. "Which I suppose refines your reading even more."

"Great. So not only do I not get answers, but I'm left with existential questions instead."

"Ah! I've had training for this!" the LifePrint said. For some reason, its tone made me see it as puffing out its chest.

"Yeah?"

"I'm supposed to say, *'toughies for you.'*"

"Wow, great training," I said, though, admittedly, that lifted my spirits a little. I had to think about something else, anything else, to avoid thinking about big important questions on the topic of my humanity and life goals. Especially now since I didn't have a life anymore, just an eternity. "Do you know the way from here to whatever office deals with illegal activity on Earth?"

"I do!" it said. "I mean, I think I do. Follow me."

The bot drifted down the corridors, and I followed close behind, stuffing the tears back into their sockets. This was definitely not the time for a deep talk about my future. I had to stay focused and keep my eyes on the prize, all the clichés there to remind me I had work to do.

"'Tada," said the LifePrint, leading me to a glass

door marked *Earth Assets and Relations.* "Can you open it? I would, but my creator never made me to be able to open doors."

"Of course he didn't," I muttered, reaching for the knob and pushing us both into the waiting room beyond. Other than me and a very bored-looking, albino-skinned alien, there was no one else there. The stranger peeled one brown camel eye open, grunted, then forced the other open as well. His head was the size and shape of a bowling ball and had large, doe-like eyes the color of hot coffee. It was precariously balanced upon a long, spindly neck that seemed like it would tip over the second he dozed off again.

The room we were in was the saddest waiting room I had ever seen, sadder still than my memories of the DMV. A dismal, bladeless fan shoved in the corner of the room seemed to be stuck and made a loud, grating noise. The alien stared at it intently, as if judging whether figuring out what was wrong with it would help him fight the boredom of a dull day. He fumbled with a wrench on his desk, as if ready to slam it when the time was right.

"And this is Carl," said the LifePrint. "He works at the desk. Say hi, Carl!"

"My name isn't Carl." The secretary shuffled uncomfortably in his seat.

"Ah. My mistake. You just really look like a Carl," it replied. "And trust me, I was programmed to know a lot of Carls."

The secretary peeled his eyes off the little bot, landing them instead on me. I offered up a weak grin. Come on, Sally Webber, you can do better than that.

"Good day, ma'am." He tipped his head forward to greet me, and, for a second, I thought it would fall off his neck. "How may I assist you today?"

"Hi. I know I don't have an appointment," I said. Did they even take appointments? Was there a hotline? No matter. "I need to speak to the person or persons who deal with tourist activity on the planet."

"Lady, everyone in this station does that."

I took a deep breath and breathed out. What would Blayde do when faced with that kind of brushing off? I needed to channel her if I wanted to be taken seriously.

"Oh, more specifically, I need to find the person who deals with tourists murdering locals," I said, showing as much teeth as I could muster. "And be quick about it. Lives are on the line."

"Fill out the light blue form over there." He indicated, pointing at the left side of the desk. "There are pens at your disposal."

It was oddly reassuring to know that even on a high-tech alien space station, alien administrative procedure moved at the pace of a concussed garden snail. I made my way to the pile of blue papers, took out a page, and began filling it out, diligently answering every question I could.

"You're not who I thought you were," said the LifePrint, hovering over my shoulder.

"Am I supposed to dismiss you or something?" I asked. "You know, you don't have to stay with me."

"It seems I do if my first reading of you could be so off," it replied, somehow flustered. "Now, if you were to see a table covered in frogs and ducks, which would you reach for first?"

"A broom to push them off?" I grumbled, returning to my form. "Can you stop asking questions?"

I brought the form back to the desk, handing it proudly to the secretary. A form that he promptly took and placed on top of what I had thought was a decorative piece of furniture but was actually a stack of identical blue forms.

"Please allow six to eight years for processing," he said. "We will get back to you as soon as possible."

"Years?" I spat. "But this is urgent! I'm on a mission here from the FBI."

"Oh, you don't say?" replied the secretary. "Please. You have your own office. You know better than to come here for a civilian matter."

"But I am a civilian," I stammered. "A civilian from the FBI. From Earth."

He sighed heavily, pulling himself to his computer. "Name, species, and planet of origin?"

"Agent James Felling, human, from Earth."

"From Earth?" He looked surprised. "Born...?"

"Both parents also humans from Earth, if that's what you're asking."

He lifted the phone to his ear, now staring at me

intently. "Yeah, get me Foollegg." He paused, still looking at me. "Which Earth agency again?"

"FBI. Sort of. You know who I am."

"Foollegg?" He spoke rapidly. "There's a woman here who needs to speak with you. She's... Well, it's a Code One. An earthling has made it to the Agency."

FOURTEEN

INTERSTELLAR ADMINISTRATIVE PROCEDURE, VOLUME ONE

THERE'S NOTHING MORE IMPRESSIVE THAN A GIANT reptile trying to speak English, its long, forked tongue flickering through every syllable. Literally forked. It had four prongs rather than a snake's two, and that was the least strange thing about it. Okay, fine, I had seen more impressive things, but this one was simultaneously flattering, which was new in my book.

"Mrs. Felling?" asked the woman—though I wasn't quite sure she was a woman or if her species even had the gender; I probably should have asked—her accent coming through even with my translator, which was taking a nap again. It didn't have anything to do when people actually spoke English to me. "Specialist Foollegg. Welcome to the Agency."

Foollegg matched her secretary almost identically. Her long, spindly neck seemed too fine and fragile to hold the massive ball of her head, which was slightly more angular than her colleague's. Her skin was pale and dry, almost like a lizard drained of pigment. As if to add support, a silvery necklace climbed up her neck, stunningly delicate like the appendage itself. Standing, her chin was a good foot over my head, while her shoulders reached mine.

And she was wearing a suit. A women's blazer, which was probably why I jumped on the whole feminine vibe. Heck, it looked too much like Felling's suit, flooding me with guilt all over again, the stolen ID burning a hole in my pocket.

I tried to stop thinking about all the reasons I shouldn't be here and focused on the reasons I should, but I was hypnotized by the alien eyes, the all-too-familiar brown eyes of a doe, blinking slowly as she took me in, pursed lips holding back her true reaction.

"Agent Felling," I said, bowing at the middle. Habit of having spent some time in the Alliance, I suppose. She returned the greeting. If she was impressed, she gave no sign. "It's an absolute pleasure to meet you."

"This all must be quite the shock," said Foollegg, ushering me into her office. She cast a quick glance at her colleague, who was all too content to return to his little computer. "And you must have a story for me, no? No one from Earth has ever made their way here before, we did not think it was possible. And where do you think you're going?"

I ground to a halt, but she wasn't talking to me. Instantly, her accent was gone, and it hit me she had switched out of English. No, she was talking to the little robot who, for some reason, was still hovering a foot behind my left shoulder.

"I've not completed my secondary scan," it replied, and I could swear it sounded terrified. Though whoever programmed a scanning flying security bot to have his voice crack when it's afraid has a terrible sense of humor.

"You must be frashing kidding me," Foollegg muttered at the ceiling. "Look, your job is to scan, it takes all of a few seconds. What is their species? Where have they been? Are they in disguise? Do they match anyone on record? Then, move on."

"I am programmed," it said, with a little more confidence than I expected, "to get to the bottom of who a person is. Species, words, records—none of that tells you who a person really, truly is."

"Roger," she said, shouting back the way we came, "call somebody up here to reprogram this LifePrint, will you? It's got a glitching existence complex."

"No," the bot said, and there was no denying the break in its voice now. "No, please, I've only just begun. I can learn. I can do better!"

"Better to lose a day than a few months of memory. You'll be in shipshape in no time. Now," she said, her accent reappearing like the flick of a switch, "where were we?"

Foollegg led me into her office, and I gasped. I couldn't help it. The back wall was entirely made of glass and had the most astounding view of the moon I had ever seen. Craters spread out like the wallpaper of a science museum lobby. Only this…this was real. Like a kid in a candy store, I was already pressed up against the glass, hands splayed, watching the moon move oh-so slowly beneath us.

"It's a beautiful rock, is it not?" she said, and I peeled away from the window. Goodbye, moon. "It's a shame your people haven't returned for a while. While it makes out job easier, we do only want the best for humanity."

"As do I," I said, trying to shift my brain into secret agent mode. *Come on, focus, Sally.* "Which is why I'm here."

"Yes, yes," said Foollegg, indicating a seat with a hand so flat all her bones must have been crushed by a steamroller. "I do have quite a few questions as to how that came to be."

"I guess we have quite a few questions for each other," I replied, forcing a smile. "I should probably mention that this meeting is informal, to say the least. None my people know I'm here. I was desperate for answers and followed them here. I will not breathe a word of this to my superiors. All I want is a little help from the Agency to hunt down a serial killer, and it will be as if none of this ever happened."

Foollegg smiled, her thin lips pointing up so

vertically she could have been a fish. She pulled the flat, three-fingered hand over the pale expanse of her scalp, sliding it down to play with the long fishtail braid hanging from the back of her skull. Recognition flashed for a split second. Hair like that, though darker. The Downdwellers. I pushed them out of my mind.

"I am glad you said that, as we are not ready for first contact, though you may have gathered that already. The mere fact you came all this way on your own shows your dedication to catching this criminal. We will help you as much as we can."

I breathed a real sigh of relief. "Thank you. I hope this spirit of cooperation will accompany our species through a fruitful friendship. Even if it is not official as of yet."

"We want nothing less than friendship," said Foollegg, lips pursed. "May I take it this is your first time meeting what you would call an alien?"

"It is not," I said, pulling at my clothes. "The ship I requisitioned was from a family of tourists who, unfortunately, had a bad reaction to Earth coffee. My branch of the FBI deals with covering up incidents like those, and we helped them get the care they needed. They were the ones to alert me to your existence, and I borrowed their ship, as well as their clothes, to come here. Though I wasn't quite sure what you would be wearing."

Foollegg barked. Was that a laugh?

"I would gladly trade you," she said, tugging at her suit. "I put this costume on for your benefit."

"That was very kind of you," I said, and I meant it. If I had been the real Felling and meeting someone so utterly alien for the first time, them wearing a suit would be a true kindness.

"The serial killer in question must be quite the terror if you had to resort to all this just to gain information."

"It was the only viable option when it became obvious he was not human."

"And what are you hoping from us, exactly?" she asked, tilting her head slightly to the side. Instinct made me want to hop over the desk and pick up her head, stop it from tumbling off the neck, but it miraculously stood still.

"It's simple, really," I said. "It turns out this extraterrestrial is none other than my now ex-partner, former agent Dustin Cross." I crossed my hands on the desk, leaning in, seething. "Catching and containing him is proving impossible with the resources we have. Your agency, however, is made for this precise situation."

Basically, do your job, enabling assholes. All of this could have been avoided if the Agency kept an eye on the alien tourists they sent down to the planet. Heck, the freaking Youpaf had managed to get through their net, and they hadn't done a thing about it, no matter how pre-contact we were. Just shrugged and thought, *Oh well, the Terrans can handle it. It didn't make much sense.*

"Catching this killer would be in both our interests," said Foollegg. "If it truly is an off-worlder committing these heinous acts, then we would want him contained. Your prisons are not made with them in mind, and should the word get out about his true nature, we may have a pre-contact riot on our hands. None of our governments want that. As for us, the Alliance could shut us down if they heard one of our tourists has been arrested by humans. It would look bad for us. You have kept these deaths out of the press?"

I nodded again, thinking it best to keep my mouth shut. Things were starting to bubble in my stomach, things that shouldn't get out here and now.

"Four girls were brutal murdered," I said, trying to drag that dagger in. "By a man I thought I knew and trusted."

Come on, Foollegg, feel guilty for the murderers you let into my home. Why didn't they do anything about the Leechins, instead letting Felling's department deal with them all by themselves? Seemed like a problem that would be in their interest of solving, seeing as how, hello, they wanted to remain pre-contact and all. They must have heard of the murders; they knew what was going on. Why they refused to do anything about them seemed downright vindictive.

There were so many cracks in their story, no amount of silver could ever make it pretty. And yet, there Foollegg was, smiling, gentle as a doe. She shook her head, her neck swaying as if in an invisible breeze.

"Do not worry," she said, patronizingly soft. "If he is one of ours, he will be off your planet before the day is done."

"Thank you," I said, once again keeping my tongue tightly under wraps. *Not the place or time for an outburst, Sally Webber.* Yelling "how could you" usually wasn't a good idea when they had something you want. "We do not know exactly what Cross is, but I have here some of the bacteria he left behind on the victims. Would that be enough to find him?"

Foollegg took the little bottle gingerly, shaking it and holding it up to the light. She frowned.

"Is there something wrong?" I asked, and her neck stiffened.

"No, no, this is just very peculiar," she said, gritting her teeth. What a terrible liar. "Here, LifePrint, make yourself useful, will you?"

I turned, startled to see that the bot was still hovering behind my shoulder, silent as space.

"Wait, you're still here?" I stammered.

"I have not completed my assessment," it replied. "That, and it was boring waiting in the lobby."

"Bots don't get bored."

"This bot does."

I sure hated that programmer. Derzan should rain holy hell down on his terrible sense of humor.

The LifePrint drifted over the desk to Foollegg's side, extending one of his metal hands to take the sample. Luckily, its analysis didn't involve asking the jar any probing questions that could shatter their mental wellbeing.

"Well, I can tell you the bacteria came from a being in the Tallag system, but their colonies spawn over four planets, and I cannot get more precise than that."

"Then what is your use?" snapped Foollegg, not in English.

"If this being were alive, I would ask it what underwear they prefer," said the LifePrint. "That would determine which planet they call home."

"But as you can see, the being is dead, so asking is—"

There was a moment of tense silence, a silence so thick I would have needed Blayde's laser to burn through.

"Oh? I'm meant to finish your thought?" asked the LifePrint.

"Aren't you programmed to keenly assess everything there is to know about a person?"

"If I wanted to reach my full potential, I would need access to a bar."

Foollegg, exasperated but holding it together like any true professional at her level, turned back to me.

"Tallagans are mostly liquid," she explained.

"Really. Back on their planet, it doesn't make much of a difference since they have shape in their own atmosphere. Couldn't really walk around Earth looking like themselves. Hell, they couldn't really walk at all without a form to stretch around. Give them a human body, and you can pour their essence into it like a cup. You'll be relieved to know that we don't allow this behavior from our tourists, which is why we don't allow Tallagans through our Agency. Not to mention, your atmosphere gives them cancer if they are not in a proper vessel."

It took all I had not to gag. "Then why is this one here? If the air is killing him?"

"Why do criminals do anything?" She shrugged. "Seriously, if you know, any insight is appreciated."

Before either of us could respond, the phone on her desk rang. A chorus of bees singing "La Cucaracha" while inside an Instant Pot filled the room, musically devoid of any rhythm of reason, yet somehow oddly catchy.

"Need to take this," said Foollegg, spinning her chair so she could face out toward the moon.

The LifePrint drifted my way. "Can you believe the nerve of this one?" it asked, scoffing. "Can't tell apart Tallagans? Excuse me, I just scanned over fifty million strands of genetic code, compared them to the entire scope of the known universe, and returned you the right solar system in less time than it takes to say thank you. And yet I'm the useless one."

EARTHSTUCK

Foollegg spun quickly in her chair, her face now so pale it was practically transparent. She murmured her agreement a few times, rising hastily to her feet and grabbing a small, black pistol from her desk drawer.

If she had a ray gun, I wanted one too.

It hit me, then, that the odds of some other terrible thing happening in this station today were astronomical. And I can say that; I've been to space. I'm there now. Statistics show that the odds of there being two guns on an airplane are smaller than those of being struck by lightning. The logic being that if you want to be sure there wouldn't be a gun on your airplane, you should bring your own. Just to kick statistics' ass.

Zander and Blayde were in the Agency, and Foollegg was looking at me like I was the rookie who'd enlisted five minutes before war broke out. The odds of there being a second gun on this station were astronomical. As it was, the siblings were the only possible answer.

I didn't need to fake the worry on my face. "What's wrong?"

"We have two wanted criminals in the terminal. You must have heard of Zander and Blayde? The Iron and the Sand?"

Zander would have hated to hear his name that way, but sure, yeah, I did know them. They were crashing at my parents'. Good buds.

"There are rumors... legends, even," I replied, playing dumb. "You're telling me they're actually real?"

Foollegg corkscrewed her neck. Probably her equivalent of a nod, seeing as how an actual nod would probably snap her neck clean in half.

"They're real, all right," she replied. "The worst terrorists the Alliance has ever seen. Beings of immense power and little to no moral code. Every time we think they're dead, they come back and hit us with an even more heinous act. Just two years ago, they destroyed the fifth moon of Callah. Burned it to a crisp and reduced it to a solar ring. And they're *here*. On this station. *Now.*"

Burning whole planets didn't sound like something on Zander's to-do list, but it was a disgusting enough story to make me visibly shudder. "No!"

"It's an all-hands-on-deck kind of situation," she continued. "Are you with us?"

I nodded hastily. "Gladly. What do we do?"

"What kind of weapon do you have?"

"Look, ma'am, this is kind of first contact from an Earth government with an alien corporation, unofficial as it may be. I really wanted to come on good terms. I mean, if I had barged in here, gun in hand or even in a holster, what would that say about me or the people I represent?"

"I like you, Felling," she said, reaching into her desk and—score!—grabbing me an actual laser gun. She must have had some trust in FBI training to have prepared me adequately for an alien shoot-out. Unfortunately, the real me had no idea what to do in such a situation. "You have what we call... *washing machine detergent.*"

She grinned as she stretched out the words, the rasp of her alien tongue evident.

"What does it mean?" I said, feigning ignorance.

"You've got spunk. Pizzazz. Jazz hands," she said. "Now, if we get separated and you come upon these criminals first, shoot to kill. Knocks 'em out for about five minutes. Just enough time for us to get them in cuffs. Can't escape our cuffs."

I nodded. No words were necessary. Plus, I expected that if I did try to talk, it would end up with me laughing like a lunatic.

But, hey, I had a laser gun. And I got to shoot at things. My mother would be so proud.

FIFTEEN

YOU CAN'T WIN NOTHING AT THE SPACE ARCADE

YOU KNOW WHAT I LIKE? LASER TAG. I mean, I liked it a lot as a kid. All those flashy lights. That terrible smell of sweat-soaked foam. The thrill of shooting your friends square in the chest, defeat on their faces. Victory tasting so sweet, sticky like Kool-Aid.

The *Space Station Earth Cinema Cool 10-D Complex, now with more funk experience* was laser tag on highly illegal intergalactic steroids. The entrance took up an entire floor of the main terminal, a gaping hole of a mouth so large and dark it might have been an actual black hole. Flashing neon lights formed and reshaped along the outside walls, urging travelers to stop in for a visit.

"Hey," said the wall, forming a humanoid figure out of neon LEDs when I stepped too close.

235

"Hey, yourself," I replied, keeping one eye on Foollegg, the other one soaking up everything this station had to offer. I was supposed to be off-world for the first time in my life, after all. I needed to look appropriately distracted. Not a problem.

"You like balls?" asked the wall.

"I beg your pardon?"

"You can throw all the balls in *The Space Station Earth Cinema Cool 10-D Complex, now with more funk experience,*" the wall urged, neon hand waving me over. "Into hoops. Into holes. Into portals. So many prizes!"

"I'm good, thanks," I said. "A little busy here."

"But I want you inside me!"

"Well, that's the first time I've been on this side of the exchange," I said. "Besides, we're here to get people *out* of you."

"Aww, no fair," it said dejectedly. "What's the big deal if they want to be here?"

"It's a long story, wall."

"Who are you calling 'wall?' I'm the *Space Station Earth Cinema Cool 10-D Complex, now with more funk experience.*"

"I'm sorry. Sa—Felling. Nice to meet you."

"Pleasure is all mine," it said. "Now, are you sure I can't interest you in a quick game? Tell you what, I'll double every ticket you earn within your first hour inside."

"You heard the woman," said the LifePrint bot.

"She doesn't have time for your silly games. Now, shoo!"

The neon wall frowned then fizzled to darkness, off to bother another guard. The little bot looked smug with itself, awkwardly long arms folded around each other.

"What are you still doing here?" I hissed.

"My assessment of you is still incomplete," it said. "You keep moving."

"What else could you seriously need at this point? A stool sample?"

"Can you provide one? That would be grand!"

"Get out of here! Shoo!" said Foollegg, striding up and swatting the air where the LifePrint had been a split second before. "I apologize, agent. Sometimes, our AI programs are a little too finicky for the work they were intended for."

"Finicky? Me?"

"Get!"

Foollegg was smartly dressed now, no more uncomfortable Earth suit. Instead, her crisp, white Alliance uniform was covered in a tight bulletproof vest and armored plating covered her thin, exposed neck. My own body armor was tight and constricting, but I was thankful for it all the same.

Before I remembered I didn't actually need it. But fake it till you make it, as they say.

"A LifePrint found them *immediately,*" she said, exaggerating the words for the benefit of a not-soresourceful LifePrint, the one still within reach, no matter how many times she had tried to send it away. "It's like they weren't even trying to hide. And how did they get here?"

"There's a rumor," I said, shivering for effect, "that these two... people... can disappear in a breath. Reappear in another."

Foollegg corkscrewed her neck. "Yes, and they are capable of much more. These two criminals are the bane of our existence."

There was an odd thrill from hearing that your boyfriend is badass, outside confirmation that, no, it's not just you who finds him formidable but also crappy interstellar government agencies.

Something less thrilling was being a part of the line of armed security intent on making sure they never left the Agency. And the whole planet-into-ash thing.

"But why are they here?" asked Foollegg, her voice lowering to where it was barely audible. "What do they want?"

"Apparently, there are many games involving balls," I said, my voice equally low. "You can throw them into hoops, into holes, into portals. I have heard there are many prizes."

"I meant on the station, but thanks. Maybe the two most-wanted criminals this side of the galaxy came here to shoot the breeze, sure."

Our eyes met, and in that second, something became awfully clear. For one, she had used some pretty specific basketball terminology, which I mean, she shoots, she scores on that one.

But I was the one who had answered her non-English question to herself with a polite and well-articulated alien response.

Foollegg pursed her lizard lips. I was screwed. One word from her and I would surely be arrested, a suspect for who knows what. But if she wanted to call me out, she didn't have the time. One of the agency's security team rushed to her side, wearing the kind of look on his face you'd have if you found bedbugs in your hotel room.

"We have confirmed the siblings are inside," he said. This man wasn't the same species as Foollegg. He was closer to human, though his body was so bulky he could as well have been the Hulk. He cast one quick look over me, but I wasn't worth his attention. "Shall we send in the retrieval team?"

"I first want to know why a threat like the Iron and the Sand would be playing video games in a place that is on high alert for them. I think they want to be caught. It could be a trap."

"That, or they let their guard down," said the security officer. "Either way, we need to apprehend them before any civilians get hurt—or even know about this."

Foollegg glanced at me. If she had wanted to do something about the translator, now was the time.

Instead, she inclined her head and asked, "Are you with us?"

I nodded. "Of course. Earth will always do its part."

"I do warn you. The rumors of these two are entirely true," she said. "They will not go down without a fight. Shoot first, ask questions later." She turned back to the guard. "Stook, divide your men through the complex. We need you to move through the holopods and escape rooms. Webber, you take the arcade row."

Possibly the only aisle in the entire complex that resembled an arcade on Earth. Foollegg split her resources well. I took a breath, holding out the ray gun as if my life depended on it. Back to my wonderful movie training. I adjusted my grip, keeping my finger extended and off the trigger. Took another breath.

I was hunting my boyfriend. Neat.

"They won't leave the station until they get what they came for," said Stook. "Even so, be wary of their short-range teleportation. Watch each other's backs."

Stook shouted orders to his men, though I couldn't hear him over the buzzing in my ears. I couldn't let the Agency catch Zander or Blayde. Handing them over to the Alliance was the worst thing that could possibly happen.

But I couldn't be seen with them either. That would

put me on the Agency and Alliance's scoreboard too. It might already be too late for that, though.

The *Space Station Earth Cinema Cool 10-D Complex now with more funk experience* swallowed me whole. The dark light inside was dizzying, like living in a neon nightmare. The floor lit up in bright patterns and lights, shifting and moving beneath our boots, giving the impression of walking on bioluminescent lily pads. There was no up or down, only dark space with blue and pink stars leading the way.

I lost the other agents before I lost myself. I must have been in the right area, though. Classic arcade games were all around with chirpy, pixelated cartoon characters urging me to come and play. Colored banners everywhere, flashing neon lights left and right proclaiming the fun one would have while wasting pocket cash. My feet led me forward almost against my will, edging me to find the siblings before the officers of the Agency would. The little mascots followed me as I walked down the aisle, screaming for my attention.

Until their screams died, along with the lights.

I was in space once again, darkness cascading over me like a blanket had dropped over my head. *Breathe, Sally.* I felt the tingle down my fingers and toes, the panic threatening to toss my body away, to bring me someplace else, anywhere else but here.

Deep breaths. Already, my eyesight was adapting, the silhouettes of the game machines coming out of the dark. I was grounded once again, though it didn't change the fact that I was a terrible secret agent. No amount of superhuman eyesight would solve that.

Something cracked under my foot, which I lifted to see a pair of broken hexagonal spectacles.

"You okay?"

A soft whisper, and then he was there, standing in front of me, a dark silhouette in the middle of the aisle of games.

"I am now," I replied.

I told you I was a terrible secret agent. Not only did I forget to shoot our target, but I found myself pressing myself against him, fully embracing his soft lips. Good thing I wasn't on the Agency's payroll.

"What are you doing here?" I wrapped my hands around his neck, my ray gun pressing against his back. I didn't exactly have any other place to put it.

"I was enjoying a round of maxi-golf," he replied. "Until the ruckus."

"You're kidding me."

"My sister, on the other hand, has been planting fake information about us in their mainframe." This close to his face, I could feel his lips curl into a smile. His breath on my neck was like feeling the sun on my skin for the first time in years. "And she needed a sufficient distraction."

"Which I take was you?"

"Whatever do you mean? A highly recognizable

criminal trying to use a LifePrint in his game of maxi-golf? Hold on, are you drunk? Not distracting at all."

I kissed that snide smile of his. What was it about imminent danger that wanted me to put us both into more of it? I would have died a million times over just to reach my hands under his stupid hippie shirt.

And then he was gone, leaving me cling to empty air, the warm space his body had once inhabited. I took a deep breath, capturing the lingering scent of him. Oh, yes, this was definitely the kind of manhunt I could get behind.

"Agent Felling, are you there?"

It took me an instant to remember that was meant to be me, and I tried to catch my breath. I stopped in my tracks: Foollegg.

"I'm here," I said, reaching down to pick up the hexagonal spectacles from under my foot. "I might have found something."

Foollegg swooped down on me, graceful as a crane. "Here," she said, handing me a pair of night-vision goggles in a single motion. "These might not fit, but put them on anyway. We need anyone we can get. It's time to hunt these felons down once and for all."

"Did you turn off the lights or did they?" I asked. Foollegg didn't answer, which was answer enough. I slipped the goggles over my eyes, the sudden brightness almost blinding me.

"If we did, it was not from *my* orders," she said.

Stook, then, I assumed. I handed her the cracked spectacles.

"We were too late," she said, making a fist around them. The cracked glasses broke clean in two. "They're already gone. They knocked two men unconscious and stole their uniforms before we even made it ten meters into the complex."

Everything was happening so fast. It couldn't have been more than ten minutes since we stepped into the arcade. I followed her back out where the barricade of soldiers still waited for us to flush out the siblings.

"Stook!" Foollegg shouted. "Get over here!"

And then the lights went out. One by one, the lights that lit the terminal flickered off, plunging the world into darkness. The screaming began instantaneously. Wild screams filled the canned air of the terminal, sounds of thousands of feet rushed to find safety from who knows what.

"Not me!" said Stook, goggles back on as he rushed to Foollegg's side. "This must be another tactic. From *them.*"

Foollegg nodded, her neck corkscrewing so tight I thought it might snap. "Find the siblings. Find them! Strange, Hartsha, with me. We need to reestablish calm in here. Panic must be their end game. We'll use it against them."

It wasn't as dark as in the *Space Station Earth Cinema Cool 10-D Complex,* now with more funk experience. The moon cast its gentle glow over the many windows of the terminal, and combined with the glasses, I could see as clear as day. Not that I wanted to see the terrorized tourists over the balustrade. Not that I wanted to be reminded our mission had gone so drastically wrong.

As expected, I suppose, when the siblings had once again refused to tell me everything they were planning. Maybe this was playing out exactly how they wanted it to. Clever jerks.

Foollegg had forgotten about me in the panic. She rushed off with her entourage, setting gears in motion to get the station back on its feet. It was Stook I had to worry about. My first and only impression of him was that he was slightly unhinged.

The barricade had already cleared, leaving me alone in its wake. This would be easy, then. All I had to do was slip away quietly and find the siblings before anyone else did. That meant finding the shuttle dock to find our little ship. No teleporting space alien worth his weight in salt would need a spaceship, after all.

I held out the gun as if I needed to use it, pacing slowly and pretending to check every shadow with one eye as I kept track of the signs with the other. I was lucky they had evacuated this level when the functional LifePrint had called in the threat, so I met no one in the halls except for other equally clueless officers. And I was wearing their own armor. All I had to do was nod, and they looked away.

EARTHSTUCK

I reached the elevator—out of service, of course, with the luck I was having. Stairs would have to do.

With a whirr, green strips of light illuminated the floor. And then suddenly, Foollegg's voice filled the air, her face filling what used to be an advertising screen.

"No need for alarm," she said, and I had to admit her face looked incredibly soft and reassuring when you didn't see her iron neck. "This is an important message. Stay where you are. Do not attempt to move. All will be taken care of momentarily. We have two criminals loose in the terminal. Their images are now on the emergency screens. If you see them, DO NOT TRY TO APPREHEND THEM. The felons go by the names Zander and Blayde."

At this, screams rose through the hall. Their mug shots flashed in a loop on the emergency signs, their heads far above those in the crowd where children cried and screamed, their parents joining them. Some people looked confused, in fear of the situation, but not the people behind it. And one very small category of those who, instead of screaming or panicking or running, sat in their place and smiled.

Blayde, head held high, not even looking straight at the camera. From her height above the crowd, she seemed to look down and judge us. Her multicolored hair pulled up in spikes, sharper than it was now. The warrior, the immortal, the feared. The Iron.

Flash. Zander's face stared out across the terminal, bringing a smile to my face. It was him, but it was also one of his characters, so much wilder than the Zander I had come to love. Huge, hairy sideburns bordering on mutton chops slid down to frame the sides of his face, a metal stud protruding from his nose, a piercing long gone and probably forgotten. A feather was poking from his hair that matched his horribly old-fashioned shirt.

Flash. Blayde, scowling. Flash. Zander, grinning. Scowling, grinning, scowling, grinning.

Bandits. Criminals. Felons.

Heroes.

Those were the types I had thrown my lot in with.

"Did you see them?" I practically jumped out of my skin. Stook was suddenly by my side, eyes blazing. If I hadn't known better, I would have said he was another jumper.

"No," I said quickly. Maybe too quickly. Stook knitted his brows, though there wasn't any hair there, so he just twisted his wrinkles. "No, I didn't. I saw them on the screen, though. It's hard to believe they're behind all this mess."

"That they are," he snarled. He reached into his pocket and pulled out a small disk, slipping it into my hand. "Look, if you find them, you contact me first, all right? That's assuming you know how to use this. Or that they haven't killed you first."

I shuddered. There was something in his tone that was so certain. "What about Foollegg?"

"What about her?"

"She's your commanding officer. Your boss - still don't know if you're military or civilian security. In any case, shouldn't we wait for her orders?"

Stook turned to look back at the pitch-black arcade that even high-tech night vision couldn't break. "No time to wait. We have to go. There's no way we can beat these two in numbers; we have to outsmart them. You shouldn't even be a part of this with your Terran training. "

"I can handle myself," I said. "Now, if you'll excuse me, I have another floor to sweep."

To his credit, he stepped aside to let me make my way to the stairs. He might have been an asshole, but he was a professional one.

It was easy from there. The docks were closed off, but it was simple enough to find the service entrance and break in that way. Inside the docks themselves, I followed the path from memory and was pleased to see the siblings waiting in front of our trusty little rust bucket.

"What was that mess?" I shouted, and Blayde grinned.

"They won't be looking for us on Earth for a very long time," she said, beaming as she held up a flat, black circle. I had used one of those before on Da-Duhui when I was supposed to hack the ICP. "And I even managed to scramble the bounty on our heads. Alliance higher ups are gonna be pissed when they find out no one gives a shit about catching us anymore now that there's nothing to gain."

"The screaming space station seems to be giving a shit," I spat.

"We won't be worth it," she waved me off. "Thanks for playing your part, hun."

I was seething. "Just a diversion, huh?"

"Yup."

I would have strangled her if it would have made a difference. No, I take that back. I'd strangle her even if she doesn't feel it. I needed to be the one to feel it.

"Are you freaking kidding me?" I said, ripping off my goggles and slamming them against the deck. "You made me march up to the head of security and blabber my way through interagency diplomacy as a diversion?"

"Worked rather well, now, didn't it?" She grinned.

"Until you sent Zander to get caught for some reason."

"Look, their servers are incredibly well guarded," she said. "I needed an overwhelming situation to get full access. And, hey, you managed to make the Agency aware of the serial killer they should be hunting anyway. I knew you wouldn't mind."

"Wouldn't mind? I joined the manhunt for my own boyfriend! Once again, you didn't trust me with the whole plan. Oh, no. You just threw me in the lion's den as you worked your magic on the side."

"Look, if you had known it was a fruitless mission, would you have agreed to come?"

"Of course not! And now you've dragged Felling's name into all this! How will she keep up her job? Foollegg practically admitted they have Alliance personnel in every level of the government, and they can make all our lives miserable."

"But they won't," Blayde insisted. "It's not worth the trouble. Relax, will you? No one made it into the Alliance's hands. We're golden."

"You practically started a riot!"

She shrugged. "No harm, no foul."

"Yes harm!"

"No permanent damage, at least."

"It was complete chaos in there! Someone could have died!"

"I've already apologized. What else do you want me to say?" she snarled.

"I want you to tell me you heard them." In that instant, her eyes went wide, and the color drained from her face—I had struck a nerve. "Did you hear their screams? When they saw your faces, which they both revered and feared simultaneously? Did you hear the children cry? Just by showing up, you tore them in two."

"You think I don't know?"

"They averted their eyes from your pictures. They knew you. What exactly have you done?"

"I don't know," she said, avoiding my gaze. "I don't know, don't know."

Zander threw open the door to the shuttle, and I almost shot him right then and there. Because my man—this adorable, handsome danger-to-himself-and-others—was now entirely blue.

"You're *blue?*" I sputtered. His skin was blue, his fingers were blue, his hair was even a darker shade of blue. "Why the hell are you blue?"

"Zander and Blayde!" A voice boomed through the dock, "Turn yourselves in now, before it's too late!"

The large dock doors slid open and Stook strode in, gun in hand, the entire Agency security at his heels. The pompous ass had his chest puffed out in pride, as if he had somehow already won.

I spun on my heels. Once again, the tingle at my fingertips was back, the tug of another world stronger than ever. I planted my feet firmly on the ground in this place, in this present.

As terrible as it was.

Before I could say a word, before I could even gasp, Blayde's arm wrapped around my back, and I felt the cool, thin pressure of a knife against my neck. My gun was snatched from my hand and kicked clear across the floor.

And I'd never once gotten to shoot it. Boo.

"Take another step, and the Terran dies," she shouted, pressing the knife into my skin. I felt it break under the touch, blood carved from my body. The sense of betrayal was short-lived. This was a ploy and a good one. Still, I cried out in pain; I was beginning to be quite the talented actress.

"Don't tense up," she whispered, so close to my ear it made the hairs raise. "The first time, it's the panic that gets to you, I would assume."

"What?" I stammered, but I knew what she was going to answer. My body tensed. Of course, she gripped me tighter. This wouldn't be acting.

"If you injure her, you lose all your chips," said Stook, and Blayde laughed.

"You think I care? I could leave here now and never return. I don't even need the ship; I just like having my own fridge. For little snacks, you see."

"She's bluffing!" said someone from behind, and Stook raised his hand, fist closed. Not very promising.

Blayde drew the knife deeper into my throat. I shouted more from panic than pain. Not that it felt painful, exactly, but deep-rooted instincts were ingrained for a reason. I thrashed against her grasp.

"Blayde," I muttered under my breath, wildfire energy coursing through my veins, "if I knew you were this kinky, I would have played patsy long ago."

"Sorry, babe, you can't handle me." She slashed my throat.

SIXTEEN
MURDERED, REVIVED,
AND IN DIRE NEED OF A COCKTAIL

YOU'VE PROBABLY HEARD THAT CLASSIC QUOTE about the rumors of one's death being greatly exaggerated. Mine were spot on, if only for about five minutes. The next five, though, I had to fight to keep them that way.

There's just something about breathing, isn't there? Despite the fact I no longer needed it to live, I still did it how-many-times per minute. I could technically hold it indefinitely, but old habits die hard, it would seem. Good thing I died with my eyes closed. I'd never tested how long I could go without blinking. So, when I woke up from death, it took everything I had not to gasp and exclaim, "I'm alive!"

"She's dead," announced a familiar voice. Stook's, by the sound of it. "Humans don't survive this much blood loss."

"A shame, really," said Foollegg, her toe coming into sharp contact with my ribs. "Managed to find a ship and make it all the way here without tipping off a single one of our plants. That takes washing machine detergent."

"This makes things easier," said Stook. "Now we don't have to terminate her ourselves."

"That was never an option," Foollegg spat.

"It was the only option. In two days, we would have been on Fox."

"She was smarter than that. Took orders well." There was a heavy sigh. "This whole situation stinks. Why were the siblings here? Now? We must issue a report immediately."

"And her?"

"Throw her out the airlock. We can't send her back to Earth. We'd have war on our hands. Remember trying to get them to shut up about Roswell?"

Screw you, too, Foollegg. Off into space I was tossed once again, the ringing in my ears already overwhelming all other senses. I had been in the vacuum of space twice before, so one could say I was used to it. The first time, I had almost died. The second time, I already had. A bit like now, really. Hello, cold of the universe. Hello, uncomfortable bloating. It's me again. Don't freeze off my toes, please.

I watched, eyes stuck open, as the sleek, white

terminal fell away from me, all windows and glittering spires. A gorgeous feat of Alliance engineering.

If all I could see was the terminal, that meant the moon was right behind me, wasn't it?

Oh shit, I was heading toward the moon. Not that I could turn around to see it. I had nothing to grip, nothing to change my altitude. Did Foollegg seriously think it was a good idea to toss my remains onto a barren space rock? I wasn't even sure if bodies could decompose there with the lack of bacteria and all.

Putting aside the amazingly cool image of becoming a moon mummy, I had bigger issues to deal with. Namely, getting rescued before I hit the ground. That's if I didn't burn up in the thin atmosphere first.

Luckily, that wasn't up to me. I drifted into a darkened hull and hit the wall, door sliding closed around me. Like a tadpole in a river, I had been scooped up. A rush of air flowed in, and suddenly, I could hear again, all the whirrs and grinding of an old, squeaky ship.

Back to air, to sound. The small space felt cozy and warm compared to the untamable cold outside, a small comfort you'd never think you'd miss until it was ripped away from you. I licked my lips, tasting the air on my tongue once again, like catching snowflakes and letting them melt into fresh-water goodness.

Ah, and gravity. You're a dear.

"How are you feeling?" Zander popped his head into the airlock, holding the pressurized door open for me. Eyes wide, body blue. So natural, it was as if he were born with it.

"Holy stars above," I sputtered.

"What?"

"Well, you turned yourself blue, for starters. Care to walk me through that?"

"What they do is give you access to basically a shower, only instead of water you have—"

"I meant the thought process behind the sudden change of skin."

"Well, it's quite simple," he said, clearing his throat for no particular reason. "They wouldn't expect me to be blue."

"No one would have expected you to be blue!"

"You see? It works!"

And before I knew it, his stupid blue lips were kissing mine. I would never get tired of this, no matter what color they were. I wrapped my arms around his warm body, soaking in the heat. I didn't realize my jaunt through space had left me so cold. I needed to thaw, and I had just the heater to help with that.

He pulled away all too soon, frowning. "I'm sorry about my sister."

I shrugged. "You know, it was kind of a compliment. If Blayde didn't want me to come back, she would have done a better job of keeping me dead."

He rolled his eyes, which were, thankfully, not blue.

"I meant about her not filling you in on the full plan. She kept me in the dark too. I'm sorry we keep dragging you into this."

"Dragging me? I'm the one rushing to be by your side." I squeezed his hand, and we walked toward the cockpit together.

"I hope your trip was worth it," I called to Blayde, "because Foollegg was no help at all."

"Well, without the Agency on our backs, we're free to hunt down Cross on our own," she said, focusing on piloting our ship. "We don't have to worry about him drawing them to us. Now he can only draw us to him."

"It's going to be difficult if he's changed his identity." I frowned. "We know who he is, what he is, and what he's capable of—but we still have no way of finding him."

"I can help with that," said an annoyingly familiar voice. "But will you *please* hold still? I'm not done with you yet!"

"Oh shit," I spat, but sure enough, there was my LifePrint buddy, letting himself out of the overhead compartment.

"Sally? What the frash is going on?" Blayde slammed the computer shut, but Zander was faster. How he had gotten out of his shirt so quickly I would never know, but he had tossed it over the LifePrint in less time than it took for me to blink.

"My vision is compromised," said the bot. "Please remove the obstruction."

"Zander!" I shouted.

"What?"

"I have scanned the obstruction. It is a shirt. Earth, circa 2017. January. Mexican cotton. A hint of coconut butter. May it please be removed?" The bot's small hands grabbed at the air over the shirt, but the elbow joints were too stiff. No matter how hard the little bot tried, its efforts were in vain.

"It's a LifePrint, Sally," Zander said, ripping the bot from the air. Its arms flailed wildly as it lost its balance, dropping into the shirt like a stone. "It's probably alerted the Agency to our presence!"

"All my stunning evasive maneuvers, all wasted," said Blayde, slamming the console. "Thanks a lot, Sally."

"Hey, I didn't know it would follow me here!" I stammered, reaching for the flailing bot. "It doesn't know anything. First day."

"It's dangerous, Sally."

"Not this one," I replied, shaking my head. "I'm literally the only person it's ever tried to scan. Can you, I don't know, just let it go?"

"It'll know who we are!"

"I don't think it will," I said, reaching. "Hand it to me. I'll deal with it."

Zander shook his head but handed the shirt over

anyway. I reached in and extracted the LifePrint, setting it gently in the air between us.

"Motherboard!" it said, whirring to life. "You're the Iron and the Sand!"

"Zap it, Zander," said Blayde. "And zap it good."

"Hey, LifePrint, over here," I said, slipping between Zander and the bot. "You still haven't told me the results of your scan."

"No, they are still incomplete."

"Then you really can't trust your scans to be correct about the Iron and the Sand, can you?"

"Yes, I can," it replied. "You do not need my programming to see that. They radiate smug, nosy interstellar know-it-all."

"Oh, really?" said Blayde, and I could hardly hold back a laugh. It was right on that front.

"Is that really what you're picking up on?" said Zander. "It's not my handsomeness? Or my need to fry your circuitry?"

"LP, you can't be serious!" I spat. "I thought we were friends."

"Any contact with the Agency was unwilling on my part, let me tell you," said the bot. "And what did you just call me?"

"Zander, shoot the bot and be done with it, will you?"

"Gladly."

"No!" I stepped in front of the LifePrint again.

"Seriously? Sally, why are you defending this thing?"

"I don't know! All I know is that I have no idea who or what I am, and it's literally this bot's job to find out, so could you put off killing him until I get some answers?"

"Sit the frash down, people!" said Blayde. "We've got so much company, we need catering!"

There are some moments that are so cool, they deserve visual effects and musical themes. Like when your boyfriend grabs you with one arm and straps you down in the copilot's chair, even as the ship is rocked by explosions. It's enough to get your heart racing, if you had a fully functioning heart.

The LifePrint yowled as it hit the windshield, toppling onto the console. Blayde cursed as she swatted him away. Instinctively, I grabbed the bot, wrapping my arms around the spherical body and bringing him safely to my lap. Its long, spindly arms hung limply over my legs, jerking every few seconds, as if it were neither dead nor unconscious, just tremendously terrified. Could robots go into shock?

The thing about space is that it's big. It's ridiculous on so many levels. It's maddening that we have to come up with fanciful imagery to make sense of the distances out here. It's so ridiculously big, you could fit every single planet in our solar system in between the Earth and the moon. That's how stupidly far apart they are. And yet that entire space is completely empty, no convenient asteroids for us to hide behind, à la *Star Wars*. Though we should be thankful for that. Any asteroid that close would bring us the same fire-and-brimstone death the dinosaurs got.

We had nowhere to hide. The only thing we could do was win. We were against Alliance ships, armed to the teeth, while flying a hippie barge. I couldn't for the life of me remember why I even wanted to come out here.

We bounced as another impact hit the belly of our ship. I grabbed the LifePrint to stop it from rocketing toward the ceiling, straining at the seat belt.

"We can't take much more of this," said Blayde, gruffly, yanking the controls back, sending the nose of the ship lurched upward. Earth disappeared from view. My stomach went from lurching to twisting, and my body followed, pushing hard into the seat to keep from flinging against the wall.

"Move over. I'll fly," said Zander, reaching for the controls. Blayde swatted him away, hissing like a cat.

"No! The last time you flew a ship, you made it sentient!"

"That was an accident!"

The ship shook again, sending us spinning round and around and around until Blayde regained control, firing counter-thrusters with a slap of her palm. Zander threw himself onto Blayde's lap, wrestling the controls from her hands.

"Let me go!" Blayde shouted. "Get your own damn ship!"

"I'll get us out of here! I'm inarguably better at it."

"Only because you're usually the reason we're being chased in the first place!"

As our spin began to slow, what did I see out the window but half a dozen sleek, white ships. They couldn't have shouted Alliance louder if they had a bullhorn with them.

The LifePrint let out a small, terrified whirr in my lap. I slid my hand over his eye, wishing someone would have the decency to do the same for me.

Zander grasped the joystick with one hand and the gearshift—probably not an actual gearshift—with the other. Despite being entirely draped over his sister's lap, he suddenly seemed in his element, his eyes riveted on the ships before him, determination tracing every line of his face.

"If our ship explodes before we get to Earth, you are so dead," Blayde muttered, crossing her now-useless arms over her chest impatiently.

"Threaten me all you like. I've heard it all before."

"And you love it."

"Not really. Whatever gave you the impression I like being threatened with murder?"

"Zander!"

I couldn't help my scream. One of the Alliance ships was flying straight toward us. I didn't need to be a sci-fi nerd to recognize the plasma guns raised and ready to shoot. Shit, they were big and glowing red, which was the universal sign of hot and dangerous and not to be screwed with.

Zander didn't seem fazed by any of it. Our clunky shuttle somehow pirouetted at the last minute, letting the bursts destroy the ship on our tail. One ship down, and we hadn't even fired our first shot.

"I don't know if I should even be asking this," I said, "but do we have guns?"

"Um, no," said Blayde. "All we have is Mister Fancy Pants and his fancy ass flying."

"You say that like it's a bad thing," said Zander. "My flying is the fanciest there is."

I sure hoped so. I didn't want to end up in ice chunks, drifting aimlessly in the void of space between Earth and the moon. For eternity, on top of it all. Eternity was a long time to be a blasted piece of space ice.

You know what they say: Shoot for the moon, die in space. Feel free to skip forward to the next chapter. If we survive, we'll hopefully be in one piece there. If not, it's going to be one sad epilogue. I wonder who they'll get to do the narration. I vote Morgan Freeman.

I peeled my eyes open again, just long enough to see the crazy bright explosions out the window. The ships were assuming a new formation, the five of them bringing their noses together, like some sort of showstopper in an air show.

"Um, what are they doing?" I clutched the LifePrint tighter, my little emotional support bot.

"I have absolutely no idea," he murmured, "but it's absolutely gorgeous."

Which was when their tail ends lit up in gorgeous flame, and all our jaws dropped.

"Zander, it's a burning ring of fire," said Blayde.

"I can see that."

"You sure? Because I'm not quite trusting my eyes right now."

My guts twisted as the feeling of being a caged animal returned. The circle advanced on us. I dug my heels into the floor, bracing for impact.

"Shit, they're going to try and light our plasma tail," she said.

"You think I didn't notice?"

"No, I'm just narrating for the viewers back home," she said, pressing her head back into the seat. "Can you hyperdrive through?"

"Does this ship look like it has hyperdrive?" His fingers clutched the controls harder, like they would give him the answers if he strangled them out of them.

"They're going to burn us alive?" I stammered. "In space?"

"If they manage to ignite our exhaust tail, it'll run into the fuel lines and blow this ship to interstellar come," Blayde explained.

"Then dump the fuel," I said. "If they can't get into the fuel lines, there'll be nothing to burn, right?"

"We'll be stuck in space," said Zander. "Drifting until they retrieve us."

"Or you aim properly," said Blayde. "Shoot this ship like an arrow."

Zander's face lit up, and he rolled his shoulders. "This is either going to get us home, or we're all going to be exploded space ice. Let's hope for the former."

"I thought you said you were the master of fancy ass flying?" I said.

"By that, he means flying by the seat of his pants," Blayde snapped.

"Shut up or I'm not saving anyone."

There was a moment of silence as the entire cabin held their breath. Breath none of us had to breathe, a moment of stillness as the ring of fire rolled toward us, bright plasma against the night sky.

Zander punched it.

The ship blasted forward, straight at the center of the Alliance ships, punching through the ring and clear onto the other side. A move that would ignite our own ship if we couldn't dump fast enough and cut off our own plasma tail.

They had no time to change direction. No one would expect a retreating ship to fly at them, after all. They flew right into the patch of abandoned fuel we had left for them.

In space, no one can hear you scream. You also

can't hear explosions. But we could see them, a red glow reflecting against the cockpit walls.

"I think we lost them," said Zander, after a few minutes of silence. The three of us—and the bot—reeled from the shock of what had just happened, the knowledge of what we had done to escape.

I peeled my eyes open, relieved to see my beautiful home planet. Of all the space rocks in all of space, our rock was the nicest rock. The emotions I felt upon seeing the moon were dialed up tenfold, hitting me like a punch in the gut. This was my home. Every single Terran who had ever lived or died—barring very, very few exceptions—had done so right on that rock.

"You were right," I said, wiping a tear with the corner of my wrist. "That was some fancy ass flying."

"I have finished my assessment," said the LifePrint.

"You have?"

"And I can conclude that you are an excellent specimen of humanity. From Earth, so a Terran human, if you want to get specific," it said smugly.

"That's it?"

I was human. I was Terran. I looked at my hands, so empty now that I had dropped the bot. They were their usual shade of tanned peach, smoother than before but still my hands. Human hands.

If the LifePrint didn't find me different deep down inside, then why was I still not happy? Why did I feel so un-human? So un-Sally? Who was I if everything pointed to me being myself, except for, well, myself?

"I have completed my function," said the LifePrint. "I must return to my post now."

"Oh, hells no," spat Zander, grabbing the sphere from its hovering place in midair. "We just escaped that place. We are not taking you back. *Veesh,* we don't even have the fuel to return."

"I apologize," said the LifePrint, "but seeing as how my function here is complete, I must ask to be returned."

"I can't return what's defective," he started.

"Defective?" the LifePrint sputtered. "Me?"

"Did you miss the part when your 'perfect human specimen' rose from the dead?"

"No, I did not. But that does not change the fact that she is still Terran. Even if her cells are more tenacious than most."

"I don't think he's defective, Zander," I said. "And you know who can pick out Tallagans from a crowd, even from under their skin wraps?" I pointed at the LifePrint. "This guy!"

"That is true," said Blayde. "You know, Zander, this bot could be the answer to our problems."

"What will you have it do?" he asked. "Scan the entire population of the planet to find Cross? It took three hours just to tell you you're human, *possibly* from Earth, so I'm pretty sure Cross will be dead long before we get a scanner on him."

"In my defense, you are a very complex human."

"Why, thank you, LP."

"That is not my name."

"Yeah, but it's quicker to say than LifePrint," I said. "If you don't mind a nickname."

"Okay, this is getting way too corny for me to deal with," said Blayde. "Plus, we have much bigger sharks to sizzle."

I felt the hair rise on the back of my neck. "Did the Agency send more ships?"

"Worse," she replied. "Let me remind you all we burned the last of our fuel back there."

"Oh, wonderful," said Zander. "Blayde, scooch so I can land us."

"Nuh-uh. You get Sally's lap this time. I need to focus."

Zander said nothing as he eased himself onto my knees, and I wound my arms around him, a makeshift seat belt. Except that he was quite large, so now I couldn't see a thing.

"Can we reach St. Pete?" I asked, though with Zander's shirt pressed up against me, it came out muffled.

"Not the one in Florida, no," said Blayde. "And, yes, I do know *some* cities. The good ones mind you. The drink in that town—but I'm getting off topic. What I meant to say was that landing wasn't the best word for what I'm about to do."

"Blayde," I hissed, "stop being coy and just tell us."

"Well, the landing gear is done for."

"Wait, what? We're crashing? Where are the sirens? Alarms?"

"Kaput as well," Blayde replied. "*Veesh,* the alarms are the only silent things on this bucket."

I let out a heavy breath, dropping my forehead against Zander's side. At least I couldn't see the fire of re-entry or the dizzying heights of falling a hundred miles to Earth.

"We're going to have to make a jump for it," said Zander.

"And the ship?" I asked. "We can't let anyone find it, no matter how busted it's going to be."

"Going to let her crash into the sea," said Blayde. "Even if it's found, it won't be revolutionary to the human race."

"We're just going to open the door and jump?"

"That's the spirit!" said Blayde, slapping her brother on the arm. He hopped on his feet, freeing my legs. "Come on, get up. In a few minutes, we'll be a whale chew. Do whales have a preference on their chew toys?"

Blayde rose from her seat, steady despite the shaking floor, leaving the flashing lights of the console for someone else to deal with. In one swift motion, she scooped up the duffel bag, ripped the LifePrint from his perch on the coat hooks, and stuffed him deep inside.

This was not a gentle landing. We were burning up like a meteor. No, we *were* a meteor, streaking through the night, shedding fire as we rushed toward the sea.

Blayde forced open the airlock, tossing the duffel

over her shoulder as the fire abated. With a laugh, she leapt from the open hull, disappearing from view.

"Shit!" I said, feeling my legs go weak. "Shit, shit, shit! I can't do that!"

"There's nothing to worry about," asked Zander, reaching for my hand. "You've done this half a dozen times before."

"Yeah, but last time we jumped out of a spaceship, we ended up having to take a train."

"See? Easy! You've done it before. And we already know we're on the wrong side of the planet. So, don't worry and just jump with me, okay?"

We stepped toward the airlock, the pressure door slamming in the wind. He squeezed my hand tighter. "Just trust me."

I closed my eyes. I didn't have to see this part, after all.

Air hiccupped around me as we jumped and fell, jumped and fell —and, just as suddenly as it began, we were standing on terra firma, surrounded by giant ferns and a very chummy snake.

"Hey-o!" Blayde yelled, appearing high in a tree. "You two make it down in one piece?"

"I thought you said we were near St. Petersburg," I said. "I don't think there's a rainforest in Russia."

"I mean, yeah, we're near St. Petersburg in the grand scheme of things." She hopped down to the jungle floor. The duffel bag squirmed behind her. LP had survived the leap.

"So, where are we really?" she asked.

"How should I know?"

"It's your planet. You should know, right?"

"I've never been to a rainforest, Blayde."

"Right. Rainforest. Sounds promising. Is that near Florida?"

"Not any that I know of."

And then the snake started to ring.

SEVENTEEN

JUNGLE BOOGIE WOOGIE

WHEN CHOOSING YOUR RINGTONE, TRY TO PICK one that's appropriate for any situation. Wind chimes, for instance, is a classic. Works anywhere. Just sounds right. And go ahead and get geeky if you have to. But after today, I no longer recommend the TARDIS sound. Once you hear it escaping the mouth of a thirty-foot snake, it kind of loses its appeal.

"Why, hello there, little one!" said Zander, crouching low to meet the snake face to face. "Are you able to point us in the direction of the closest town or village?"

The snake hissed. Its chest continued to wheeze, the TARDIS still failing to make an appearance. Zander reached out to stroke the snake's head, but it snapped back. Not the friendly type.

"Sally, was the *Doctor Who* sound effect based on a live creature?" he asked.

"No, Zan, that's not what it's meant to sound like at all."

"I might not be a local, but I think that animal is having trouble breathing," said Blayde. "Maybe it's choking. Are you choking?"

She, too, crouched by the snake, suddenly the sweetest little interstellar vigilante you ever did see. She reached out for the snake, and, just as with her brother, it wasn't appreciative of the gesture. With one massive chomp, the snake bit off her pinky.

"That is a snake," said LP proudly, drifting over Blayde's shoulder. "A reptile local to planet Earth."

"I could have told you that," I said. "And, Blayde, it's not going to answer you."

"Well, it's definitely not going anywhere, either," she said. With one massive swipe, she grabbed it behind the head, shoving her hand down its gullet, retrieving a small, black pod: my phone, covered in the intestinal juices of a rainforest reptile. She shoved it in my hands as the terrified snake plunged back into the jungle. "What do we say?"

The pinky on her hand was about the size and shape of a baby's, all bright pink and tiny, with a nail so adorable you could eat it. She ran a hand through her hair, pinning it back into place behind her ear, her useless pinky striving to help but only jiggling against her scalp.

"Thanks, Blayde," I said, pulling up my missed calls. "Now all I need is a bag of rice before the snake guts ruin it."

"A thank you would be nice, too, if you can spare one," said LP, waving.

"What for?" she asked.

"For identifying the local fauna for you!"

I had missed a lot in my short time in space. Approximately twelve missed calls from my parents and another four from Felling, who had somehow been the one to call me from inside the snake. Except I shouldn't have signal here in the middle of the jungle at all.

"LP, what kind of snake was it?" I asked.

"Does it matter?" Zander, who was staring off into the distance where the snake had disappeared, finally made his way back to us.

"It might help us narrow down where we are," I said. "Do you know how many jungles there are on Earth?"

"It was a reticulated python," said LP, and there was no mistaking the smugness in its voice now. "Found in South Asia from the Nicobar Islands, India, Bangladesh, Burma, Thailand, Laos, Cambodia, Vietnam, Malaysia, and Singapore, east through Indonesia and the Indo-Australian Archipelago and the Philippines."

"Well, that sure narrowed it down," said Blayde, arms akimbo. "Not close to Florida, I presume."

"Pretty much literally the other side of the planet," I replied.

"We'd better get on our way soon," said Zander, "if we have any hope of getting back to our dear Agent Felling before Cross's trail goes cold."

"What trail? Cross could be anywhere right now," I said, stuffing my phone into my pocket, hoping it wasn't in the snake's guts long enough to start a meltdown. "We broke into Area 51, and all we have to show for it is a portable body scanner."

"And a very good one, I might add," said LP. "One who identified both a human and a reticulated python on its first day."

"Yes, yes, we're all proud of you, LP. But we need more than that to bring down Cross."

The phone rang again, the eerie breathing of the TARDIS filling the jungle floor. All eyes were on me—any monkey having stumbled on our little party, suddenly quiet and entranced.

I pulled the phone back out of my pocket. I should not have had signal out here, deep in the jungle somewhere in Asia, yet my phone proved me wrong, ringing its cheerful ditty despite the laws of telecommunication.

"Hello?" I said, the only voice in the entire jungle.

"Sally?" Mom sounded giddy and excited on the phone. Which wasn't what I had anticipated what with how we had left things last time.

With the mail-order Russian bride.

With me hanging up on my way to the moon.

Shit.

"Heeeey, Mom. Sorry, my phone ran out of battery."

"Oh, it's fine, honey," said Mom. "We didn't want to bother you and your little friends."

"Mom? You sound tipsy. Is everything all right?" The time zones ran amok in my brain, and I rephrased that. "Isn't it too early to have a drink?"

"We didn't sleep! Svetlana took us to all the local happening places. We played tourist in our own home."

"They are happening!" said a Russian-accented voice in the background.

"You went out to sample the Florida nightlife?" I asked incredulously.

"Your dad has really got the moves!" she replied. "After we told Sveta that Blayde wasn't going to be her husband, she was devastated. So, your father and I got it in our heads to help her find a better match. Instead, we got her to love herself."

Sveta? Nicknames, now? Oh boy. "That's great, Mom, but I'm sure that doesn't help with her visa trouble."

"Oh, we've got her covered. We're adopting her! You're going to have a sister!"

"What?"

"I am sister to American girl!" said Svetlana,

probably even more excited than my mother was. "God bless America!"

I had to hang up then because both my father and her had burst into singing 'America the Beautiful,' and Mom joined in, her voice joyfully off-key and her mouth too close to the receiver for comfort.

"Blayde, your ex-fiancée is now my future sister," I said, still trying to wrap my head around the news.

"*Ex*-fiancée? *Veesh*. She could have at least told me she was thinking of breaking up."

In that instant, the phone rang again. Zander let out a laugh. "Wow, you're popular!"

"It's Felling, shit." This weird phone voodoo was scaring me. The roaming bill was going to be enormous.

"What the hell did you do, Sally?" Felling's voice was frantic, her tongue slipping over words as they tumbled out her mouth. "Why have I been sent my own death certificate?"

I told Blayde there was a cost to stealing identities, but did she listen? Never. Did I go with it? Sure, I did. Felling had practically bought me first-class tickets because she was sure taking me on a guilt trip.

"There was… an incident at the Agency," I replied. "But don't worry. It all ties back to us three idiots, and they think I'm dead. So, if anything, it's a case of mistaken identity."

Felling let out a heavy sigh, though it was less of a

sigh and more a punch of air being shot out of her. "Did you at least get them to help with Cross?"

"In a way," I said, making eye contact—emphasis on the singularity of that eye—with LP, who lifted his hands into the air like it was a party. "They… lent… us an instrument that will help us catch him. It's a pretty powerful tool."

If the bot could have blushed, it would have. It shoved its hands higher into the air, the stiff elbows only allowing so much give.

"You'd better hope it's powerful enough for it to make what you did worth it. I've been putting out your fires for hours. Breaking into Area 51, I understood, but the show you put on? Seriously? I thought you wanted to fly under the radar! Instead, we're talking *War of the Worlds* scenarios."

"Well, I doubt we could have just asked for the ship," I said, glaring at my partners in crime. They may have masterminded the effort, but I was the one who had to take the phone call.

"And where is that ship now? Need I remind you that it's United States property and belongs in the hangar where you found it?"

"Well, that's going to be a little difficult."

"Oh no."

"We kinda crashed it."

"You crashed United States property?"

"Don't worry," I said quickly. "The craft won't fall

into the wrong hands. It's deep under the ocean somewhere."

"That's not the point. I brought you into this case, so I expected a tiny bit of responsibility on your end. Instead, I end up with having to explain why I supposedly died in a freak scuba accident while my— surprise!—extraterrestrial partner is running around killing people. If I don't get results, they can, and will, fire me. And probably put me in jail as well. Sally, you can't go around stealing ships and then crashing them. I think that goes without saying."

"Hey, need I remind you that we're the ones doing you a favor?" My phone was in Blayde's hands before I could react. She must have heard both sides of the conversation over the lull of the jungle. This place was not happy to have a screaming match between its trees.

"Now, listen here, bud," she snapped. "You asked for our help. We told you we'd follow our methods. Our methods get results! So, sit back and let us do the job you hired us to do or we'll go back to our holiday, dull as those are. Do you understand?"

There was a pause. Then Blayde handed the phone back to me. "She doesn't like me that much," she muttered.

I took the phone, holding it gingerly to my ear. James sounded even more exasperated than before. "Sally, just get back here as soon as you can, all right?"

"I'm not even sure where I'm at right now," I

replied. "Somewhere in southeast Asia, according to the python."

"You speak snake, now?"

"No, the LifePrint told me."

Felling let out another one of her signature sighs. If she kept deflating like this, there would be nothing left of her.

"Just get back as fast as you can. I'm in D.C. trying to save our asses. Cross is still out there, somewhere, and his trail is getting colder by the minute. Oh, and I'll have a bacon cheeseburger with small fries."

"Wait, what?"

"I'm not sure what time it is in your corner of the world, but it's the middle of the night in D.C., so make it snappy." She then hung up on me, which stung more than I'd like to admit. I shoved the phone deep into my pocket.

"Well, first things first, we get out of the jungle," said Blayde, clapping her hands together gleefully. "And reach Felling before she grounds us. And Sally? Don't lose our only asset, will you? You claimed it, so it's your responsibility."

I took LP's dangling hand and found myself feeling like a girl with a balloon, albeit my balloon's tail had very pointy elbows and the little girl was lost in the middle of a jungle while a vicious killer was still on the loose halfway across the planet. This girl needed ice cream.

The last time I had been in a rainforest-type

situation, it had been on the planet where we had met Nim. Or was it on the island none of us had known was Atlantis? Was a Krimoge cluster considered a real forest?

It was an overwhelming feeling to be in a jungle on my own planet. Whatever had happened to me up there, be it experience or my new biology, it had shifted my perspective on everything. My memories felt like silent films, black and white and unspooling at an uneven rate. This, right here, right now was 4-D cinema with Dolby surround sound. My life was running on such high definition that I was overwhelmed by the sights and the colors. My eyes would catch on a brightly colored bird and watch it soar through the air and through the thick branches, picking it out even as it slid behind the dense foliage. Then, like a spring, my eyes would pull me across the expanse, spotting instead a monkey, watching its small, golden body leap across the most extreme gaps in the trees, following its golden buddies.

I felt disgusting wearing the tight bulletproof vest over a loose hippie dress, the neck of which was covered in my own blood and had dried stiff even with the onslaught of sweat. The only thing I would possibly want was a shower. I wasn't dressed for hiking in the jungle. I had to toss out the body armor, stuffing it into the duffel bag along with my overly flowy dress. Now I did look the part of a jungle explorer, wearing a sweaty, white undershirt smeared with mud on top of already ragged jeans that was covered in dust from the Nevada desert. At least I didn't have to wear the tie-dye alien shirt.

No one told me detective work required so many costume changes.

· · · · · · · · ● · · · · · · · · · · ·

Blayde led the way as we trudged deeper into the jungle. Well, it felt like deeper. In reality, we were hoping for a town over the next ridge. Zander was always the one to throw himself up trees, climbing hand over hand like a monkey until he reached the canopy, always looking down with a shake of his head. Nothing.

We had wasted a day walking in the jungle with nothing to show for it. Night was already beginning to fall, and still not a village in sight, not even a road. I trudged onward, hungry having missed dinner and whatever meal I lost to time zones, breakfast or lunch or both. My feet slipped on the damp ground, each step becoming more like a feat of gymnastics than the last. I was amazed I was still standing at this point.

"Can we please take a break?" I begged.

"Why?" asked Blayde, not even gracing me with a glance. "We make better time if we keep moving."

"Look, I'm tired, I'm hungry, I'm thirsty, it's getting dark, and we don't even know where we're going."

"She's got a point," said Zander.

"She's got to learn to get over it. Exhaustion, thirst, hunger, those are all just states of mind. Control it."

"But a lack of direction isn't a state of mind," I said, sitting in the middle of the foliage and crossing my legs.

"Don't be a child," said Blayde. "You need to learn to get past these emotions. To forget about them completely. They're of no use to you now."

"I need a break too," said Zander, taking the duffel bag off his back and plopping himself down beside me. This was enough to have Blayde spin on her heels, grabbing the duffel before it hit the ground.

"No, not you, too," she spat. "I was afraid of this since the beginning! Now it's always going to be two against one."

"Blayde, come on. We've been marching all day," said Zander.

"And we'll march all night if we have to," she snapped. "It's not like it's ever bothered you before."

"We have to stop making everything into an argument," he said. "Let us take a break, just to gather our thoughts."

"What thoughts are there to gather? We're lost; we keep walking until we're not. That's it."

"Please, Blayde."

"I thought Felling needed us. I thought Cross was out there in your home country, Sally, ready to strike again if he hasn't already."

Blayde glowed with anger. Or maybe it wasn't her

glowing. Maybe it was the small light coming from deep inside the trees, somewhere far behind her. She stopped her tirade, turned back, and frowned.

"Do pythons carry torches?" she asked.

"No, no they do not," I said, pushing myself to my feet.

"Yay! People!" said Zander. "That or fire snakes, so I'm hoping for the former."

Thankfully, it *was* the former. A man emerged from the shadows, carrying with him an LED lantern. He smiled as he reached us, grinning from ear to ear.

"Miss Blayde, Miss Sally, Mister Zander," he said. "I'm so thrilled to have found you here. Come, we have to hurry."

I practically leapt out of my shoes when he said my name. I glanced him over again. Nope, no idea who this was. His hair was cropped short to the scalp, and he was dressed comfortably in loose jeans and a faded sweatshirt. Some complete stranger wandering the jungle in the middle of the night who knew exactly who we were and where to find us. A colleague of Felling's? Southeast Asian branch of the secret not-FBI she was a part of?

"Hold on, who are you now?" asked Zander.

"I'm a friend," the stranger replied. "Though I suppose you don't know that yet. Timelines and all. You told me to bring you this. And by the looks of it, you need it. Now, follow me. We don't have much time. Meedian is waiting for you."

He turned, tossing a small bottle over his shoulder.

It landed perfectly in Zander's hands, his blue skin wrapping around the brown glass.

"What's that?" I asked, glancing over his shoulder. And Zander just... laughed.

"It's Blue-Be-Gone," he said, tears of delight running down his face. "Someone out there's looking out for me, and it seems to be me."

"Is he human?" I asked LP. My hand was still firmly clasped around its small, metal appendage, keeping it from drifting away. Not that it had anywhere else to go what with the Agency being at least 400,000 kilometers from here.

"Everyone here is human," LP scoffed as we trekked through the jungle behind our new friend. "Well, except for insects and the worms and the—"

"Yes, but you said I'm human," I insisted. "And I'm not... exactly. Is he entirely human?"

"I'm not sure what you mean."

"You know I can hear you back there, right?" the stranger shouted back at us, still keeping a fast pace. "And, yes, I am human. From Earth. From Bangkok, if you need to know."

"Oh! Are we in Bangkok now?" asked Zander, clapping gleefully. "The last time I was here, I remember it being a city. Though I'm no longer sure if it's past or present, come to think of it."

"We're not even in Thailand." Our guide laughed. "We're in Malaysia. Kinabalu. You told me you were going to be lost, but I didn't believe it until now."

"Hold up—we're definitely the ones who sent you to pick us up?" said Blayde.

"Meedian will explain everything. I am here to get you out of here."

"Meedian? Who's that?"

"As I said, he'll explain everything."

"And what about you? Do you have a name?"

"Sunan. Sorry, I didn't remember to introduce myself. I am glad you're finally meeting me."

All of this was just too surreal. Or maybe it hadn't stopped being surreal since we landed in Nevada. All I wanted was a hot meal and a nice long bath.

"LifePrint?" I asked, my voice low.

"Yes, Sally?"

"You will tell me if we ever run into someone non-Terran, right?"

"That is my job, Sally."

"Is it, though?"

"It is now," it said. "To be honest, I have nothing better to do."

EIGHTEEN

MEETING AN OLD FRIEND FOR THE VERY FIRST TIME

UPSIDE: YOUR BOYFRIEND IS NO LONGER GOING TO be blue. Downside: The de-blueing process involves him scrubbing himself with cotton-candy foam, singing alien show tunes as he goes, blue bubbles drifting in the breeze and smacking us in our faces.

Knowing that future me had been the one to send Sunan, I was thrilled at the thought of everything they had set up for my arrival. Food. Bath. That bed I was dreaming of.

After so long on the dirt, walking on a paving seemed weird; out of nowhere, a path appeared, as if built just for us, and soon the path met a road, one paved with asphalt and lit on both sides by little solar lights. In no time at all, we had reached a small village, colorful houses all in a row filled with the silence of sleep. We reached the largest house of all, a brown, blocky thing with a large, almost quaint American sign outside, white with worn, red letters marking that this was the apothecary.

Sunan pushed the door open into the bright interior, leading us through and taking us from night to day. Every space that wasn't filled with wares was taken up by candles, giving off heat as well as their soft, red glow. Together, that soft light was amplified a thousandfold, making the room feel like a hug from your least favorite, but still beloved, aunt.

In the back, almost right up against the wall, a display case stretched out the length of the store, cutting customers off from the rest of the massive house. The glass was filled with curios of any kind, not just herbal: animal skulls, radios, and a Nintendo Switch all occupied the same shelf, next to a cup of green goo that could very well have been Flubber.

"You were supposed to wait here," Sunan chided, switching off his lantern and setting it on the counter. "I couldn't have missed my temporal mark even if I tried."

"My bladder, however, did," said a voice from the back. "They didn't care to warn me of that, now, did they?"

"*They* are here, Meedian," said Sunan, "so stop with the theatrics and show yourself so I can sleep, all right?"

"Fine."

Wooden beads that had blended in with the decor

in the back of the store gracefully parted, letting through a large man in rich orange robes. His round face lit up when he saw us, bursting into a wide smile and striding with his arms held wide.

"Miss Sally! Mister Zander! Miss Blayde! It is so wonderful to finally see you again and for you to meet me for the first time, I'm sure. I'm sorry these introductions will have to be rushed."

At this point, none of us were following. We got the gist of it—I mean I know I did, not sure about the others, but they dealt with much weirder on a regular basis anyway—but meeting someone who already knew you was a strange experience. I was sure I had never seen this man before, and by the looks the siblings were giving each other, they hadn't either. Even though he was a stranger, I could tell he was trying his hardest not to be hurt by our blank stares, forcing a smile through it all.

"I take it you're the man to thank for this?" asked Zander, holding up his empty box of Blue-Be-Gone.

"Not a man," said the LifePrint, but our host was already talking over it.

"Oh, *pssh,*" said Meedian. "It was nothing. You placed the order. I simply got it in your hands. And you paid cash, which was a bonus."

"Miss Sally," the LifePrint buzzed excitedly, "you told me to tell you if we ever run into someone non-Terran."

"Yes?"

"He is non-Terran," LP squealed. "I'm doing it! I'm doing my job!"

"I would have told you that," the man huffed. Suddenly, his head was floating above his torso. Instead of a neck, there was a body that I could only describe as a baby dinosaur's, all small and chubby and leathery like a croc's. It was also a vibrant shade of pink.

"You're a Uniphage," said Zander, awestruck.

"Hey, I was supposed to say that!" said LP, all enthusiasm gone. It attempted once again to cross his arms but remembered halfway through the gesture that its elbows wouldn't allow it, so he windmilled sadly.

"I've never seen one of you off your home planet before," Zander continued. "I didn't think your species did any traveling."

"I'm the exception," said our host, throwing his hands up in the air. "A quite exceptional exception."

"And who exactly are you, then?" asked Blayde. "Because, sure, I get it, future us have been bothering you or whatever, but does that mean we never get a proper introduction?"

The stranger smiled wider. "The name's Meedian. In a word, I'm a man who knows how to get things."

"How so?"

"I can get any off-planet item you need, if you have the money." He pulled out his card, thin and light aluminum, with words engraved in a darker tone on its surface. *Meedian Gray, the go-to guy to go to,* followed by some coordinates that must have been the location of his shop. "Food from home. Cosmetics. But sometimes weapons. Identities, names, passports, IDs, jobs. I've made quite a handful for you three, that's for sure. No point in hiding any of this from you, seeing as how when I met you, you knew more about my business than I do now."

"And when exactly does that happen?" she asked. "Or did? This is frashing confusing."

"I said too much," he said, shaking his head slowly. I was impressed with such a human gesture, knowing what was hidden underneath his robes. Were his tiny clawed hands seriously running the controls for such a mundane movement? "You gave me specific rules when I first met, about not revealing your future. I try my best, but you've put me in a difficult position since I have to carry this entire conversation by myself. "

"Let me get this clear, then," said Blayde. "You met us before we met you?"

"Don't stand so far away. Come on in; I don't bite!" He waved us forward, but none of us moved. "Time travelers, you know, never meet in the right order. We've had this conversation before, only the roles were reversed. Cliff Notes: You first came to me about ten years ago. I had just moved to Earth and opened my shop, and one day, you three wandered in here cheerfully proclaiming how glad you were to see me. We had a conversation much like this one, only... reversed."

"Look, you don't have to trust us," said Sunan. "Just believe us. We're your friends, and we have been for years. And when we first met, you had known me for centuries. Give us a few minutes, and I promise you'll see we're not a threat. It's more important that we get you to Washington. "

He slipped behind Meedian and motioned for us to follow. It hit me then that the whole time the conversation had been unfolding, I had been on the outside looking in. Part of me didn't believe I could be one of this man's past-future friends and that I would truly know Sunan for centuries.

The storeroom was dark, and Sunan didn't go through the trouble of hitting the light. The shelves were stacked high with red boxes, none of them labelled. He led us farther back, but instead of taking us through the doorway to the stairs, he stopped, closed it, and turned the handle as if to unscrew it. This time when he opened it, the stairs were gone, and a world of wonders awaited us instead.

"Welcome," he said, "to the Sibling Museum."

The room before us glowed white under the bright LEDs, which flickered on in sequence, illuminating an entire strip the length of an airplane hangar. Every wall was covered in pictures, and not just those from Earth. Old, wrinkled pages protected under glass, shelves of weapons and jackets and art, books upon books upon books—a library shoved in a shoebox scale.

And at the very back, hovering delicately in the air, was a hologram of the universe, the intricate web of galaxies filling the air. Sunan handed Zander a remote with a huge grin.

"What's this for?" asked Zander, awestruck.

"This is a map of the known universe. At least, those in contact with our civilization and those with a recorded history or with remnants of cultures past. And if you press that button there... yes, that one, go ahead."

Suddenly, the universe was connected. Red lines crisscrossed over hundreds of worlds, joining galaxies together. The image started to pivot, zooming into a small galaxy I slowly recognized as my own, the Milky Way, where the lines were more numerous and of a different color.

"What is this?" Zander asked, his voice barely a whisper.

"This, this, my friend, is you."

Sunan paused for dramatic effect, but he couldn't stop himself from grinning. "The colder the color is, the longer it's been. Every piece of history I find that depicts you and your sister, I input into the map, which adds a dot. The lines are what I could find in the journal, what you two documented. Time travel is hard to track and harder still to represent in three-dimensional space, so I had to take some liberties.

You only see space here, which place came before, which after. Since you didn't know you traveled in time until very recently, I've input dates from what I myself could connect through fiction or legend, and you have a map."

"Is this... this is my journal, isn't it?" said Blayde, reaching up to touch the red tail of her travels.

"You like it?" asked Sunan. "It's been my life's work since meeting you. I call her Suzy."

"I gave you my journal," she said, turning around to look at Meedian, her eyes wide. "I trusted you to read it."

He nodded. "It's still incomplete, sadly. Some of the older accounts are vague, so I can't tell where you went and when. You did, however, start this journal over here." He pointed to a space closer to the center of the galaxy. "And documented less and less as you ran out of pages."

"And you didn't... you don't have any of the journals that escaped the Berbabsywell Library, do you?"

He shook his head, and her shoulders dropped. "Sadly, no. And whatever cycle you had—willingly giving Nimien your journal, then somehow gaining a new, identical one over and over—was broken when you confronted him. No more mystery journals."

They knew about Nimien and the journals. Read Blayde's journal. This wasn't a trick. This was real.

"So, the two of you have been... what exactly have you

been doing here?" asked Blayde, taking in the museum fully. "Documenting our lives, collecting weird stuff?"

"We get people the things they need," said Sunan. "In your case, we store them too."

Meedian picked through a crate intently before pulling out an old, worn pack of playing cards. "I got hold of this around the same time your package arrived. Look at this."

He spread the cards out on one of the glass display cases. On each card, there was a mug shot or zoomed-in picture taken from a distance. Blayde snorted.

"Alliance-issued toy on the capital planets," Meedian chortled. "*Know Their Aliases,* the Iron and the Sand version."

"No kidding." Blayde was glowing—actually glowing—for the first time since I met her. She rifled through the cards, grinning from ear to ear. I didn't think her smile even extended that wide. "Our fifty-two best costumes. Wow, they packed at least ten jokers in this deck. Sixty-two best costumes, then." She shuffled through the cards, giggling like a child.

"You see this boa?" she asked, holding up what my mind was telling me was the seven of hearts, but my eyes saw instead a red planet with a feisty bachelorette party tiara. "This boa saved the entire planet of Theosse."

I took a closer look at what I could only describe as party Blayde, dressed in a neon yellow jumpsuit, her cheeks painted in bright blue holographic blush.

Around her neck, though, was no feather boa but a kind of hefty, brown salamander. I made it a point to focus on her forehead, avoiding glancing down, dare I find another pirate version of Zander or one where he'd grown out a terrible beard.

"Of course it did," I replied, tapping the spot behind my ear where my translator chip sat, hoping it wasn't on the fritz.

I was a little apprehensive of the Sibling Museum. Was I allowed to see photos of future me? I thought we were supposed to have rules about these kinds of things. Maybe there wasn't a threat because I was so sure to forget them. This day was too long already.

I did like the punk art, though. Part of the wall was sectioned off for displays of different t-shirts—so many different armhole arrangements, holy cow—with different colorful pictures of the siblings arranged in faces of resistance. Not sure if they were a fashion statement or a political one or both. Either way, I was crushing hard on the fractal revolutionary Zander.

I stared down at the cards on the table, the sixty-plus different faces looking up at me, the people my friends could be. But they were always eternal—one of the few constants in this ever-changing universe.

Blayde turned to Meedian, genuine tears filling her eyes. There was a silence then, the kind of contemplation that came from irrevocable twists of fate. Like stumbling across your entire history—or what was left of it—in the basement of a Malaysian apothecary a day's walk from where your spaceship crashed.

Like seeing yourself included in the history of your two closest friends, seeing a room equally divided between a duo and a trio.

I was going to be a part of this for a very long time.

"This is fascinating," said the LifePrint, drifting around the room. "I don't have half of these aliases in my database. What a wealth of knowledge."

Blayde's head whipped up faster than a chipmunk on coke. "You didn't turn off the bot?"

"Was I supposed to?" asked Zander, leaping at LP, who zipped away just as fast.

"Didn't you hear what it said?" she snapped. "It's going to update the Alliance database!"

"You brought an Agency LifePrint? Here?" stammered Meedian, his chubby baby body slipping back into his human suit.

"Well, if this all happened before and future us didn't do anything to prevent it, then it's going to be okay, isn't it?" I asked.

"Unless future us can only do what they themselves experienced and can't change the future!" said Zander, taking another leap at the LifePrint, who swooped away with dashing dexterity.

"You missed me," it said. "Please refrain from attacking me. It hurts my feelings."

"You don't have any feelings."

"I know, and that hurts my feelings too."

Blayde reached for a shelf, pulling off a blanket of some kind. This time she leapt, catching the LifePrint gently inside. Its arms thrashed around weakly. Meedian screamed.

"That's priceless!" he shouted. "Don't you dare get a tear in it! Do you know how difficult it is to get the matching Blayde bed set? Even out of the plastic, it's worth its weight in uranium!"

LP stopped fighting immediately. "This is truly unpleasant," it said.

"Let it go, Blayde," I said. "LP's not a threat."

"And how do you know that?" She reached into the blanket, retrieving the bot with one hand, holding it like a sullen pomelo. I couldn't take my eyes off the woven tapestry, Blayde's scowling face apparent in the features of a blue amphibious dragon. "It may be out of range of the Agency now, but what happens when they get it back? Their database gets a serious upload. I only *just* managed to divert their attention from us here!"

Meedian delicately extracted the blanket from Blayde's hand, folding it with all the reverence of the shroud of Turin.

"So, we disconnect it entirely," I stammered. "I don't know! Just don't hurt it."

"Hurt?" Blayde scoffed. "It's a bot, Sally. It doesn't feel hurt."

The LifePrint thrashed and screamed in her arms.

"No, don't, please. I'm programmed to not like the dark!"

With a quick twist, Blayde had split LP in half. With its eye now divided down the middle, the light went out and the little bot's arms sagged uselessly at its side.

"Don't look so heartbroken," she said. "We'll turn it back on when we need it again. Right now, it's a liability."

"Well, now that all this is taken care of," said Meedian, returning from wherever he had stashed Blayde's merchandising, "you have to get to D.C. Right now. Your friend is in danger."

"Our friend?" asked Zander. "Which friend?"

"Felling!" I stammered. "Is she okay?"

"She will be," said Meedian hastily. "We have a hopper outside waiting for you. You couldn't tell us anything more. Rules of time travel forbid it. All you've said is that she's in danger, and you need to get to Washington right away."

"This way," said Sunan. "As much as I want to show you more of the map, we'll have time for that later."

He led us out of the museum, closed the door, turned the knob in seven different directions, and opened it again. When it opened this time, we were in a massive stone courtyard, lit by the same solar LEDs that lined the town's roads.

And in the middle of the courtyard was the clown-car equivalent of a hopper.

"Oh, you have got to be kidding me," said Blayde, dropping her head into her hands.

"Kicks some punch in the higher atmosphere," said Meedian, slipping out of his shop and following us outside, cardboard box in hand. "But the best part is, it has an autopilot feature, so you can send it back when you land."

"What? So that the next version of us can have their turn?" she asked.

The hopper, impossibly, was smaller now that I stood next to it. This wasn't a ship. It was a toy jet plane, the kind billionaires' kids flew once on their birthday and then got bored with half an hour later.

"I admit it wasn't built as a ferry and I barely fit myself, but it's small enough that the Agency won't see it on their radars. You could fly around Earth three times, and they would think you were a very determined pigeon." He took in all our disgruntled faces. "It won't be a long flight, I promise. Time is of the essence."

Blayde got in first, shoving herself flat in the back, a sleeping LP in her arms. And that was it. No more room available.

I climbed in anyway, her arms a seat belt around my waist, our heads so close together we could share secrets at a slumber party. The little bot's body dug into the small of my back. Zander placed the duffle bag gently in my arms and clambered in last, knees pressed against the controls. But we did, indeed, fit.

"Maybe if we got rid of the redundant wigs, we could fit better?" I suggested.

"Every wig is an important wig," said Blayde.

"And one last thing," said Meedian, stuffing a box into my arms, wedging it between Zander's back and my shoulders, "your future selves placed this order two weeks ago. Anti-bacterial cream from Alliance medical centers. You said someone would be needing it."

"Meedian, you are a lifesaver," she said, trying to extract her hand to shake his, but I was sitting on it and Zander on me, so neither of us could move. Meedian waved us off.

"Oh, *pssh,*" he said. "I'm extremely glad this went so well. The first time I met you, I blew your face off, so this is definitely an improvement. I hope I made up for it."

"I suppose you have," said Zander.

"I'll tell you that you said that next time you stop by," he replied. "Now, go. And don't you dare break my ship."

He brought the hatch down, pushed, and it bounced right back up. He frowned, tried again, and the thing bounced once more. He scowled.

"Oh! I've got a note for you, Sally," said Sunan, handing it to me in between Meedian's bounces. "I've been holding on to it for a while now."

"Thank you, you two," I said. "Looking forward to seeing you again."

"Us too!" heaved Meedian, throwing all his weight on the hatch. With a click, it snapped shut, leaving all our heads crushed together at an odd angle.

We were so pressed together that I hardly felt the acceleration of our takeoff. All I could do was focus on my breathing, hoping my back wouldn't snap during the short half hour it took to fly to Washington D.C. The last time I was here, I had saved the world. There was quite a bit of pride that came with that. Quite a lot of comfort.

I felt nothing but relief when we landed, the hatch clicking open so that we spilled out into the field, fresh air replaced the sweaty funk we had been breathing for what felt like an age. No sooner had we piled out, the ship beeped a cheerful jingle like a washing machine at the end of its cycle and took off into the air.

Leaving us definitely not in Washington D.C.

"Lovely capital," said Blayde. "Very quaint. I like the natural feel. And the fact you can't see any buildings."

"You must feel very proud of your nation," said Zander, reaching for my hand. This time, I didn't give it to him.

"Not the capital," I sputtered. "We're lost. Again."

He sniffed the air. "Smells like America."

"We have a smell?"

"Everywhere has a smell," he replied. "What does your note from the future say? Are we even allowed to know?"

In all the excitement, I had almost forgotten my future self had given me something to read. I unfolded the tiny piece of paper, more than slightly unnerved to see a warning scrawled in my own handwriting. A warning I definitely didn't write.

Five years early, it read, and I frowned. "Five years? Five years until what?"

Blayde glanced over my shoulder, keeping her hands to herself for once. Admittedly, they were a little full with the duffel bag and the bot at the moment.

"It'll make sense soon enough, I suppose," she said. "And as much as I want to talk about what the hell happened back there, apparently, we're on a time crunch. Can we get a ride?"

I fished my trusty phone out of my pocket. Full bars, though that no longer meant anything to me. I wondered how much I'd racked up in roaming charges while I was away.

"Right, so we're in Maryland," I said. "At least, that's what my GPS is telling me now that my data's working."

"Is that close to Washington?" asked Blayde, kicking up dirt with the toe of her boot.

"We could be." I zoomed into my map. "Yes! We're right by the end of the green line. Meedian must have wanted to avoid capital airspace. Just means we need to text Felling to pick us up."

Which became the most natural thing in the world to do after having been to the moon and back again: just text your Agent Mulder to come grab you.

The scary thing is when Mulder doesn't respond.

NINETEEN

NOT THE GREATEST PLACE FOR AN
ALIEN MARKET SCENE

OUR TRIO OF HALF-HIPPIE, HALF-UFO ENTHUSIASTS, covered in mud from the Malaysian rainforest — thank Derzan that Zander wasn't blue anymore— were far from being the strangest people on the D.C. Metro that day, even factoring in the robot. No one even glanced our way as we huddled on the plastic seats, trying to work out a game plan as we zoomed below D.C.'s monuments.

"I hate public transport," Blayde muttered, tinkering with LP. Her hands were stable, even as mine trembled as I clutched my duffel bag of mysteries. "If it turns out Felling is avoiding playing taxi, she's going to find herself on the next transport to the spice mines of Katari. She'd probably make a better miner than secret agent."

"Blayde," I hissed, "don't say things like that. Felling is my friend. Our friend."

"A friend you were avoiding," she said. There was no malice, just frustration, as she sorted the rainbow wires of LP's little digital brain. "One you were hiding us from. And a friend whose partner tried to turn us in to our enemies."

"I misjudged her," I said. "And she needs us right now. She means enough to us in the future that we had Meedian send us right to her."

"But not enough to give ourselves the actual details to save her," said Zander, slamming his hand against the plexiglass window. "Wouldn't we have given ourselves more information to track her down than just a city name?"

"I trust you," I said. "So, I trust future you too."

"I'm not sure you should," she said. "Who knows what future me wants from us."

With that, LP's eye turned back on, bright and beautiful and alive. I couldn't explain the relief that flowed through me at the sight.

"Oh, hello," he said, giving up all pretense of hovering. Its arms bounced lazily up and down. "Have you brought me back to the office? Or should I consider myself stolen property for good?"

"You know, I thought most bots would be happy to not be under the Agency's thumb," said Zander. "I hear working conditions for them are not the best."

"I can't say," it replied. "It's still my first day."

We came up right on the National Mall into a bright and sunny winter's day. The lawn stretched long before us, a beautiful shade of green, the museums cutting sharp angles against the cloudless, blue sky. Behind us, the Washington Monument rose up and up, and I wondered if I could find that sushi place again, the one we had huddled in with the president while the world was ending. If we weren't here to save our friend's life, I would have called it a great day for touring.

"What is it with your nation's obsession with malls?" asked Blayde, glancing quickly up and down the green. "That's a lot of malls."

"Those are museums," I muttered, fishing my phone from my pocket as it dinged. A message from Felling. No, not a message, a location. "The National Mall is the stretch of lawn. Anyway, what would she be doing at Eastern Market?" I asked, more to myself than to anyone else.

"Maybe she's hungry?" asked Zander. "The emergency is that we've forgotten to feed her."

"She must be held there against her will," I said, showing them the text. "She did a location share, didn't write anything. Like she was trying to send this off as quickly as possible."

"Like someone is with her," said Blayde. "Cross? The Agency?"

"Is she driving past it or is she there?" asked

Zander. And at the same time, his sister said, "It could be a trap."

"Either way, would it stop us from going?" I asked.

"I say we avoid anything with a trap," said LP. "Even if it's mildly trap-shaped, we should not go there."

Blayde shoved the bot into my arms, spinning him so that his eye faced outward, toward her. It was sulking and turned off whatever antigravity it had, making it dead weight in my arms. It was like carrying a boulder up a mountain.

"Listen up, you little neuron. You're not a part of this group. You don't get a say in where we go. Your job is to figure out who's from this planet and who isn't. Don't say a word unless you spot the Tallagan. *Capisce?*"

The bot remained silent. Blayde's brow furrowed.

"This either means he knows exactly what I'm asking, or I got his wires crossed and he's now a potato," she muttered. "Right. Which way is east?"

"We can just take the… never mind."

Blayde was already off, following the throng of people up the mall toward the Capitol building. I couldn't have gotten her back into the metro even if I had her bound and gagged. It was lucky that Eastern Market was actually to our east or we would have been chasing her up and down the mall all day.

Zander offered a hand. "You know what? I *have*

been here before. Were there bears in your past or your future?"

"Bears?" I asked. "What kind of bears? No, I don't want to know. Not really." I reset LP on my hip, his silence more than a little unnerving at this point. "This time travel thing is starting to drive me crazy."

"Tell me about it," said Zander, putting his arms down when I refused to relinquish the bot.

Eastern Market was just that: a market to the east of the Capitol. I'd been only once before and had been pretty let down. Despite it being listed on almost every tourist site, it really was nothing more than a market with overpriced cheese. Though today, it was bustling with activity. Brightly colored stalls with local artists on display, pretty pieces from all over the globe. The smell of something delicious and deep fried wafted over us, making my stomach rumble. I hadn't eaten in what could have been days at this point.

"You know, this is pretty tame for an alien market," said Blayde, having found the place before us and already scoping the territory. "Usually, they're all about hawking their spices."

"That's inside," I said, pointing out the building. Blayde frowned.

"So where are we meant to find Felling?" she asked.

"The app isn't any more specific than this," I replied, showing her my phone again—a challenging move with LP in my arms. "We're going to have to find her the old-fashioned way."

"Great," said Blayde. "I'll circle the north. Zander, you take the south. And Sally—"

"Sally stays here with the LifePrint," he said, quickly cutting her off. "In case Felling comes by."

"I'm not staying out here alone," I spat. "Felling needs us. She's my friend, I can't just—"

"Sally, please," said Zander. "We need you here."

"Why here, exactly?" I said. "There's literally three roads she could run down. The only reason you don't want me to move is that you're scared, aren't you?"

He said nothing. Blayde rolled her eyes in her patented way, grabbing him by the shoulder.

"Come on," she said, yanking him forward. "Sally, keep that LifePrint scanning the crowd. We can't have any surprises."

"Sure, sure," I muttered, as Zander looked at me apologetically. He couldn't even bring himself to say it. They marched down the row of stalls, fading into the crowd, leaving me angry and poised at the corner of the road.

So much for Zander accepting that I was different. I couldn't be both immortal and breakable, yet he was somehow balancing that paradox like a champ, blinders on, ignoring everything we had been through today.

"You're still with me, right, LP?" I asked. It said nothing. How could it, with Blayde's parameters still in place? It wouldn't be able to talk unless there was a Tallagan in front of it.

Dead weight in my arms. Still sulking.

The market was full of activity today. I wasn't even sure what day of the week it was anymore, but it was busy, parents with kids in their hands. How similar it looked like the Agency. How many of these normal, lovely people were tourists from more than just out of state? How many people here were eyeing the soda can art because it was both a snack and a collectible on their home world?

I'm sure LP could tell me, but it said nothing still. And so I waited, nerves shot, watching the throng of people move up and down the rows, hoping to high heaven that Felling was here and safe. With my stomach rumbling as effective background music.

"Any luck?" asked Zander, appearing by my side, either through stealth or his own brand of not-magic. He very delicately handed me a hot dog.

"Oh god, thank you!" I sputtered, moving LP over to my hip so I could accept the gift. My stomach rumbled, and he laughed, even as it made my face glow like a stoplight. I thought we weren't supposed to feel hunger anymore. But I was too hungry to ask.

One bite, and I was in heaven. There's something majestic about the simple nature of a hot dog. But as I lifted my eyes from the food, I caught the gaze of a very huffy warrior, pouting from across the market.

"Does Blayde want one too?" I asked.

"She's probably mad we're taking a snack break," Zander muttered.

Her hands flew about her face in a flurry, Zander nodding all the while. Their own secret sign language, one even my translator couldn't pick up.

"So?" I asked.

"I'm telling her this is probably a red herring," he replied, brows furrowed in concentration. "She's wondering what fake fish have to do with this."

"Guess some things don't translate," I said. "But she does raise a good point. How can a fish be fake?"

"Now she's saying something about ice cream."

"What?" I returned to my hot dog. "I'm pretty sure she's flipping you the bird, my dear."

"Of course, punching a stranger can mean many things, least of them ice cream," he said. The man who was now tumbling to the ground behind Blayde's shoulder definitely wasn't going to forget. "I think I have to go."

And then he was gone and so was my hot dog, though the latter was my own fault for eating it so fast. Zander and Blayde had found a clue—maybe. Or equally possible, the man they were now hauling to his feet was just some creep. It was D.C., after all.

My phone rang, which almost sent me out of my skin. I should have been used to it by now. This was a more likely scenario than the jungle, after all. I scooted LP to my other hip, feeling like a tech-savvy peasant washwoman, and slipped my phone out of my pocket. My gut twisted as I saw the caller ID. Felling.

"James, are you okay?" I asked, before the call even went through. I should have known better than to expect her on the other end of it.

"This should keep the siblings occupied for a while," said Cross, sending a shiver down my spine.

"You're really terrible at this whole distraction thing," I said, glancing up and down the market. If he knew I was alone, he could see me, but I for shit couldn't see him. "Really? You don't think we know this is a trap?"

"Oh, sure," he replied. "But a trap for whom?"

I felt a chill roll through me. Where were Zander and Blayde? I couldn't see them anymore, couldn't signal them even if I wanted to. So much for being the lookout.

"Where's Felling?" I sputtered. "What have you done with her?"

"Oh, she's fine. She's taking a nap for a little while. You don't need to worry about her. Not if you do what I say."

Where were they? Where was anyone? Could Cross see me or not? Why weren't Zander and Blayde emerging from the market? My skin was cold, and my belly was in knots. I was alone.

"What do you want?" I didn't want to ask those words, but they came out all the same. Felling had only been doing her job; she didn't deserve this, any of this.

"I want you to cross the street. Can you do that for me? And don't you dare signal the siblings. I can see everything. Now, walk south. Then take a right."

I hefted LP back up and did as he asked, casting glances back over my shoulder. Cross tutted.

"What did I say? No signaling."

I crossed the street, turning right at the intersection, and walked toward a bookstore with old paperbacks clogging the windows. I could still hear the market behind me, smell it. Cross had to be there, hiding in the crowd.

Only LP hadn't seen him, so there went that theory.

"Walk into the bookstore," Cross ordered. "Walk downstairs."

I clutched LP tight to my chest as I swerved between the stacks of paperbacks rising along the walls. The bookstore was literally floor to ceiling books. The usually calming scent of old pages was overwhelming, cloyingly so when it mixed with the adrenaline running through me.

Figures this guy wanted to use a bookstore to intimidate me. Too many distractions.

I ducked down the rickety staircase into the somehow even more stuffed basement, passing no one on the way. A labyrinth of shelves was there to greet me, but no Agent Cross in sight. He could have been anywhere.

"Go to the back corner," he said, finally cutting out the creepy heavy breathing. "Wait for me there."

He hung up on me then, my phone flashing Felling's name for a brief second as the call ended. I shuddered. I shouldn't have been scared. I was immortal, after all, a fact I kept trying to remind the others. But they had left me weaponless and skill-less, going up against a man who was a literal Man in Black.

But while I was immortal, Felling was not. If I had to take a bullet for her, it was a small price to pay. I'd already died today, after all.

The stairs creaked as Cross climbed down them. Of course, he hadn't been watching me from the basement. The upstairs window, stuffed high with paperbacks, would have been the perfect vantage point.

"What have you done to James?" I asked as he rounded the shelves to face me. He looked worse for wear since the last time I had seen him only a day before. His skin was pale, hanging limply off his frame, like he had aged a span of thirty, forty years in a single day. I gaped at him.

"Don't have to look so happy to see me," he replied. His hand went to his hip, and my throat tightened. A basement was a great place for a murder. No one to hear the shot. No one to find the body.

Wait. I'm immortal. If he was going to kill me, he wasn't going to leave me here.

Shit.

"I am!" LP fluttered to life in my hands, his jinx over. "Tallagan here! Tallagan here! Haha I found him!"

Cross raised his hand and shot LP clear through its bright blue eye. The poor bot didn't have time to move out of the way—nor could it, with the shelves so close together. There was nowhere it could have gone, even if it tried.

"Oh no, not again," it said as it collapsed to the ground.

"LP!" I screamed, rushing to it like I would a wounded friend. The light in its eye flickered and went out. Once again, far too soon. I looked up at Cross.

"You didn't have to do that," I spat.

"It's not alive, Webber," he said, still clutching his gun, the heat off its muzzle close enough to singe. "You don't have to pretend to feel sorry for it."

"I liked it. Far more than I ever liked you. You're an ass, you know that? For years you—"

"Kid, I'm not here for a lecture," he said, sighing heavily. "If you want to see Felling alive, you're going to have to shut up for this part."

I didn't need to ask.

With a heavy sigh, I died from a silent shot to the head.

TWENTY

I IGNORE MY OWN ADVICE, SO CALL ME A DUMBASS

IF YOU CAN NO LONGER REMEMBER HOW MANY times in your life you've woken up bound to a chair, then you start to wonder where everything went wrong.

When the first thing that hits after gaining consciousness is a retched, moldy smell, you know very well you don't want to open your eyes. You don't want to know what's out there. Sometimes, it's better to keep your eyes shut and pretend you're in a reverse Febreze ad where everything smells bad but still looks amazing.

If there was one thing I learned from the other times I had been knocked unconscious—sure, this time I had been outright killed, but I was at the point in my life where that meant the same thing—it was to take this time before the captor realizes you're awake to understand your surroundings. Even before testing my restraints and seeing if I could get out on my own, I needed to know what I was going to attempt to escape from.

Okay, cement floor. It was winter, yet the room was somewhat warm. We must have been underground, unless someone was choosing to heat an abandoned basement.

Or maybe I was in someone's home and they just never washed. Which I guess was always a possibility, yet somehow a tad more gross.

Now, to test the restraints and do so quietly. I tugged at my wrists, feeling the plastic zip ties digging into my skin. Surely, I could break them quietly enough to slip away from this place undetected.

If there was any time for my panic button to activate, it would be now. *Come on, jumping skills, take me anywhere but here.* It was just my luck that I was now too calm to get out of my own way. But Felling was here somewhere in this monster's clutches. I couldn't leave until she was safe.

My body betrayed me because, sure, after the day I just had, what wasn't going to go wrong? I started to cough, a strong cough I could not contain. It erupted from me as I expelled air in sharp gusts.

It just would not stop. I opened my eyes to find myself in a tiny room, feeling a twinge of relief when it became obvious I wasn't in someone's gross house. My eyes would adjust to the dark, but my body was too focused on coughing to deal with my vision right now. Somewhere there was a movement in the shadows, and, suddenly, Cross was striding toward me, a look of worry on his face. He looked somehow worse now, his skin so white it practically glowed while the sheen of sweat made everything even brighter.

With a clang, a small, silver-colored item jumped from my throat onto the ground. My coughing died down, my breath steadying as the man lifted the debris off the ground.

"Well, look what we have here." He lifted the small piece of metal to his eye. "I always wondered what would happen to an immortal with a bullet through their brain. Result? The bullet is expelled."

"You probably don't want to touch that," I said. "It's basically puke."

I was surprisingly glib about being held captive by a serial killer, immortal or not. Though maybe it came with the territory: I had, after all, already died twice today and hadn't gotten a nap in between. It was a little unnerving how quickly you get used to that.

"Well, it's no longer your problem now, is it?" he said, pocketing it. "I trust you're fully recovered?"

"Are my brains hanging out? No? Then I suppose I am."

He nodded to himself, crossing the small room to an old, forgotten table in the corner. He slipped off his jacket, folding it gently and placing it before him, almost like a display.

"Being immortal, I expect you might have some experience with removing brain matter from wool."

"Um, no. That's not exactly taught in immortal school."

"Shame, I did love this jacket." He sighed, turning his attention back to me.

"Where's Felling?" I spat. "If you hurt her, I—"

"Do what you're told, and no harm will come to her," he said, showing far too many teeth.

I rolled my eyes, leaning deeper into this confident persona I adopted. "Look, are you going to tell me what you want or not? We can keep wasting time, but it doesn't look like there's much of you left."

"You can't seriously be doing this."

"Doing what?"

"You know, the whole 'now that you've got me, tell me your whole plan.' I mean, it works in movies. Not in real life."

"Did I ask for your life story?" I laughed. "I don't give a crap. I just want Felling safe. And even if I did, it's worked for me at least once before, and it makes for damn compelling storytelling. Or at least heavy handed exposition."

"This isn't a movie," he said, rolling up his sleeves past his elbows. If I had a heartbeat, it would have stopped, right then and there.

"Exactly. Let's just get this over with."

Instead, Cross took his chair, spun it around, and sat on it backwards, facing me in a terrible imitation of an intimidating interrogator. Except he was the one doing all the talking. Maybe my charming personality was keeping me alive for once instead of getting me in trouble, so I forced myself to give him one of those terribly awkward smiles, the kind that said, "hey, I feel you, bro."

"I knew even before I landed that I could never go home," he began, and I realized in that moment that mansplaining transcended species. "There were people back on Tallaga—three—who would kill me the second I set foot back there."

"But our air is toxic to you," I said. Should I have stayed quiet? What exactly was the etiquette on evil rants? "I was told cancer is a side effect of prolonged exposure."

"It was too late. I had spent all the money I had on forging my new life here. I didn't even have enough for a ride off this rock. I managed to connect with others from my world, and they turned me toward a local flesh peddler. Certain types of human cells allowed us to continue living and breathing on Earth, so long as they were consumed regularly. He grew them in his lab, and we had enough to get around without harming anyone."

"So, what happened?"

"The Agency happened," Cross scoffed. "Busted the peddler for selling to illegals. Suddenly, our entire supply was gone. Some of the other Tallagans managed to get off the planet, others were picked up in an Agency raid, and I, I was the only one who tried to continue living a normal life here."

"And that didn't last long."

"What was I supposed to do? I was desperate. I couldn't leave the planet; I couldn't afford it. I couldn't give myself up to the Agency since they'd put me behind bars for a decade. My last available option was to try to get by. I didn't... I didn't know what I did would kill them."

Further evidence Foollegg was a massive liar when she claimed to have no idea Tallagans were here at all. Or maybe it was her ego thinking they got them all in one go. "You ate women's spinal cords. You didn't think that might not be in their best interest?"

"They were perfectly healthy! So healthy! What's the loss of one's limbs if it means someone else can continue to live?"

"I don't suppose you asked them first."

"Well, I asked the first donor," he said. "And after a long discussion, she agreed I could at least try. She wasn't meant to die."

"And the next woman?"

He shrugged. And that was as heartwarming as his story was going to get.

"Then Felling tells me that you're back," he said. "We had just finished cleaning up the incident with the Youpaf, and neither of us expected you to come back so soon, with the siblings in tow, no less. And I saw a way out: give you up to the Agency, who would tear sky and Earth apart to reach you, and gain a pardon for all my past crimes. The only problem is you're a bit hard to present on a silver platter."

"And then you slip up and have to go on the run anyway," I said. "What I don't understand is what you want with me. The Agency thinks I'm dead. The Alliance doesn't even know who I am, let alone care. Turning me in won't get you anywhere."

"What makes you think I'm going to turn you in?" he said, smiling wide, revealing two glistening rows of white teeth. I shuddered. I knew he had more than just human teeth in that false mouth.

"You do realize I'm far from being a perfect specimen, right? I had chicken pox as a kid. Measles too. I heard that stays with you even into your adult life."

"Have you forgotten the most important part?" He grinned, regaling me with far too many ivory teeth. "The power of immortality trapped in a weak, little girl."

I tried not to get offended—not the right time. "So, that's what you're looking for? Immortality?"

"Who isn't?"

"Well, I can name quite a few people, myself included. Not too thrilled with the whole dying family thing."

"I killed you a few minutes ago. Would you have liked it better if you had stayed dead?"

"By definition, I probably wouldn't have minded either way. Plus, it would mean I wouldn't have to sit through your insufferable monologuing. And seeing as how I'm going to die in a few minutes away, what's the point of coming back for that?"

"Have you seen my body?" he spat. "Have you seen how it decays? It doesn't have much time left. I want to live. I can't imagine anyone not."

"Well, you're not the one tied to this chair."

"I'm confused. Are you saying you want to die?"

"I'm confused too. It's just really odd having a conversation about forced organ donation. What are you waiting for? You need me to stay still while you drink my spine like a straw? Is there meant to be a ritual?"

"Oooh, I like this. Like I need to guzzle some Mountain Dew and do a little dance to absorb your power. Should I wear face paint?"

He lifted his hands to his jaw and unhinged it. There was no other word for that terrible motion, that clicking of bone against bone. But worse came after when the skin began to melt off his face, a perfect imitation of melting Nazis from *Indiana Jones*. Trust me, not a movie scene you want to see in real life.

"Oh, this?" He pointed to the melting area, in response to my wide eyes.

"I didn't ask," I said, practically gagging.

"This skin wrap is rather nice, and when I need to go underground, I'll rip this one off and get another. Loads of resellers out there. Plus, I'm done with this identity."

"Again, I didn't ask. Also, I'm done listening to your stupid rant you weren't going to give in the first place. Oh, come on now!" I shouted. "Help, help! I'm down here! Help!"

A low thump echoed from far beyond; someone could hear me. Felling? I had no way of knowing, but if she could hear me, she was closer than I thought.

"No one is around for miles," said Cross, reaching up to snap his jaw back in place. The melted skin wrap remained limp on his chin. "So, don't waste your breath. I'm going to check on our mutual friend, and if I hear a peep out of you, chances are she won't be alive for long."

With that, he walked toward the rusted metal door and slid out without a second glance my way, leaving me I was trapped in the dark.

Well, this was lovely.

I tugged my wrists against the zip ties. I could pull as much as I wanted—the plastic digging into my skin didn't bother me much more than flies landing on my skin—but I didn't have the strength to snap the plastic all the way.

I resigned myself to the fact that there was no way out of the chair. At least, not with the physical strength I had. The chair was heavy and metallic; this baby would not break, no matter what I would do with it. My only way out was to jump. I gritted my teeth, closing my eyes and focusing on home. *Come on, Sally Webber, you can do this.* Believe in yourself. You were a literal goddess. You can get out of this stupid chair.

I had done it before, too. But right now, I couldn't get Felling out of my mind. If she died because of me, I would never forgive myself. My mind bounced around the room, unable to grasp a place to drag myself to.

I wasn't going to stand for any of this.

Or sit, either, but I didn't have many options with that.

I realized quite suddenly that I was sitting here seeing myself as a damsel in distress when I really had to save myself on this one. If all went well, I would have captured a killer and saved my friend before anyone even figured out where I was.

But first, I had to get out of this damn chair.

I could write a book with all the things I learned while tied to a chair. Maybe this is a new form of mindfulness meditation. Did I feel zen? Not particularly. But I was feeling damn insightful.

Insight number one: You should have listened to your dad when he first went through his conspiracy nut phase. Back then, he had offered to teach me how to break out of handcuffs and zip ties. That would have been a huge help right now.

Insight number two: The mind will conjure all sorts of images to distract from oncoming doom. The lack of sleep mixed with the wave of nausea that came from one of these hostile situations were muddling with my mind. I had to think straight if I was to get out of this. Right now, I was sure I was hearing the entire theme to *Star Trek: Enterprise,* and it was glorious.

I sang along, my hands straining at the plastic ties around my wrists. At least my fingers were free. I slid my hand into one of my back pockets, wishing, dreaming for something of use to be there. But I never kept anything back there, ever.

Desperate times called for desperate measures. Even if it meant prodding my own butt for answers.

Dang, that's a catchy tune. The theme song kept going in my head, and I was signing along, louder and louder.

There. My fingers wrapped around a small, almost unnoticeable hairpin. The kind you used to hold back a strand of hair that was bugging you without being too noticeable. The kind I never had the need to use, the kind I lost too often when I did, the kind that was small enough to save my life.

How could they have gotten in my jeans?

Only they weren't my jeans. Well, they were, but for the past week, they had been Blayde's. I had pulled them out of the duffel in need of something to wear. And left in the back pocket was one lone, forgotten hairpin she had used as part of her hippie getup.

I sang louder now, bolstered by my find. I was going to get out of here. But what good was a hairpin when faced with plastic zip ties? These weren't like handcuffs; there was no lock to jimmy open. Barrettes were nothing when you didn't have a lock to break.

With a scream of frustration, I flung my arms back. I was boiling, rage filling me, the heat wafting off me in steaming geysers.

The zip ties snapped apart like store-label plastic.

I stomped my legs. The ties there broke apart as if they had never been bound at all. I was shaking now, trembling with the knowledge that there was a dangerous strength within me.

So much for being just human. Only human, but with many upgrades, it seemed. Super strong and super badass and pretty terrified, thank you very much.

I picked the hairpin from the ground where I had dropped it, slipping it back in my pocket as I made my way to the door. Fortunately, it was unlocked. I pushed it open, checking if the coast was clear, and exited the room where I had been held captive, walking up the stairs.

I was wrong. This was not the basement of an old bookstore: it was the stockroom of a Starbucks in an abandoned mall.

I held back a laugh. Are you kidding me? I hadn't seen so many malls in so few days in my entire life. Blayde was right. What was our obsession with them, exactly?

And this one was a very large, fancy, and expensive-looking shopping mall at that. A chandelier lay fallen in the middle of the hall in front of me, glass surrounding it, a lone, forgotten, faux-crystal tear having landed as far as the top step where I was standing now. I was surrounded by tall shoots of bamboo in pots, probably intended to hide the entrance to the basement. The only light illuminating the room was from the moon outside and the occasional headlights of the cars slowly passing by outside.

Well, this was going to be easy. Now all I needed was to find Felling before Cross came back to check on me. A directory would be helpful, specifically one that pointed toward effective hiding places. For once, can we just have a big billboard saying, 'Bad Guy right here?' It would make things much easier.

I froze, hoping to fade in with the shadows. A figure swept by, impossible to recognize in the near darkness, gliding behind the overgrown plants and down the cleverly concealed staircase. As soon as it passed, I took off at a dead run, sprinting down the street-wide corridor between the abandoned shops. I reached the end with a skid and with wide eyes found the door.

Wood, padlocks, chains, and nails held the doors

tightly shut, a barricade against intruders that resembled the feeble attempts at protection in a zombie movie. Nothing I could do would get me through that. I would have to find another exit. And fast.

A massive department store was to my left, so I ran that way, staying near the wall to keep hidden from sight. Who would have known my knowledge of retail would save me now? The loading dock shouldn't be too far from the back, so it was the best option for now. The place was empty, shelves askew and bare, but it had obviously served as a place to party for some who had found a way into the old mall. I had reached the back corner in a few minutes, old beer cans and cigarette butts littering the way.

And there, in the middle of it all, the hilt of a weapon I hadn't seen since it had been slipped into my duffel bag. Why it was there, I had no idea, but it was. How it got there, I really didn't care. I picked it up, pressing the switch to release the beam of light.

The saber hummed with life, heat flooding through me. The warmth of safety. I had a way to defend myself now. I had a chance of getting out of here in one piece.

And I knew very well that laser sabers didn't just fall from the sky. Someone was looking out for me.

And that person was, most likely, me.

Time travel is flipping awesome, you guys.

TWENTY-ONE

LEAVE YOUR ABANDONED ROOMS
THE WAY YOU WANT TO FIND THEM

FINDING A SECRET AGENT HIDDEN BY ANOTHER secret agent was proving more difficult than previously assumed. Then again, I generally didn't go around assuming how easy one is to find, so maybe no bar was ever really set.

I needed Zander on this one. No: I'd done worse—or better—alone before. I didn't really *need* him. But then again, there was one agent to find and another to arrest, so two hands were better than one.

This was all very confusing. I was supposed to be the immortal hero now, and I couldn't even use my supposed superpowers to avoid thinking about how hungry I was. The hot dog had been burned off by whatever energy I needed to bring myself back to life.

No. Find Felling. That's what's most important.

Get her out of here. But even if I did find her, how was I going to get her out? I couldn't freaking jump.

Any good heist needed a getaway driver, after all.

So I did what I was best at: meandered around a creepy location until I stumbled upon the action. Or, at least, a clue. Or until the action found me. I was sensing a theme here.

Seconds ago, I felt so safe. Secure. All thanks to the small, metal weapon in my hands. But everything was wrong. The mall was empty, except for a few birds who found their way in broken panes of glass in the sunroofs. Every once in a while, the flutter of their wings made me spin on my heels, laser extended, scared that it was Cross there to take me back to the basement.

But I was not going to give him the chance. I wasn't going to let him steal my cells and poison me in the process. I wasn't going to let him get by with another murder on his hands, even though I would then count twice, since he had already killed me that day.

Now, where could she be? I had been hidden in one of the stock rooms beneath the mall itself. Definitely the best place to hide someone you didn't want found. If Cross had access to the entire place, then the best place to stash a kidnapped secret agent would be directly opposite where he stashed me.

I made a beeline for the farthest point from where I had been hidden, trotting the broken fossils of the mall underfoot. The ominous ruins of an old sunglass hut, now sans sunglasses. The once-beautiful mall fountain, now full of empty bottles, coughed up a putrid stench. Clearly, there was a way in and out of this place. I just hadn't found it yet.

That, or Cross had closed it up, trapping us inside with him. What kind of sick game was he playing?

I was getting freaking tired of this. How many people wanted to manipulate me for the sheer thrill of it? At least Nimien had an actual plan. This whole rat-in-a-maze thing just seemed to be entertainment for messed-up Cross. I was just lucky this wasn't one of those semi-underground city malls that D.C. and Arlington were somewhat known for. I could get lost in those for days.

The antipode of where I had been stashed turned out to also be a Starbucks. Figures you needed two in a space as large as this. I let myself through the staff-only door and walked down a flight of stairs to the old abandoned basement where, surprise, surprise, my secret agent bestie was tied to a chair.

Okay, maybe I was overestimating the relationship. She was my closest friend who happened to be an agent, but maybe she wasn't my best friend who was also an agent. Not that any of that mattered right now, seeing as how she didn't look all that alive.

Her face bloodied beyond belief, Felling was tied to a chair just as I was, head lolling to the side in a way that screamed to get her to the hospital right now. I didn't think; I just ran, ran to her side, holding back tears at the sight of her, feeling for a pulse I couldn't dare hope was there.

I was right to dare. It was thready, but she was alive, dammit.

"You're okay, you're okay," I said, the best lie I had told all day, as I wrapped my arms around her. She let out a low moan, the barest sound she could possibly utter.

"Don't try to speak," I said, letting her go for just a minute so that I could undo her restraints. I had to use my teeth on the zip ties, seeing as how a laser saber would have cut off her hands whole.

What had he done to her, run her through a ringer? She must have put up a terrible fight for her to be in such a state. She was strong; she was James Felling, secret agent of the Men in Black, and she was going to pull through this.

"Sally?" she uttered, and I let out a sigh of relief.

"Yeah, it's me," I said. "I'm getting you out of here."

"'Tr-ap," she said, sagging forward as I helped her hands shake free.

"I know," I replied, placing a hand on her knee as I swung to her front, trying to find the best way to relieve her of her ankle restraints. "Cross shot me. He gave me the whole spiel, you know, about wanting to turn in Zander and Blayde to the Agency for his own freedom and stuff. But then I got away! You see? It's all going to be okay. He doesn't control us the way he wants us to think."

"No," she hissed through bloodied teeth. Her hands on my shoulders, her whole weight hitting me. "This trap."

My skin went cold. Shaking, I helped her back up into the seat, propping her against the back of the chair where she could breathe a little easier. My hands were shaking. My eyes focused on her, only her, not wanting to guess at what was hiding in the dark around me.

Her pulse was stronger than I gave her credit for. She wasn't dying; she only looked so.

"Don't let him in," she begged through gritted teeth.

But it was too late—Cross was already here.

He had been all along.

Sometimes, no amount of deep breathing will be enough to calm your nerves. And maybe that's the point. I felt my guts grow cold. How, I didn't know. Usually they were supposed to stay warm, but instead they were making me freeze. It was all in my head; I knew it. I wasn't meant to feel cold, not anymore.

"Found you," a voice breathed on my neck, raising every hair at my disposal.

I turned around slowly. Incredibly slowly. As slow as slow could allow. Looming behind me was Cross, larger than life, synthetic skin still melting off his frame and over his gap-toothed grin. I thrust my arms out, shielding James.

"Why didn't you kill me?" I stammered. "You could have. The teacher, your fourth victim, she had no idea when you snuck up on her. If you really wanted to suck me dry, why haven't you done it already?"

He said nothing, only widened his grin into a snarl, lips melting like putty over his yellow teeth. His eyes were expressionless; whatever control he had over them was already gone.

"You're driving me insane," he replied, seemingly happy, glad. "I want to see you scream."

"My god, you are such a creep," I snapped. "You know what I did with the last creeper who held me against my will? I killed him, and I blew up his home and his life's work. Oh wait, I also did that to the *first* creeper. Life's like that."

I thought saying it would help me feel pride, accept what has happened, but instead I felt like an ass. Even more so when Cross snarled through his dislocated jaw. Blowing people up wasn't so easy to get past.

Felling coughed behind us, and I felt the ice inside me get colder. Just how badly had he hurt her before thrusting her into that chair? There was so much blood, more than I wanted to believe I was seeing. The coughing was bad. He must have hurt her ribs, her lungs.

"Dustin," she hissed. I threw my arms out wider,

casting a larger protective net. "What happened to you? You were never… a killer."

"And I wouldn't have pinned you as easy prey," he replied. "Seems like we're both mistaken tonight."

Don't you dare insult my girl like that, I wanted to say, but I kept my mouth shut. He wanted to get a rise out of me, out of Felling. I felt her hand brush against my hip and stood still, waiting for her to make her move. Whatever it was, I wasn't going to let Cross see.

"You monster," I spat. "You could have taken this body after you killed me the first time. You could have killed me again just minutes ago. You're liking this. You want to see Felling suffer. You- you know what? No insult is going to cut it. You're more messed up than words can properly insult."

I think what he was trying to do with his mouth could be considered snarling, but it was hard to tell with the putty-skin now dripping down his lips and clumping at the chin like water in the rain. It was hard to keep a steady demeanor when a melted face was right in front of yours. To make himself more intimidating, if that was even possible, he pressed the barrel of his gun under my chin, lifting it so that I had to meet his gaze. Gross, his eyes were melting, too, now.

"Yet now, I have the upper hand, and in a few minutes, I'll be out of your life and off the radar."

"Then why haven't you already?" I spat. "Not that I don't appreciate you dragging out this time of ours."

"Don't step all over my fun," he hissed.

"Think about this. You want to live with humans. This act will remove every last bit of humanity in you." Not that it hadn't already, but I needed time. I could feel Felling fumbling at my back. She was up to something.

"But I'm not human, don't you get that?" He opened his jaw, the mouth clicking as a separate set of teeth, these completely alien, extended from the human orifice. Four large, talon-like teeth set around the esophagus, itself ringed with a small circle of sharp teeth.

My god, so many teeth.

"I do."

There was no recoil from turning the laser saber on. There was no sound, all of it muffled by the skin of his belly, no noise escaping as I killed him. He gasped and dropped his weapon, looking at me in shock. I stepped back as he slid down the luminous beam of the weapon, his mouth gaping wide as the plasma burned away at his insides.

I tried not to think of what I had just done. I felt empty, sick. The body crumpled on the ground in front of me, the alien appendage clinging helplessly to the human corpse, gruesome enough for me to feel the most disturbed I had ever felt in my life. I turned off the saber, ignoring the hot, sticky blood running down the hilt and my hands.

"Step away, Sally," said Felling. All hint of struggle

was gone from her voice. I turned toward her, watching as she wiped the blood from her face. That, at least, was real. The rest of it? I wasn't quite sure.

"Are you okay?" I asked. She held up a phone, her phone.

"I fished this out of Cross's pocket," she said. "Your friends know where we are, but you need to step away from the corpse."

A strange, green liquid trickled from the dead creature's mouth, a thick slime that ran quickly over the cracked tiles. It seemed to know where I was, turning in my direction and seeping down the floor to reach me. At that point, I was so jumpy that the green slime scared me to the bone.

"Dammit, Sally, why aren't you moving?" Felling hissed. She tried to move her own legs, but they were still firmly tied to her chair. She managed to scoot away, but I was still frozen in place.

The slime started to climb my leg. I brushed it off, but it slid over my hand as if it weren't there. It was like trying to wipe water off in a storm. It just kept coming, kept climbing up my leg, reaching over my knee, my hip, my chest, my neck. I dropped my laser saber in terror.

I couldn't run anymore. I was petrified as the slime forced itself into my mouth, my gag reflex kicking in but being completely unhelpful until the slime was gone. I was left standing alone, lightheaded.

"Sally!" Felling screamed. She threw herself into

the air, coming down on the ground with a wood-shattering force. The chair split into its resultant parts, but it was too late.

I could feel it as it tried to take control of my mind. My senses were suddenly heightened—my hearing louder, my sight sharper—as the creature changed a few of the automatic synapses. I could feel him making himself at home in there, a monster in his own little car, trying out all the fancy, new features.

"Fight it, Sally," said Felling. She took a step toward me then backed off, as if unsure who was in control. She looked so scared—scared of me, of what I had become.

I wanted to vomit. No one was allowed in my mind but me. Someone up there, playing with the controls, it was repulsive, turning me inside out with disgust. But how could I fight what was literally me?

"Last Friday in three weeks' time, I saw a spotted, striped, blue worm shake hands with a legless lizard," I said, my mouth moving beyond my control. Parts of my mind flared up like little Christmas trees as Cross tested them out. Speech was a good one. I could feel he was happy with his new home.

"Fight him!" Felling shouted. "Fight him! You are so much stronger than that asshole, Sally. You can force him out!"

My hands flew up in rapid sequence. "The Macarena." "YMCA." Not graceful by any means but still recognizable. He was gaining on me.

And then, a patch of brain I had never felt before. My atoms, reaching and stretching, reaching for a place that was anywhere but here.

"No way am I going to let you jump us anywhere!" I snarled.

I threw up on the floor, that sad and lonely hot dog adding to the putridity of the place, my throat tingling slightly as the gastric acid burned the side of my throat.

Felling laughed, pounding her fists against her thighs. "You can do this, Sally Webber! Kick his metaphysical ass!"

I fought against the intruder, trying to push him out, but I knew this was not going to work. With extreme difficulty, I managed to lift my leg, dragging it upwards and dropping it back on the ground, putting my weight on it and repeating the sequence.

Slowly but surely, I began to walk away.

This wasn't the first time that I exited a Starbucks with my brain on autopilot, but it was definitely the first that I left while followed by a laser saber-wielding secret agent and stumbled right into the waiting arms of my alien boyfriend.

Starbucks, man.

"Sally!" Zander practically shrieked, wrapping his arms tightly around me. I could feel his warmth, but it was as if he were hugging me underwater, the touch muffled by something damp and all encompassing. "We got your text. We found you. Oh, thank the stars you're safe. I will never forgive myself, never. I… I'm so sorry. I shouldn't have left you alone. Where is he? Where's Cross?"

I wanted to say something, to let him know this was not me. This was not right. Even now, inside my brain, the being that was once Cross was hatching a plan I wasn't entirely privy too. But it involved the jumping part of my brain he had just discovered and a whole list of friends who would love to have Zander signed, sealed, and delivered to their doorstep.

I had control of my tongue; Cross had control of my lips. "Hmmmrrrmmm," was all I could say.

"That's not Sally," said Felling. Out of the corner of my eye, I could see her. Bloodied but not beaten, standing in front of the Starbucks with a laser saber in hand. She flicked her thumb, and the light arced to life, filling the empty space with the crackling hum of plasma on a leash.

"What are you—" Zander stammered. Blayde intervened first, ripping him away.

"Cross is in her head," Felling continued.

Meanwhile, I just stood there, rooted in place like some damn tree, unable to move either way. Wait, I wasn't the one mad about that. Shit, Cross's thoughts were becoming my thoughts. He was infecting me, taking over me.

This couldn't be happening.

"Sally, are you hurt?" Zander took a tentative step toward me, brows creased in worry. He looked a decade older. Still nowhere close to his real age, but the stress there made my heart hurt. At least I still had control over that.

And I was not relinquishing that, even after my last breath.

"He's... in...me, Zan," I forced out, piggybacking on every bout of nausea, every lapse of Cross's focus. Taking over a body was difficult work, after all. It was still my body, not for the taking.

It was my body, and there was one thing it was good at: dying, but not really.

"Who is?" he asked, cocking his head sideways.

Come on, Zander-freaking-no-last-name, Mister Sand. Show me why the Alliance fears you so much. Put two and two together and get this asshole out of my head.

"The... thing. You need.... to shoot me, Zan. Now."

Out of nowhere, my hand flew up and slapped me right across the cheek. I laughed, the sound muffled by my unresponsive lips. Cross was turning his attention away from taking over and fighting back.

"Sally." Why did he have to look like a puppy when he said that? He knew very well what I was. This wasn't a difficult task. Even Blayde was standing back, nodding. She would have done it already if she didn't know how much it would destroy her brother.

"Kill, Zan." I spat. "Only way."

Zander was shaking his head no, Blayde was shaking her head yes, and my arm was flying through the air to both their wide-eyed stares. Cross and I looked down at the stump of my lost arm, to the limb on the ground, leaking green onto the floor.

Odd. I smelled like sizzling bacon. Not a realization I was thrilled about.

"Felling!" Zander screamed, just as the crackling plasma drove through my chest and destroyed my heart.

Good old Felling. A friend until the end. That was three deaths in a single day: must be some kind of record. I collapsed forward to Zander's petrified scream, my vision going black before I hit the ground.

Death number three was probably the middle child of my deaths of the day, at least in terms of drama.

TWENTY-TWO

LET'S STAND AROUND THE BONFIRE
SINGING KUMBAYA

I CAME AWAKE ON THE COLD, HARD GROUND, feeling the rush of endorphins flood through me as my senses came online. Another thing they don't tell you in Immortal School: your body is so happy it's not dead, it floods your brain with happy neurotransmitters, and for a split second, you feel as if your entire body is floating on a cloud. Just pure joy at being alive. Coupled with the relief of not having to share your body with anyone else, which in my case, was a bonus.

Then it all comes crashing down when you see your dismal surroundings again. When your hands feel the burning edge of broken glass. I reached up to one of the laser saber wounds on my chest—or at least, where it should have been. My UFO shirt was now soaked in blood, but my chest was closed, fresh skin waiting under my fingertips.

Felling. She had done what I asked, no question. Maybe she was the friend she had always claimed to be. Maybe it was time to repair that relationship.

There were voices around me. I let out a silent breath. Not that I needed to breathe, not really. I just liked the taste of air, even here, even with the taste of smoke. Something, someone was burning.

And it wasn't the smoking former hole in my chest.

I let myself listen to my surroundings, unable—no, unwilling—to get up and face the music just yet. I had died so many times today and deserved a little break - that and I didn't want to see Cross's discarded corpse burning on a pyre.

I could feel everything around me. I could feel Blayde, stoking the flames, a silent vigil over the discarded skin wrap. I could feel Zander and James in deep conversation at the fireside, feel the tension of their aching bodies. And I knew that if I wanted to, I could join them without walking a step.

I could go wherever I wanted. Anywhere at all.

"I just saved her life," James was saying, anger bubbling to the edge. Zander was less reserved, a master of whisper-shouts.

"By burning a hole through her."

"Something you were too cowardly to do. I told you she's stronger than you give her credit for. Look, the hole's already closed up."

Blayde's voice joined them. "Stop it, both of you," she said. "You did what had to be done. Felling, you need to get Cross's remains to the Agency. Once we're gone, go back to your office and make a big fuss about your baggie of green goo. Someone will be watching. You're going to make a new friend today."

There was a pause, filled with only the crackling of the flames. I didn't want to move. Not quite yet. Neither did they, it seemed.

"You know, you never did tell me," said James.

No one answered. I relished in the silence.

"This is the point where I ask you *'what,'*" she said.

"What?" asked Zander, finally.

"Exactly. Only I'm the one who's meant to be saying it."

"I'm not sure what you're getting at, Felling."

"Shanghai? Come on, it's not every day you visit Earth. What put the two of you in that alley?"

"I told you," Zander replied. "I felt drawn there by mystical voices beyond my understanding."

"Really?"

"No. Like always, I just pop up in places randomly. You just happened to need a hand. So, how have you been treating yourself for the past fifteen years? You seem to have a promising career."

"Yeah, yeah. We moved to the States after the incident. Dad and I. He thought I was crazy, you know, telling stories of a mysterious pair of immortals who saved both our skins. The team of psychiatrists agreed with him: post-traumatic stress. Dad got it into his head that the more studies I'd do, the more common sense I would have and the delusions would dissolve over time. Instead, with all those resources at my disposal, I found more stories of you."

"As one does."

"I passed my exams with perfect scores. I entered the FBI, worked my way up, then demanded the strange and supernatural cases. I debunked most of them as hoaxes or just another crime hidden by falsehood. Turns out, *Scooby-Doo* is more accurate than we ever give it credit for. But some cases gave me indication of... more. Eventually, I got put on the interdepartmental task force trying to coax together a coherent view of aliens among us. And eventually, I found you, which brings us to now."

"So, now what? You found us. You saved the planet too. Just last week! You must be proud."

"Two weeks ago."

"Frashing time, pff," said Blayde. "Anyway, you found us and saved the planet. Twice now, technically. Life's work. Yet you don't seem all that happy."

"Happy?" She spat, crossing her arms over her chest. "Why would any of that make me happy?"

"I mean, happiness might be subjective and all, but saving the world is supposed to, I don't know, what's the Earth saying? Spark joy?"

"You know who saved the world? Sally did. She

was willing to die to save the planet, and no one will ever know."

"You're upset because Sally doesn't get a parade?"

"It sounds like high school drama, doesn't it?" James laughed. "Sorry. It's just not every night you get to catch up with the man from space who literally saved your life."

"This is a new one for me too," said Zander, "and you did just kill my girlfriend."

"Truth is, I thought meeting you again would make me happy," she continued. "Instead, I'm frustrated. I spent the entire day trying to cover your ass after you broke into Area-freaking-51. Then I got kidnapped by my partner, who tried to kill me before I killed him by proxy. Not how I expected to work with you."

"I'll make it up to you," said Zander hopefully.

"But you know what happened before we saved the world? For a minute, Sally and I were friends. I finally had someone I could talk to about your existence who didn't find me crazy. Then suddenly, she's dead, and it's all my fault. Now she's the opposite of dead, and I'm pretty sure it's my fault too. And my only space friend won't talk to me because of it."

"Felling, you do know it wasn't your fault Sally died that night, don't you?" Blayde interjected. "It was orchestrated by one of her exes. The whole thing."

"Even the night we met," said Zander. "He put everything in motion."

"This lie won't make me feel better," James scoffed.

"It's not a lie. It's…we all had a terrible, terrible thing happen to us. Sally's still coming to terms with everything. Even Blayde came back different."

"And you? You're coping?"

There was a shifting of fabric. "Someone has to."

"I'm not sure you are," she said, shaking her head. "And if you were, I would be worried. And as Sally's friend, as little as she cares for me now, I want to be mad at you, you know? Because you left her. She was devastated, and then you come back. Oh, just an accident! Haha! And she falls for you all over again. And then you leave again. Again. She was furious! You hurt her so much, abandoning her again and again. And yet you waltz back into her life, curse her with immortality, and she takes you back *again.*"

"Your point?"

"She's head over heels for you," said James. "It's not healthy."

"I'm out of here," said Blayde. "I'm going to check on our little undead one."

"Relationships take work," he said. "And we're working on ours. We just haven't had any time, seeing as how we're running around trying to solve a murder for you. Remember that part?"

"I at least realize that Sally and I were only friends because we had *you* in common. That search for you drove us together, and we were the only other person who could even count as a friend we could share this with. Ever stop to think she's only with you because you're the only man she can be with?"

"You don't know what you're saying."

"She's taken to you because you're shiny and new. You're the only person she can date and who can't grow old and die on her and—"

"Let me stop you right there," he spat. "This is Sally's life we're talking about. Neither of us can guess at her choices. She's happy."

To that, James laughed. "She just found out she can't ever die. I'm not sure she's happy about that. Tell me, did she proclaim her love for you before or after she gained immortality?"

"I think you need some sleep."

"Yup, because I'll always defer to you, the immortal expert of the universe."

"Should we have taken you to a hospital?" he asked. "You have a concussion?"

"And you're an alien," she stammered. "We both contain the secrets of the universe."

Blayde's hand tapped my wrist gently. "I know you're alive," she said. "You breathe louder than a chain-smoker."

"I don't wanna," I replied, trying to keep my voice low. I didn't want to get in whatever mess Zander and James were on about. "Come be dead with me?"

She stretched out along my side, not saying a word. Together, we stared at the ceiling, watching the orange glow of the bonfire dance back and forth far above us.

"Are you okay, Blayde?" I asked.

"Never better."

"You sure?" Part of me wanted to reach for her, to grab her hand, just to hold her skin and tell her she wasn't alone. But this was Blayde, and immortal or not, I could lose my head over this.

"Sally, you don't have to worry about me," she said. "I'm not your sister."

"You're worse," I replied. "You're my friend."

She turned to me. For the first time since I had met her, for the first time I had ever known her, she smiled. I had seen her smile already, but this, this was a smile of a whole different sort. It was as if a heavy curtain had dropped, and behind it there was this soft Blayde, like the stranger who had been living in my apartment after our return from the library. That Blayde had never smiled at me before.

Oh, screw it. I took her hand, and she squeezed back.

"I mean it. You don't have to look out for me," she said. "I always heal. Always. If time doesn't scar this over, it will instead help me forget. I mean, you know this too. No matter what happens, I go on to live another day."

"It doesn't mean you have to keep it all to yourself," I insisted. "You can throw yourself into your work—for lack of a better word—as a distraction, but it's not going to help what's going on inside."

"But it does," she said. "It reminds me I'm the same person I've always been. Even after all this shit we've been through, I'm still me. I can still solve a stupid serial murder case on a planet I know nothing about. I can still break into government facilities on strange worlds and fly off into the sunset. I won't let what happened change me."

"But what if... what if you can't help it?"

She squeezed my hand tighter. "You saw the museum, Sally. You're there too. Whatever happens today, tomorrow, you're going to be around for quite a long time."

"That's what I'm scared of." I may have lost my anxiety, but I had gained something else instead. Now when I looked ahead, I didn't see emptiness. I saw vastness. I didn't know which void was more terrifying.

"Immortality sucks, my dear," she said. "But you get over it. Then it sucks again, but you get over it again. It's not perfect all the time, but it's not entirely awful either. Not when you've got good people with you along the way. Just because something isn't finite, it doesn't mean it doesn't matter."

She pressed her shoulder against me, and I pressed back, soaking in her warmth. I realized then that I loved this woman. Not in the same way I loved Zander, no, but in this deep part of me that realized I could never live without her. And seeing how long I was going to live, that feeling was more intense than any I had ever felt before.

Even as that thought became clear, another one bubbled to the surface. The image, clear as day, of Marcy as an old woman, her hair white, her body bent at the waist as gravity and age brought her back to the ground where she would spend her own eternity.

"Do you understand now?" she asked. "Why I was so against having you come with us in the first place?"

I didn't respond. I didn't need to. I knew exactly what she meant.

"Zander loves you. I could see it the first time I saw you together when you walked down that hallway, ready to tell him off for giving away company secrets. Do you remember? He looked up to you, and I was standing close enough to hear his heart shatter. Because he realized that now I was there, he was going to lose you."

"He was always going to lose me. He knew that from the start."

"But for a little while, he forgot. When he was with you, he forgot. And while we forget a lot of things, our own eternity is rarely one of them"

"Also," I said, "your accidental Russian bride is going to be my actual sister now. How does that work?"

Blayde let out a laugh. "Way to change the subject."

"It doesn't bother you at all?"

She shrugged. "Remember, I have no baseline for normal anymore."

I laughed and realized too late that everyone could hear me. Too bad. "Can adults even adopt another adult?"

"How should I know? It's your planet."

"Who are we suddenly talking about adopting?" asked Zander, waltzing into my field of view, all smiles.

"Yes, Zander, the three of us are going to co-parent Felling," I said.

"Because that went well the last time," said Blayde under her breath. "Shall we get going? I don't know about you, but I'm looking forward to meeting my future ex-wife."

That was the end of the man once called Agent Dustin Cross. While his Terran body burned to ash in a mall, his green, goopy consciousness lived on in a Ziploc bag, heading back to Felling's mysterious HQ, the woman giving us only passing glances as we all said goodbye.

We'd be having a real talk soon. But tonight, if only tonight, we'd all go our separate ways and pretend none of this ever happened.

TWENTY-THREE
EVEN AFTER ALL THIS,
THE END GOAL IS ALWAYS FLORIDA

MOM WAS OPENING THE DOOR FOR US BEFORE WE even got out of the car, rushing in to hug me the instant my foot hit pavement. She looked us over in shock, opening her mouth to say something, but was interrupted by Galli, who ran out to join us, her whole rear end wagging in excitement.

"Where on earth have you been?" she snapped. "I should ground you, young lady."

I laughed, hugging her tighter. "It's been a long day."

"Two days. The next time someone bangs on our door in the middle of the night, we're putting in earplugs and leaving them outside. You hear me?"

"Loud and clear," I replied. "I'll be doing the same."

"Well, are you coming in or what?" She turned to

the siblings. Blayde was clutching LP in her arms, its long hands dragging on the floor without the bot conscious enough to lift them. She had fixed it in the long ride back down the coast, but it wasn't entirely up to snuff yet. "Sally, please don't tell me you did all this just to go to a con."

Well, she sure made things easier for me. "It was a very important con."

"You ran off just to go to a convention?"

"We got really good last-minute passes," I muttered.

"Just wait until your father hears about this," she said, crossing her arms. "He's a little busy right now, though."

Much to my surprise, the living room was packed with people, each seated on sofas or on the floor, watching a man standing beside what had been a bookshelf when I had left, but was now a bare wall with a PowerPoint presentation covering it.

"Your father's conspiracy group," said Mom. "Be careful. Don't bring up aliens unless you're willing to have a half an hour conversation with them where you can't get a word in edgewise."

"You're kidding me," I said, finding Dad in the crowd. He smiled and waved. "Why can't he meet with others online? Like a normal conspiracy theorist."

"It's a generational thing."

At that, the entire room groaned. I realized then

that all eyes were on us, which should have been expected seeing as how we'd just busted into their super-secret meeting.

"Close the door!" said someone from the back.

"Honey, you know we don't call ourselves that," said Dad. "But please do close the door."

"Fine, truthers," I said, rolling my eyes. "Dad, this is really upsetting."

"Come on, Sally."

"Dad, why is there a TARDIS projected on our wall?"

He didn't answer. Galli bounded through the attendees, which gave us enough room to slide through the crowd, avoiding their pointed glares. I managed to reach my dad and kissed him on the cheek.

"If you have nothing nice to say, don't say it at all," he said.

"Sorry, Dad, it's been a long day."

"She went to a convention!" Mom spat.

"Without me?" Dad frowned.

"That isn't the part you're meant to be angry about, dear."

"Sister Sally!" A tall blonde woman bounded out from the kitchen, lacing me in a tight hug. "I am so glad we finally meet!"

"You're Svetlana?" I asked, hugging her back. I had completely forgotten about my spontaneous sister, but that was a whole other pickle. "It's so nice to finally meet you!"

"Sveta, please. We are sisters now. And you must be Blayde?" she asked, turning to Zander.

"No, that was me," said the real Blayde. "Hi. If you still want to get married, I'm game."

"Will you four be quiet?" snapped the presenter. "I'm trying to speak here!"

"By all means," said Zander, sweeping out of the way and dropping himself on the floor by my father's feet.

Svetlana squeezed my hand and slipped back into the kitchen, as comfortable here as if she had lived in the house longer than I had. I didn't know what to think of her. This complete stranger had breezed through this house, bringing my parents a much-needed breath of fresh air, but I knew nothing about her, her intentions, or what kind of life she wanted here.

Maybe this was one problem I didn't need to be a part of. I sat down on the ground next to Zander, the two of us framing my father's legs, and the presentation went on.

"Who's the speaker?" I whispered up at him.

"One of my friends from church, Danny Gilman," said Dad. "He's the most knowledgeable of the group."

"He's an astronomer or a physicist or something?"

"Well, he has a telescope. But he has the most free time on his hands and does all the research."

"Cool," I said with a smile, looking at the people who sat in the living room. Not one, it seemed, was under sixty. There were definitely worse ways to spend their time.

"So, where were we?" Gilman asked his audience.

"The government trying to conceal the truth about the hoax?"

"Yes, that's where." He switched slides to show a group of people in patriotic tourist clothes trying to grab a bite of sushi. "I obtained this photo from a close friend, who managed to take it in one of the restaurants across from the White House. As you can see, the men and women are in heated discussion over the incidents. To the president's left, one of his most trusted *war* generals. He was not planning a cover-up. He was planning a war strategy with the ship. Not the way a president would act if there was a hoax."

"Can you see me?" I whispered to Zander. "Bottom right corner. Next to James."

"Huh, fancy that," he said cheerfully.

"Next slide." Gilman ordered, then continued with his tale. "According to one of my sources, who would prefer to remain anonymous, a covert operation was organized with an undercover agent, actor Alejandro Vasquez, and the alien being aboard the ship. We believe that was a trade done where they took

Vasquez to their planet and left their agent in his place to spy on our planet."

I snorted. I got a few glares, but the eyes all eventually returned to the speaker.

"The next photos are a time-lapse of the same spot. This is the spot the ship hovered over for fifteen minutes before leaving the planet. I decided to do research into this spot and got my hands on a file from a camera in the vicinity. First, we see a lady of the night speaking to Vasquez. It is safe to assume that the woman is the undercover agent, or possibly an alien in deep cover. The cameras go blank for the next fifteen minutes. When they come back on, we have this." He used his laser to highlight an area of the still. "A pool of blood. Human or extraterrestrial?"

"What comes next?" one of the ladies asked, her excitement evident.

"Nothing for the next week. There is a woman who comes to the spot every two hours or so, just to meander around." He froze the feed, bringing an enhanced photo of the man. Gasps rose from the crowd.

"But that's..." one of the older ladies of the group asked, her hand rising to her face.

"Yes. It is the public face of the hoax." Gilman juxtaposed the still with a screen capture from a press conference. "A certain Agent Jameson."

"Doesn't know how to stay out of the spotlight,

that one." Blayde snickered, returning from the kitchen with her arms full of little pigs in a blanket. One of the strangers made a little hum of agreement, as if Blayde's comment had been incredibly insightful.

"Is there more?" the lady urged.

"There is. Oh, thank you, Laurie." He smiled as my mom offered him a plate of macaroni and cheese, which he ate standing up as the other members helped themselves to the warm food. "One week later," he said between mouthfuls. "Wonderful as always, Laurie. One week later, we have this."

He played the video. The camera had a frame rate of one shot per second, so it was jumpy, but it was easy enough to see three people appear out of thin air. I felt the concentration of oxygen in the room drop, as loud intakes of air could be heard through the house.

"It's the girl!" my father said, shocked. "Sally, are you seeing this?"

"Yes, Dad," I replied quickly, watching myself on the screen.

The film stopped, the presentation continuing to show an enhanced photo of my face, though still covered in the hasty makeup.

"Is that blood?"

"It could be. It can be many things. The girl is most likely an undercover alien spy who was beamed down from the mothership."

"But if the mothership's in space, shouldn't the satellites pick it up?" a man pointed out.

"The ones who control the satellites are in on it too," said Gilam.

Zander snorted loudly. I think I may have as well.

"Do you have something to add, young man?"

"No, no, sorry. Carry on."

"So, what does this all mean? For us?" a member of the audience asked.

"The aliens could be anyone. We need to be careful who we trust," Gilman replied, a look of confidence on his wrinkled face. "The only people who we know for sure are human are the people inside this room."

I felt uncomfortable in the house, in need of fresh air. I made my way out the back door to the beach, bursting out in the dark of the evening and digging my toes into the light sand every once in a while. I walked down the coast far enough so that the sound of the street faded away and all that could be heard was the crash of waves on the shore by my feet.

But something was wrong.

Not in the sand. Nothing was wrong with the waves, nothing with the beach. Nothing with the cluster of dark palms and trees that grew close together to create a dense, dark forest.

I dropped down, ignoring the rough sand on my jeans. The moon was high, a beautiful orb of white, a familiar place I had been just a single day ago. And something in the back of my brain, a small sense I had gained after the encounter, told me that I could go there now if I wished. I knew the distance; I could see it. I could jump there.

I could jump over the moon.

I heard footsteps down the beach. I turned my head, watching the figure approaching, knowing well enough who it was. It wouldn't take long for him to reach me, so I said nothing as I let the water kiss my toes.

"Hey, Dad," I said quietly.

"Hi." He sat down next to me, watching the sky with me. "I sent everyone home."

"Thanks."

"They really bothered you, didn't they?" he asked. "I'm sorry. I really am. It was fun being able to talk to other people about these… these mad things happening in the world. It's so easy to fall into the fantasy. But those images… they were too real for me too."

I smiled, shaking slightly. I should tell him. This was the perfect time, wasn't it? That all his conspiracy friends were right? That his houseguests were also planetguests? Tell him that the only child he had left would be around forever?

In the silence, he pointed to a constellation. "You see Orion's Belt?"

"Those three stars, right there?" I knew the stars, or, at least, I had a vague memory of their names. I could hear each of them calling to me, each light-years away from each other, each with their own worlds, their own little beginnings and endings.

"Yeah. You know why they called it Orion's Belt?" I shook my head. He continued, "Can you believe it's a love story?"

"Really?"

"Yeah. Orion was kind of a big bragger, a man with too much vanity for one man. He was an archer, a good one. One day, he was taken by the beauty of Artemis, the goddess of archery. He fell head over heels for her. Instead of his usual tricks, he let go of his trail of one-night stands and humbled himself in front of her, asking for her to teach him her skill. He learned and didn't brag or flaunt his ability. And Artemis was taken with him, for she knew his history, but his change softened her heart. They fell in love."

He paused, waiting for me to interrupt, but I didn't. There was something soothing about listening to a story, to just let him talk without needing to speak. I was afraid if I opened my mouth, I would say something I would regret.

"Artemis's brother, Apollo, did not approve of his sister's talk of marriage. One day, as Orion was swimming in the ocean, Apollo challenged his sister to an archery match. You know those ancient Greeks: she could not refuse. The target was the black spot in the sea, a few miles off. Apollo missed. Artemis hit right on target. It was only then that she realized that the black spot had been the back of her betrothed's head."

"She killed him?"

"Yeah."

"Is this the real story?"

"Yup."

"Oh, those Greeks."

"In despair, she used her power to make him into a constellation in the sky so she could see him every night. She made a vow of chastity and continued on with her life."

"And the belt?"

"What about the belt?"

"You were telling me why the belt was named Orion's Belt."

"Well, because it was his."

"Come on."

"Seriously, that's the story! You can't become a constellation and watch the world for all eternity without a statement piece."

"Dad, come on. I thought the belt was part of a love story."

"It was. It is. The goddess was immortal. She could never live with him forever. The arrow is symbolic: although it killed him, it also permitted her to make him like her. They can see each other forever, even though they're miles apart. And though the world changes, they will always be eternal. And she made sure that he got to keep his belt."

"You a poet now, Dad?"

"I try," he smiled. "You are somewhat in love with that Zander boy, aren't you?"

"Yes, Dad. I am."

"Why didn't you tell me earlier?"

"It's a bit of a recent development."

"Well, if you want to talk… Well, I guess I'm here. I mean, you never really needed to talk relationship problems with your old man before, did you?"

"It was less awkward when John was around."

"Yes, yes, it was."

We sat together in silence, looking up at the stars. I thought of the dream that had taken over my thoughts—John dying when I could never die. Death was such a simple thing for me to overcome now. It wasn't fair that it wasn't the case for him.

And my parents. They would live and die on this rock, and I would keep going, slowly forgetting my past until there was nothing of them left, not even memory.

Or it would be like Meedian. Maybe I would always be able to come back and see them, a me from a different time, never changing, always returning to a time when the people I loved would be there to love me too.

"So, your convention was in D.C.?"

"Yeah."

"Nice t-shirt."

"Oh, thanks." I touched the thick cotton fabric,

watching my dad shiver in the breeze. "You're tiptoeing around your actual question, though, aren't you?"

"Since when could you ever read me so well?" he said, smiling weakly. "I'm just… I don't know Zander. And when I see you two together, there's no softness there. Only tension. His sister too."

"It's why we needed to come down here in the first place," I said. "Long week. We've all been through a lot."

"Like wandering around crime scenes, I suppose," he said. I tried to keep myself from stiffening at those words. *He knew. Oh god, he knew.*

"What are you saying?" I asked.

"You realize that no matter how you dress, I'd recognize you anywhere, right?" He let out a heavy sigh. "I just want to say that if you ever do want to talk about what really happened under that overpass, you know where to find me."

We sat in silence for a few more minutes, a few difficult minutes where it was almost impossible to keep myself from blurting out the terrible truth. The truth that one day, when he would be an old man, I would still look the same. That he would probably never have the grandkids he wanted so badly. That one day, I may not find my way back again, and I would be gone, without him knowing what happened to me.

I mean, what would be the downside of him

knowing what had happened to me? Finding out your daughter will live forever would probably fill a parent's heart with joy. But my parents had no idea how to keep a secret, and this was not one with light consequences.

"Now." He got to his feet as well, facing me. "I hope Zander's not the one who's got you bothered."

"No, not him." I smiled. "Quite the opposite, I think."

"Good. Just so that's cleared up." He tipped an imaginary hat, like when I was a kid. "Good night, Sally."

"Night, Dad."

He left for the house, and I watched him go silently. He meant well. He cared. I should tell him.

No, I shouldn't.

Yes, I should.

At least I would have all the time in the world to make up my mind.

TWENTY-FOUR

I WON'T HIDE ANY SPOILERS HERE, NOPE

I STARTED TO WALK AGAIN, WALK AWAY FROM THE house, farther than I usually went when I came for a visit. I felt the sudden urge to run, to let my hair fly out behind me as I spread my arms and ran. It felt glorious, the wind against my face at full force as I pelted down the beach. I wasn't tired; I wasn't wearing out. I just kept running, running away from the secrets and the silence.

It reached a point where the grove of trees had grown too close to the water, one single tree blocking the entire stretch with its large roots. Without thinking much, I jumped to the other side, as simply as if I had been doing it my entire life, and continued my run.

It was much later when I stopped, not from

exhaustion but from reason. It was dumb to run. Cowardly. Not when I had so much going for me.

I had been so wrong. This wasn't a curse: this was something new and thrilling and incredible. A new life, so many possibilities. I had lifetimes to explore the universe, time and space at my fingertips.

Did this change make them any less of who they were? Did they change themselves because of immortality, or had immortality brought out their true natures? They were looking for home, sure, lost in space and time, but along the way, they had saved countless lives from things that would probably change the universe for the worst.

And where was I in all this?

I had just become immortal. And I could teleport anywhere, any time. I was going to live forever. And I wasn't going to live forever alone.

Soon enough, the house was in sight, and so was the man who waited in front of it. Zander waited on the beach, facing away from the ocean, watching instead the dense forest that followed the coastline. He looked up as I came, saying nothing. He extended his hands in silence, and I took them. Soon we were dancing on the beach, laughing and flying across the sand to a rhythm only we could hear.

"You can jump," he said, giddy and grinning, spinning me like a top.

"I think I've got the gist of it," I said, laughing.

"And?"

"And what?"

"Does it make up for the rest?" he asked. "Do you regret it?"

I shook my head, my hair catching in the breeze. *No.*

"Did you tell your father?"

"I can't, not yet. I can keep trying to get by with lame excuses, but the truth is, point blank, I just can't."

"It's going to be complicated, you know," he said. "Living on Earth, if that's what you want to do. After a while, you won't be able to see your friends again. Your family."

"I'm going wherever you go," I said. "If you stay on Earth, I'll stay on Earth. If you go to the stars, I'll go with you. If you decide to live the rest of eternity in a tree, I'll live the rest of my life in that same tree."

"Eternity is a long, long time," he said. "Especially in a tree. They make for terrible roommates. Listen, Sally, we need to talk."

No great conversation ever started with that. The breeze that magically lifted my hair died down. Our dancing slowed to a sway, then to two people just standing on the beach, toes curled in the sand.

"Yes, I suppose we do," I said. "Let's walk?"

We continued down the beach, passing other houses in the dark, my bare feet slipping in and out of the water. For a moment, it made me think of a world now entirely submerged. Of the two of us dancing on another beach, worlds and eons away.

"Where do we start?" asked Zander.

I nodded. "Now that's a question."

"Have you read *The Tempest?*"

"Now that's a whole other question," I stammered. "Have you?"

"No. But I read a good summary online. Felling suggested it for us. I guess it's culturally significant or something."

"What does James have to do with us?"

"She's worried about you. And I can't say she's wrong. Every point she brought up hit a little too close to home."

I nodded. "So, tell me about *The Tempest.*"

"I'll keep it short. You have Miranda, living on an island with her wizard father, Prospero. And she's never met another human being before, then suddenly, a shipwreck. This man falls onto Miranda's shores, Ferdinand, and it's what they might call insta-love."

"What does this three-hundred-year-old play have to do with us?"

"Ferdinand is the first man Miranda had ever seen. She immediately falls head over heels for him."

"So?"

"And I'm the first alien you've ever met."

"It's weird hearing you say that."

"You don't think we're like Ferdinand and

Miranda? You falling for me because I'm not from Earth?"

My hands were shaking now, and not from the cold. I didn't try to hide them. "Then maybe the only reason you like me back is because I'm the only one like you who you're not related to. Did you think about that?"

"That's cold, Sally."

"But it's what you're saying. It applies to me now as well. And I can't get the thought out of my head. I can't stop thinking about all the reasons we ended up together, and I can't help but wonder—is any of this right?"

"You know I need to ask," he said. "I gave you space. A lot of people would fake a relationship to get to see the stars up close."

"Oh yeah, of course you would know. Not once have I asked about your life before now. If you were married before. If you had kids. If you could even remember them."

"I'm sorry."

"Zander, just for your information, during the two years when you were gone, every once in a while I would think that I wouldn't care if we were together for a day, a month, a year, if one day you were gone and you would forget about me forever—as long as maybe, one day, Zander was mine. I didn't care that you were immortal, alien, or had long-term memory loss. It didn't mean a thing to me that you could live forever and I couldn't, just as long as I could have a little tiny bit of your forever."

He dropped down on the sand, so suddenly that I walked by him before I realized he was no longer by my side. I turned back, and there he was, just sitting by the sea and watching the waves crash in the distance.

"Would it have been different if we had seen where this was going before the incident at the library?" he asked, peeling his eyes from the horizon. "If I had asked you to court me the moment I felt my heart burn for you?"

I sat down beside him. "I guess it depends when it was."

"The moment I opened my eyes to the woman who had run me over," he said, dropping his head onto his knees. "Shit, I'm the Miranda."

"I think we're both Mirandas here," I said, putting a hand on his knee. He wrapped his arm around me, and I leaned in, my head against his.

"If you had asked me out then and there, I would have driven you straight to a hospital to have you checked for a concussion."

He laughed. "Okay, that's fair."

"But on another day, I would have said yes, you know," I replied. "I had this crush on you that just wouldn't go away. You were this… I don't know, this amazing guy, going around saving the world, saving people. I didn't want you to have to save me."

He kissed me lightly on the top of the head, and butterflies fluttered in my stomach.

"You asked if any of this was right," he whispered. "I believe it is. I'm terribly afraid, Sally. I don't want this to end. I don't want us to not give this a chance. To not give *us* a chance."

I took a deep breath, savoring his smell mixed with the salt of the sea. "I don't want that either. And we don't need old writers or ancient philosophers to tell us we can't."

He sighed, his breath warm against my neck. "There's no relationship like ours in all of space and time. We're breaking new ground. We need to stop looking for a rulebook where there isn't one."

"Have you ever stopped to think about last week? How somehow I died and found myself at your side across the galaxy?" He said nothing. "Because as I died, an entirely mortal death, the only thing I could think of was that I would never see you again. And then I saw you."

"And you saved me," he said. "You crossed space and time, and you saved me."

"That was a Miranda move," I laughed.

"No," he replied. "That was a Sally move."

We sat there a little longer, watching the waves pull in and out, falling back into sync with each other. It felt like pieces of a puzzle falling into place, building calm out of what once was chaos.

"When I asked you to kill me," I said, "why didn't you?"

"Oh, come now. You know why."

"I suppose I do. I didn't think that would bother me, but it does. If you want me to accept how I am now, you're going to have to do the same. I want you to stop treating me like I'm made of glass because I'm not."

"Got it," he said, pulling me closer. "I'll try to get rid of any qualms I have against murdering you when it's consensual."

I stood, brushing the sand off my legs, pulling him up with me. When before we had been two people walking together on the beach, we walked home as a couple, together, with the beach as a gorgeous backdrop.

"In the past," he started, "my experience has always been that if something is too good to be true, it usually is."

"Same. Though, admittedly, my experience is much shorter than yours."

"I can't apologize for my memory or lack thereof."

"I'm not asking you to." I squeezed his hand tighter. "We'll figure that all out as we go along."

"And I'm here if you want to tell your parents," he said. "There's no manual here. You can tell them. I mean, why not? If you want Marcy to know, you can tell her too."

"They won't believe me."

"Do you lie to them often?""

"No."

"Then why wouldn't they trust you?"

"Because of how absurd this is. I am dating a spaceman, you know."

"Well, that's their problem."

I laughed. "Really? It's that easy?"

"Maybe? I don't really know. The people I tell about myself don't tend to see me again."

Blayde sat on the back porch, eyes already rolling as she saw us coming down the beach. She said nothing as we walked past her, instead following us into the house where my mother and my new sister Svetlana were putting the living room back in order, while my father struggled to get the bookshelf back against the empty wall. Zander was at his side in an instant.

"What I do with robot?" asked Svetlana, holding up the LifePrint. "I put in trash?"

The phone rang and Mom went for it, taking it to the kitchen as the living room crowd put things back in place.

"That's mine, honey," said Blayde, sweeping past us. "Sorry, I keep forgetting the wedding is off."

"You're a funny one," said Svetlana. "We can still make this happen?"

With that, Blayde laughed, and I felt weights slip from my shoulders. All was well with the world. We had put an end to a serial killer's rampage, helped

Blayde through a terrible time, and made things official between Zander and me. We were going to be all right.

"Sally? It's for you," said Mom, handing me the phone. And just like that, the trance had ended.

"Who is it?" I asked, confused. It was getting rather late.

She shrugged, and I took the phone to my ear.

"Ms. Webber?"

"Who is this?"

"Ms. Sally Webber?"

"Who wants to know?"

"We met yesterday. At the Agency. Where you died."

I froze in shock. Foollegg. "How did you find me?"

"It wasn't hard. You didn't match the James Felling we had on file, but you left your fingerprints in my office. I actually was calling your parents to break them the bad news, but your mother said something very interesting."

"Which was?"

"*'I'll go get her.'*"

There was a sort of excitement to her voice, the kind of ravenous urgency that came with endings falling into place.

"It was also easy to find that you were not part of any intelligence agency on Earth," she continued. "Although they do have a file on you. You helped during the incident with the prison ship?"

"Somebody had to. Seeing as how you didn't."

"We don't interfere with natural disasters."

"Natural? It was an Alliance ship. An *ancient* Alliance ship, but still one of yours. You would have let billions die if no one stepped up."

"Like an immortal?"

"That's not what I meant."

"You're not who I meant."

"Will you just tell me what you want?"

"I want the Iron and the Sand. I want Zander and Blayde in my custody. I want them to finally come to justice."

"You know very well there's no way in the 'verse that you're going to get them."

"There's still time. I also have a message for you." She paused for dramatic effect. "You still have time to detach yourself from the criminals. You can come clean. There are no charges against you, especially now since we have received the message that the culprit has been apprehended. We know you helped. Know that we already have you. If you turn yourself in, and the Iron and the Sand, you'll be rewarded."

"I want you to guess the answer I'm going to give you."

"I'm going to let you say it."

"I'm not turning anyone in. You get that?" I heard nothing from the other end of the line. "But before I hang up, I have one last thing I must make clear."

"And that is?"

"The Sand is an absolute terrible name for a villain." I hung up, jamming the phone back on its hub. I took deep breaths, trying to calm my rising panic.

"Zander? Blayde? How do you feel about going for pizza?" I asked, grabbing the duffel bag from the ground by LP's dangling arms. His eye opened as I stepped by, and he yawned, rising into the air.

"Oh, hello, I didn't know we had company," he said, scanning the room. "Nice to meet you all!"

Galli started to bark uncontrollably, her little paws leaving the ground as she yipped in panic. She backed away from LP, her little body trembling like a leaf. She ran into the kitchen.

"Not now, LP," I hissed. "Zander, they know where we are."

"They?"

Blayde was immediately at attention. "We need to go. Back door. Hurry."

"I come with?" asked Svetlana, clutching Blayde's wrist. Blayde patted her arm.

"Sorry, darling. I'll be back for you."

Svetlana didn't let go. Blayde pulled a little harder, her eyebrows knotting.

"Miss Sally?" asked LP. "You told me to tell you if we ever so run into someone non Terran?"

And Svetlana shot him straight through the eye.

"Oh, come on!" said the bot, as he died yet again. My mother screamed.

The house filled with light, the windows a blinding

yellow color from the headlight of the cars parked in front of the small Florida home. Sirens wailed outside. Voices called for us, called for us to surrender, called for us to give it up. I froze in fear.

"Nobody move," said Svetlana, "Laurie, Hal, I have nothing against you. Go out the back door and don't come home until morning. I have acquired amnesty for you both."

"What is she saying?" Mom stammered. "What happened to her accent? Sally? What's happening?"

I was drifting. Blayde ripped the front door open, rushing out among the policemen, no transition between house and shoot-out, her laser swinging wildly into the crowd.

I was spinning. My body a dancer, my mind racing, unable to tell if I was supposed to be outside or in, helping Blayde or my parents. Svetlana turned her gun on Zander, shooting him through the head with one clean move.

I was screaming. Blayde was down. Zander was down. I was disconnected, lost in the scream of gunfire, in my parents' cries.

The last thing I expected were human handcuffs, human policemen, American patrol cars leading us away. It turns out it wasn't so easy to get away with the murder of a not-exactly-FBI agent in modern America.

Lesson learned.

SALLY'S ADVENTURE CONTINUES IN

INALIENABLE

ACKNOWLEDGEMENTS

EVERY BOOK SEEMS TO NEED EXPONENTIALLY more people to bring it to life, and I'm thankful to every single one for bringing out the best in every one of Sally's adventures. The biggest rewrite of this draft was smack dab when I moved up north to start my PhD, and the final edits and planning of the release right in the middle of a global pandemic. Once again, I'm made fully aware of how I cannot do this on my own.

As always, thank you to Michelle, my publisher, who made all this possible. Thank you for keeping a steady head during this madness and for steering us all into victory. Knowing I have you on my team gives me confidence like you wouldn't believe.

To Anna and Cayleigh, my editors. Thank you for kicking me in the pants when I needed it most. Thank you for stripping and polishing this book until it gleamed. It would just be a rambling mess without you.

Cora, thank you is not enough. You are so much more than

a friend. Every time I send you the next chapter of Sally's adventures, you give me the kindest, most heart-exploding replies. The love that you have for Sally, Zander, and Blayde, rivals my own. Friend, fan, cheerleader; you have made this story possible.

To my writing team: Maddie, Lisa, Emily, Heidi. Thank you for pushing me beyond what I believe I can do. For leading by example and showing me the steps to growth. When I'm with you, I'm a better author almost by osmosis!

To my family, for believing in me, for giving me the support and encouragement to keep on writing these crazy adventures.

And finally, to my wonderful Hugo, to whom I dedicate yet another one of my books. You bring the balance I need in my life. You throw out hilarious ideas without even realizing. You bring me tea when I'm so far into fiction that I've forgotten where I am. You are so much more than you think you are.

I was going to end this on a punchline, but 2020 is enough of a punchline as it is. Here's to writing book seven in the middle of a global pandemic, where everything is more absurd than what I put on the page!

ABOUT THE AUTHOR

SARAH ANDERSON CAN'T EVER TELL YOU WHERE she's from. Not because she doesn't want to, but because it inevitably leads to a confusing conversation about where she was born (England) where she grew up (France) and where her family is from (USA) and it tends to make things very complicated.

She's lived her entire life in the South of France, except for a brief stint where she moved to Washington DC, or the eighty years she spent as a queen of Narnia before coming back home five minutes after she had left. Currently, she is working on her PhD in Astrophysics and Planetary sciences in Besançon, France.

When she's not writing - or trying to wrangle comets - she's either reading, designing, crafting, or attempting to speak with various woodland creatures in an attempt to get them to do household chores for her. She could also be gaming, or pretending she's not watching anything on Netflix.

CONNECT WITH THE AUTHOR

www.seandersonauthor.com
facebook.com/seandersonauthor
instagram.com/readcommendations
twitter.com/sea_author